# THE BONE CHIME SONG AND OTHER STORIES

# ALSO BY JOANNE ANDERTON

**THE VEILED WORLD SERIES (Written as Jo Anderton)**

Debris

Suited

Guardian

**COLLECTIONS**

The Art of Broken Things

Inanimates: Tales of Everyday Fear

**FOR CHILDREN**

The Flying Optometrist (illustrated by Karen Erasmus)

# THE BONE CHIME SONG AND OTHER STORIES

JOANNE ANDERTON

Brain Jar Press
PO Box 6687
Upper Mt Gravatt, QLD, 4122
Australia
www.BrainJarPress.com

First published in Australia by FableCroft Publishing, 2013.
This edition published by Brain Jar Press, 2024



Cover design by Brain Jar Press
Cover Image: *Spine Human Bone,* bdavid32/Shutterstock

ISBN: 978-1-922479-64-8 (paperback) | 978-1-922479-65-5 (Ebook)

# CONTENTS

# INTRODUCTION

## KAARON WARREN

There are some writers who inhabit a world set slightly apart from ours. It feels familiar, smells, looks, sounds that way. You get drawn in because of this familiarity. You sink into it.

Then everything changes.

Joanne Anderton inhabits such a place. Her stories are transformative. From the hauntingly beautiful 'The Bone Chime Song' to the poignant 'From the Dry Heart to the Sea', Anderton casts a spell over us that draws us into Anderton-world and makes us believe it is all possible.

Her stories are filled with people we care about, because she cares so damn much. She brings them to life on the page, from the natural sense of dialogue ('Some yuppie wanker's idea of art,' Nathan says, in the excellent 'Shadow of Drought') to her descriptions. In 'Mah Song', new to this collection: *Mother burns fragrant handfuls of carefully preserved flowers, Father fills tiny cups of recycled tin with cheap rice wine* juxtaposed with *Cables run like mangrove roots from dozens of sockets in his shaved scalp* makes this story a classic Anderton magic trick.

She has a powerful imagination. It is a rare writer who can immerse us so completely in worlds as odd as those depicted in 'Always a Price', which I think of as Anderton's Fuck Cancer story and 'Tied to the Waste', a glorious story I first read when working with Joanne as mentor. I've never forgotten it.

Joanne understands how societies work, and how easily they can fall apart, and how much it hurts when this happens, demonstrated with great compassion in stories like 'Shadow of Drought' which mixes horror with the ordinary, tapping into the despair and hopelessness that drought brings and 'Fence Lines', where she explores the importance of safety in a dangerous world and the lengths to which people might go to achieve it.

Anderton's writing allows us suspension of disbelief, even when reading of the creation of life out of rubbish such as in 'Tied to the Waste' because her story logic is so good. Things happen for a reason, even within the context of a seemingly impossible world. In one of my favourites in the collection, 'Out Hunting for Teeth', Anderton is unsettling and deeply disturbing, yet still logical.

She has a real mastery of the surreal, is what I'm saying, and somehow manages to make the surreal seem normal.

At the heart of every story is caring. I call Anderton-world a beautiful dystopia, because even in nightmare scenarios, like 'Out Hunting for Teeth', there is still that belief in the triumph of human nature, and that belief love exists, and will exist, as long as we do, so that even when she is describing horrific things (and she doesn't hold back for the sake of the reader) there is a certainty of the human spirit that shines through.

What this means is that reading this book will fill you with horror, wonder, awe, sorrow, delight, surprise and admiration.

Kaaron Warren, February, 2013

# THE BONE CHIME SONG



Those bones were singing before Casimir brought them to me. I heard their jumbled and discordant notes through wood and calico lining, through security spells and spirit wards, as far away as the centre of town. I appreciated the warning; it gave me time to compose myself before I opened the shop to him.

He stood a little too straight, dark waistcoat emblazoned with an eye in gold thread, crisp white shirtsleeves rolled up to his elbows in the heat. His loosely clubbed hair was iron grey, and the Summoner scars across his cheeks stood out as though they were fresh.

Five years since I last saw him, and he had aged far more than he should have. The war was long over and he was married now, with three apparently beautiful children. Not that I'd ever seen them — I had no desire to put myself through that particular torture. What right did he have to come here now, looking so tired and old?

'Casimir,' I said, stepped back to let him enter, and prided myself on the steadiness of my tone.

'Zvonimir.' He entered stiffly, with none of his usual sharp soldier's step. 'I come requesting help.' I jammed the shop door open, and was surprised to see his dark Watchman's carriage waiting, surrounded by half a dozen or so of his UnderWatch Necromancers.

They scowled back at me, white robes bright in the midday sun. What could their fearless Watchman — war hero, powerful Summoner and wholesome family man — want with a poor, middle-aged craftsman like me?

A breeze from the street set my wind chimes humming, casting faint shadows through the shop with their songs. 'This would be an official visit, then?' I asked, as I ran my fingers through the coat of a spectral foal then steadied its horseshoe chime. 'I've never had one of those before.'

'Please understand.' Casimir skirted the racks of wind chimes to place his wooden box on my workbench. 'You are my last resort. I only come to you because I could think of nothing else to do.'

I smiled my bitterness, and said nothing.

Casimir, lips pursed tightly, spilled his bones across the table. I was forced to grip the edge to stay on my feet. Their song rolled chorus-like from the clatter-clatter, the empty echoes, the hollow beating drums. A song like I had never heard, terrible in its need to be sung, dominating, roaring into my brain until my fingers twitched for the tools.

'What is it?' Casimir reached across the table to grip my arm, and the bones hushed, a little, enough to allow me to think.

I shook him from my torn and singed sleeve. 'Where did you get these? What do you want me to do with them?'

'You must know.' Casimir glanced around the shop. 'Build me a wind chime. Play me its song.'

'Of bone?'

'They will sing for you.' There was a fiery light in his eyes, almost madness, something he'd never allowed me to see before.

'I don't understand.' My hands strayed. They touched split skull, smooth femur, small toe. It all hummed through me, in torn patches of melody. 'Why would you need me? Can't you just summon their spirit?'

He shook his head. 'Murder was done to this poor soul. This and at least four others on the edge of the tidal plain, to the west of the city wall. Foul, desecrating murder that twisted their spirits. The Necromancers and I have raised nothing but tortured, gibbering shrouds. But I am Watch, and I will not allow the people of my city to die unknown, unmourned, and unavenged.'

'And so you thought of wind chimes?' I drew my hands away.

'You give song to those whose voices are lost.' Casimir drew his timepiece, but did not look at its hands. It was meant as a conciliatory gesture. I had given it to him twenty years ago, and it had survived separation and war, now marriage and offspring. I did not return the gesture. I had long ago dismantled the one he gave me.

Instead, I pointed around the shop. 'I give voices to perambulators—' a melancholy six tone in copper and wood '— carriages—' iron four tone, large and deeply resonant '—and cutlery—' a glistening eight tone, still haunted by the shapes of knives, forks and spoons, that smelled like a baked dinner whenever it sang. 'Not to the dead.'

'But that is my point exactly. These bones have lost the ability to speak. You can coax music from metal and wood, so will you not teach them to sing?'

## AND THEN THE DESIGN.

*Plate: left parietal and incisors, wound with copper.*

The Necromancers did not approve of me. I would have sooner avoided them altogether, but the bones were fickle. They refused to sing from my workbench alone, and dulled my tools, slipped free of the chain and roared a disapproving cacophony in my dreams until I took them home. Back to the site of their death.

I wound wire around teeth as Casimir and I rode his carriage to the western edge of the city. He could not watch me do it. 'Must you?' he asked in a sickened, restricted voice.

'Isn't this what you wanted?' I had chipped tiny perforations into the parietal while waiting for him to arrive. The teeth, adorned now with polished copper, hooked tightly into these cracks. The song guided my hands and created its own patterns.

'Yes, but not where I have to see it.' He absently rubbed a thumbnail across his cheeks, scratching at the raised and angry looking scars. 'I have had protests. My Necromancers consider this a desecration.'

The bones did not.

They had been found on a desolate spot of land, riddled with mud and the creeping fingers of mangrove roots. Bright wards cordoned off the area: fierce UnderWatch symbols in gold swirled over lapping water, wrapped around tree trunks, and stretched fine across thin air.

The Necromancers lifted their spells for Casimir to pass through, and slammed them back down so close on my heels that the song in my head crackled. The plate vibrated, and for a moment the wards flickered. I glanced at them in surprise. The bones sung a powerful song, true, but strong enough to rattle UnderWatch spirit wards? Just what had happened to these bones?

'Is this truly necessary, sir?' A young female Necromancer fell into step beside us. Mud caked the hem of her white gown, splattered up her arms and coated her hands. Her face was red from heat and sunburn, making the scars beneath her eyes all the more prominent. 'I know you have been having difficulty of late, but we are all here to help you. We have made some progress, while you were gone these past few hours. Just send the artisan away and we will show—'

Casimir cut her off with the curt motion of his hand. She halted, bowed, but glared at me as we waded away.

'This is where they were found.' Casimir stopped at the centre of the wards. Above us, an insignia filtered hard midmorning sunlight into a softer brush of gold. 'We believe they were killed last month, just before the high tide. It's been difficult to tell. The water sucked away any evidence that could have assisted us, and it also took most of their flesh. What it left seems to have been devoured, apparently by crabs and small animals.'

We had arrived at a dry patch, the ground solid and slightly raised above the swamp. The trees around us were bare, stripped of their leaves, and coiled with rotting rope and broad, rusting chain.

'The four other bodies were tied into the trees.' Casimir pointed to four compass points, where the bark was discoloured and the chains laced thickly. 'At least, we think there were four. They were dismembered prior to being hung. Parts were missing. It was hard to tell.' The ward above us wavered slightly, as though a cloud had passed before its light, and Casimir shuddered. 'This is a hard place to die, Zvoni. We found old passages through the lower planes here, when we tried to summon their spirits. Large tracks made by ancient feet. I think this might even have been a god's death gate, and it remembers the power it once had. Bodies are older here, spirits looser.'

I couldn't even imagine such things. I would rather not. 'And my bones?'

A deep breath, and Casimir gathered his thoughts.

He pointed to the ground at our feet, the very centre of the clearing. 'Not tied to trees like the others, but half-buried.'

'I still don't understand why you need me—'

Casimir hissed between his teeth. 'Why have you decided not to trust me, Zvonimir? Now, when I need you the most?' He took a tiny blade from a pocket in his waistcoat and knelt in the mud. 'If you can't take my word then maybe you need to see.'

The blade was only the size of a large fingernail, but it shone coldly between his fingers. He pushed up his left sleeve, exposing scarred and sundarkened skin across thick muscle.

'Casimir, please—'

'No.' His expression was hard, mouth set, but in the unsteady light from the wards his eyes seemed to swim with fear. 'You need to see.'

Casimir cut fine, tiny spells into his own arm. I wanted to look away from this power born from pain, but I couldn't move. His blood dripped to the ground where it pooled into thin, distinct shapes. Something rose from their centre. Not a song, like I knew them. Not a spirit, either. A smoky, formless shade that screamed an endless 'Waaaaa!' as it grew. I pressed hands to my ears but couldn't keep out the meaningless screaming—

Until Casimir dispelled it with a flick of his blade, a single shallow cut that undid all his intricate symbols.

'There,' he said, and stood. Necromancers hurried over with white towelling to wrap around his wounds. 'Do you believe me now? Nothing I have tried will give it shape; nothing I can do will retrieve its voice. I have tried many, many times.' He pressed the cloth to his arm, and I watched it soak up his blood.

Shaking, I crouched and ran the plate — the bone and teeth and wire — across the ground. They sang, far clearer than they ever had in my workshop. At first their song was rough and uneven, like inexperienced hands across a row of large, deep bells. I knew from those notes that they would make a resonant four-tone, each tube placed like the points of a compass. But soon their song began to change. It grew terrible, broken. And it filled me. It supplanted the sunlight, the mangrove smells, the sounds of Necromancers and the power of their wards. All in pieces, disjointed snippets, discordant warbles, high-pitched screeching. Through it, I saw a shadow. Something inhuman, unreal. It stalked me, face scarred, bright blade in its hand—

And then the sunlight returned, and I was hot, and the world stank, and Casimir was frowning down at me. 'Well?' he snapped. 'Does this help? Have you got what you needed?'

I dug fingertips into the soft ground. I felt dizzy, and tired, and a distressing need to be sick. 'Give me a moment,' I rasped. Time, yes. I needed time. 'You asked me to do this. I will do it my way.'

'I did not think the construction of a wind chime would take so long.'

Something snagged on my fingers, and I pulled a strange, mesh-like object from the earth. Mangrove roots, animal bones and crab shell wound together tightly. Flat, almost circular, about as large as my palm. The song whispered, thin again. My wind catcher.

'You never took much interest in my craft,' I said.

*Clapper: Fragments of pubis and ilium, fused with imitation gold and fake opals made of glass.*

Casimir, in the dead of night, hammering against the shop door, woke me from dreams of mud and crab claws. 'Where is it?' he hissed, locked the door heavily behind him, and peered out a window into the gaslamp-lit street. 'Have you finished yet?'

'No.' The bones called from the workbench in scattered gasps of half-formed cadenzas. 'What are you doing here?'

He spun. 'What is taking you so long? Finish it!'

I realised with a shock that he was wearing a bathrobe with nothing apparently underneath it. His hair was a loose and tangled mess, like iron filings around a magnet. His eyes were bloodshot, and the skin across his cheeks rubbed raw and bloody.

I took his hands, tried to draw him close. 'Why are you here, love?' I whispered.

He shuddered and pushed me back. 'Don't call me that.'

I collected a clean cloth from a drawer beneath my workbench and held it out to him. 'You're bleeding.'

'Again?' He touched his cheeks, blinked down at the blood on his fingertips. 'I can't sleep, Zvoni. See, if I sleep, my fingers scratch. So I can't sleep. I won't.'

He did not stop me as I placed one hand on his shoulder, and with the other I held the cloth to his face. Gentle. So very gentle.

'They want me to step down, because it's not getting any better. Can't solve this case, didn't solve the last, or the one before or before. My skills are abandoning me. Spirits won't talk, some don't even rise. And I'm tired, always tired.' He was shaking, quivering beneath my hands. 'Is this old age? Zvoni? Is this what happens? Everything you used to be slipping away like unmarked time?' I threw the cloth away and embraced him, bloody face against my shoulder. 'You'll help me, won't you? They think I'm mad, coming to you. If your chimes don't work, this will be the end. My career, everything I've worked so hard for slipping out of my hands.'

There was only one way to calm him when he got like this. I guided him to my simple living quarters at the back of the shop. Kitchen and bedroom in one, with shared outhouse a little way down the alley at the back. Nothing like the grand city WatchHouse, hundreds of years old, built of marble and festooned with bright spirit wards. I'd only seen it a few times, since Casimir took its title. Mostly, I tried to avoid it.

My bed was small and heaped with blankets, difficult to fit two middle-aged men in. Still, I had practice. I laid Casimir on his side, facing the wall, and cupped myself behind him even as I drew the blankets over us. I pressed my face into his hair and breathed in his scent: sweat and blood, always, mingled with sweet hints of something rotting, something dead. A Summoner's smell. Casimir's smell.

This calmed him, it always did. I breathed loudly, drawing air enough for the two of us, reminding him that he was alive and flesh, like me, not dust and shadow like his spirits.

Here, in the dark, I had listened to him so many times. The night before he enlisted, when we were both too young to understand what war would do to him, he told me he hoped he would be killed. A bayonet was easier than this, he'd said, this *whatever we have between us*. He returned a decorated soldier, having discovered his Summoning skills in all that murder and blood. But with me, and me alone, he wept for each enemy he'd killed and each ally he could not save. Each time, it was worse. Gunpowder scars and Summoning scars and darkness like a chasm that swallowed him deeper, deeper.

*'Be grateful you know nothing of war, Zvonimir.'*

Casimir's hand crept back up to his face. I reached across the hump of his body, grabbed both wrists before he had the chance to draw blood, and held them as he muttered, again, and shook, again.

He slept, finally. I waited to be certain before I left him there, tucked him in tightly, and returned to the bones laid out on my workbench.

I looked down at my hands. Only one blackened nail, better than usual, soldering burns, notches from sharp saw teeth, chemical discoloration. My own kind of Summoning scars.

The song settled into a constant rhythm, somewhere at the back of my mind, as I took up my tools and started to work. I threaded chain through plate, added clapper, wind catcher, attached the tubes that had taken so much work to carve. The bone chime was small, after all that work, only as long as my forearm. Ugly, and strangely dark to look at.

Finished, I wrapped it in the calico it had come in, and waited out the night at Casimir's side.

*Tubes: Fibula, femur, humerus, ulna, radius. Hollowed out. Scratched with wards. Threaded with mourning bells.*

The entire league of UnderWatch Necromancers knocked on my door just after dawn. The sheer force of their disapproval disturbed the chimes in my shop and set them rattling, conjuring a mess of scents and shadowed images.

'We have come for the Watch,' the Necromancer from the murder scene addressed me with heavy scorn. 'He was not at his home, when we called. His wife appeared concerned, but after questioning she directed us here. To you. His ... *old friend.*'

I closed my eyes.

'That poor woman,' the Necromancer hissed. 'She does not deserve this. He should have kept you out of this, relinquished his post with dignity, taken up the quiet life he has earned through his years of service, not indulged in this foolish charade and his ... unnatural lusts.' She pushed past me. 'Now tell me, where is he?'

There were too many of them for my little shop. They brushed against chimes and the songs combined with my sleepless night left me feeling like this wasn't quite real. Wasn't actually happening.

'What is this?' Casimir appeared at the curtain to my bedroom: bathrobe gaping open, left cheek bleeding where he worried at a fresh scab, skin pale and clammy and great shadows beneath his eyes. 'What are you all doing here?'

'Casimir.' The Necromancer did not even try to hide her disgust. 'This must end. We have petitioned the Medium Triumvirate and informed them of your, ah, state of mind. Your inability to perform the role of Watch.'

'You what?' Casimir strode into the room, and even now he was imposing. 'How dare you!' The Necromancer took a halting step back. 'Get out of here, and we will discuss—'

'No, actually, we won't,' the Necromancer said, straightening and holding her ground. 'There is nothing to discuss. The Triumvirate are in agreement with us. Your failure to solve this case has sealed your dismissal from the post of Watch. You are to be stripped of your title, you must hand over the WatchHouse and relocate your—'

'Wait!' I collected the bone chime from my workbench, and pushed through all the white cloaks to stand beside the windows. 'But he has solved it! I mean, he will.'

Both Casimir and the Necromancer glared at me.

'I finished it.' I unwrapped calico, carefully. 'Its song is powerful. Believe me, these bones will sing.'

The Necromancer hissed at the sight of the bone wind chime. 'Foolish, sacrilegious nonsense. You have been reported too, for desecrating human remains and doing the dead gods only know how much damage to their spirit!'

But Casimir had hope in his eyes. 'You did it?' he whispered. 'Really, will it sing?'

Holding the chime out before me, I opened the shop windows, and let the breeze stream over us.

It sung a dull, hollow song. Bone really wasn't my preferred medium. But despite this, it was strong. The notes reverberated through me and around the shop, catching on every chime I had hanging, building until they surrounded us like mist. Heavy, and full of images. The Necromancers all gasped, and I allowed myself a warm flush of pride. There, let them see just what my foolish toys could do! Until shapes solidified. And we all watched as Casimir, scarred and haunted *Casimir*, eyes empty, hands bloody, drew blades down skin. Tied bodies, cut them away, left them to be dragged down into the mud and gnawed by crabs and sucked by leeches. My love. Swimming in dark spirits, covered in black wards, wreaking the worst kind of murder on this body, these bones—

Dropping the chime, I stumbled back, blind, and slammed the windows closed.

The song took its time to fade. And when the mist cleared and the sounds died and all the shop seemed hushed, muted, the Necromancers cut fresh wards into their hands. They took hold of Casimir and chained him with light, such horror and betrayal written clearer than their symbols in wide eyes and pale skin.

'I—' the Necromancer who had argued with him was shaking her head. 'I thought you were just incompetent,' she whispered. 'Not that you were hiding — not that you could—'

'No,' I gasped, stepped over the chime, reached for him. Necromancers parted around me like I was too dirty to touch. 'Tell them it's a mistake.

Tell them it's not true. It's me! I built a poor chime for you, my love. You entrusted me and I—'

But Casimir bent, and placed a long kiss on my lips. His chin was rough with his unkempt beard, and his mouth tasted faintly of blood. When he straightened, he seemed lighter. Composed. Why wasn't he fighting, struggling, denying these lies as loudly as he could? 'Thank you, Zvonimir,' he said, and smiled. 'I was right to trust you with this, after all.'

And then he was gone, surrounded by white robes and angry glowing wards.

I locked the shop, barricaded doors and latched shutters. I fell into bed, pressing my face into the bunched sheets and his smell buried so deep within them. Something hard bit into my cheek. With a frown, I sat up, and drew the blankets back.

Casimir's timepiece.

I picked it up. It ticked loudly, still warm, his heart in my hand. Slowly, I stood, and returned to the shop. I pulled out the tiny drawer I had installed beneath my workbench, and withdrew my clockwork wind chime. Built from the timepiece Casimir had given me, it tinkled the faintest of songs as I lifted it. The memory of a time when we were young.

## FINALLY, THE WIND.

On the morning of Casimir's trial I did not take the bone chime to the WatchHouse as I had been commanded to do. Instead, I took it back to the swamp where its body had died. It alone could testify to his guilt, and it would not be able to sing from its grave buried deep in cursed mud. Where it belonged.

The UnderWatch wards were still shining, but the chime broke them open with a buzz of fevered words whispered in panic and fear. I trudged to the small clearing and bent, to dig. But the wind came up, sudden and hot, stinking of rotting mud and crab shell, heavy with salt and burning spells, and even as I tried to bury them, the bone chime sang.

'*One man to defend them all.*'

I dared not look up. Mud to my wrists, but the bones would not lay still or quiet. They chimed and they rocked and they sang so strongly in my head, until I thought my skull would break with it.

'*An honour, for a soldier, to give your life like that. We drew lots, and swore to secrecy. But a tortured spirit — a dark spirit — is so much more powerful.*'

*'He volunteered. We drew lots. The first one volunteered.'*

I couldn't stop myself, the song was in my veins. 'The first one?' I whispered, and looked up.

Dark forms surrounded me, heavy shadows that did not belong in the crisp sunlight. They covered the wards, dulled them until they were nothing but etchings in smoke. Not just one tortured form, one victim, not even the four chained like the points of the compass. Many, so many. More than I could count.

*'We travelled far, for our redemption. Across god paths and through time, seeking the peace he took from us. Strange, that it would take one such as you, someone who loves him truly, who wishes him no ill, to finally seal our revenge.'*

'I don't understand.' I left the chimes half buried, and stood to face the shadows. 'Who are you, I thought Casimir killed you here, just before the tide—'

Then a single, solid figure stepped out of all the shadows, and my words faltered. Casimir, as young as I remembered him. His face unscarred, his eyes bright and not yet burdened by the secret horrors he had seen. The Casimir who had given me the watch that now hung in so many sweet pieces around my neck.

'Hello, Zvoni,' he said, and his voice was light with youth. His hair cropped and tussled. His clothes slightly dishevelled, as though he was only just emerging from sleep.

'Casimir?' I whispered, forgot the chimes, and stepped forward. But he wasn't real, not the real of flesh and bone. Just memory, just the spirit of a time and a place summoned forth by one of my wind chimes. I struggled to get myself under control. To steady the rush in my head and the pulse in my veins he always elicited. 'Why are you here? I thought you'd killed these bones, here in this spot. Desecrated their spirits and turned them dark for your own power.' That, at least, was what the Necromancers were saying. That was what they had read from my song.

'Truth is a strange thing, isn't it?' He floated forward, rested a spectral hand on my cheek. When I closed my eyes I couldn't feel it. He wasn't really there. 'Did I murder these bones in this muddy swamp a month ago? No, Zvoni, I did not.'

Hope rushed through me. 'Then we have to tell them—!'

The shadows whispered, pressed forward, and suddenly I hardly had enough air to breathe.

'Hush, my love,' Casimir's memory whispered. 'I might not have murdered them here, but I did kill them.' He glanced around at all the malevolence at his back. 'Be grateful you know nothing of war. Of the things a man must do, to survive. The sacrifices he must make to protect his homeland.' He lifted ghostly arms. 'I created these dark spirits, and you do not want to know how. What tortures it takes, to tear the light from a man's soul. Their power saved whole companies of men, their power turned the tide of battles, their power was met in turn by the dark spirits created by our enemy. But none of that pardons the horror I forced upon them.' He lowered his hands and faded slightly.

'Please—' I gasped.

'That was a long time ago. But they have come for me now, followed the paths tread by dead gods to find me here, older, weakened, ready to pay my dues. Everything has its price. Your love has cost me loneliness, their power will cost me my life.'

'You can't.' I pulled out the chime I had made from his watch and shook it in front of me. It dispelled the darkness, a little. 'I will tell them, I will make a new chime, from mangrove roots and crab shell and the gears of Casimir's heart! He is a hero, and he should not suffer now for what he was forced to do!'

'Remember, Zvoni,' he whispered. 'Everything has its price. Each slice of my knife tore into me too; each twisted soul I created warped a little bit more of my spirit. Why do you think I am here? One cannot create such horror without becoming a part of it. I have gathered these spirits, I have led them down the ancient paths for one purpose. I want peace, my love. You, who have tried so hard to soothe me, surely you would not deny me that.'

I lowered my chime and stared at him in horror. 'No.' But I remembered the look Casimir had given me, when his Necromancers took him away. He hadn't fought them, he hadn't even denied his guilt.

'You do understand.' Ghostly arms around me, soft as the warm, putrid breeze. 'I knew you would. I was right to trust you, I always have been.'

Then Casimir and his dark spirits faded.

I stood, for a long time, in that swamp, the half-buried bone chime at my feet.

When the Necromancers stormed their own wards, seized the chime and arrested me, I did not fight them either. No more arguments or sabotage or chimes. Nothing, but peace.

## AND ALWAYS BACK TO THE SONG.

The Necromancers strung him up on the stake in the WatchHouse Square, in front of his broken home, for all the city to gawk at. The body of their fallen Watchman — war hero, Summoner, family man — punished for his misdeeds. No one understood what he had done to save them, the sacrifices he had made.

I hoped he had what he wanted. I hoped he'd found peace in this punishment.

I, for one, could not go to stare at his body, the skin I knew so well, the length of his legs, the strength of his arms, all changed with death, all so wrong. Instead, I locked myself in my shop, and took apart the watch he had left me. His heart in my hands. To rebuild.

Casimir's tiny wind chime played a sadder note than mine, a deeper, minor key. But they complemented each other so well, their tunes made for each other.

I hung them both above my bed, and when the wind blew just right — from the west, heavy with a salty mangrove smell — I could feel him. Holding me.

# MAH SONG

A rain of stars heralds the descent of the Nine Lords, and the rest of my family celebrate. Mother burns fragrant handfuls of carefully preserved flowers, Father fills tiny cups of recycled tin with cheap rice wine. Later there will be sticky cakes of preserved red beans, and the entire crop of my mother's window-grown spinach served wilted, and heavily salted.

I do not join the celebrations. Instead, I go in search of Aroon. It's important to see him before the Mah Song takes him again.

He sits in his room, as he always does, plugged into a world we cannot see. Cables run like mangrove roots from dozens of sockets in his shaved scalp. They continue beneath the floorboards to intersect with the ancient optical and copper streams that twist through the ruined city.

'Aroon,' I whisper, and crouch beside him. 'Little brother.' I touch his shoulder to get his attention. 'How long before they land?' He is sitting as if in meditation, legs crossed, hands on his knees, palms up. Beneath his shirt the fan in his chest whirs gently, like calm breathing. He turns toward me and his eyes are glowing: flicking green and red numbers in his right eye, a complex array of charts in his left.

'Hello big sister,' he replies. He closes one eye and concentrates for a moment. 'Two days.' His voice is unsteady, but it's not nerves. Long gone are my little brother's childhood days, when he clung to my leg and wept each time the Lords descended. It's hard to believe he is only ten years old. He carries himself with such dignity now.

His voice is unsteady because the last sacrifice hasn't had time to settle into his body. A complex design of pins on either side of his neck, each lit by a tiny bulb of a different colour. I don't know what they do, and he has not offered to tell me yet.

My heart drops. Two days is so soon. 'Shall we walk by the river, then? I have credits enough for khanom jark. A whole one each.'

A faint smile, nothing like the grins and sticky fingers I remember so clearly. 'The taste of coconut is nothing but data,' he says. 'Chemical reactions translated by the brain.' He traces the plugs in his head. 'There's too much inside me now, to leave any space for taste. Do not waste your credits on me.' He blinks unevenly, one eye after the other. 'But that's not the point, is it? I forget, sometimes. Yes, we must walk. It's time.'

I give him the space to get ready. As he goes through the complicated process of disconnecting himself, my preparations are far more mundane. I tie back my dark hair without brushing it and change into slightly cleaner clothes. The night is humid, but the sleeves of my blouse are long, to hide the scars — old and new — across the underside of my forearms.

The result of my failed Mah Song tests.

'What shall we pray to the Lords for?'

I turn. Mother stands in the doorway, arms crossed, all her good humour gone.

'Good health,' I answer, head down. That's what the Lords are for. 'And a Mah Song to carry our prayers.'

'Or a husband?' Her tone is bitter. 'One less mouth to feed.'

I am the third of three daughters. I should have been born Mah Song — according to my mother, at least. That burden does not rightly belong to the miracle son she should have been too old to carry to term. She had me tested, over and over. My scars are ropey, like the wires the monks shoved beneath my skin when, really, I was too old and had failed too many times to try.

Aroon tells me memory is only data. The stink of the temple, the razor in a monk's wrinkled fingers, are just like the taste of coconut. If I want, I can erase them.

The inoperative nodes sewn into my arms convince me otherwise.

It's no cooler outside, but the air feels lighter. Aroon has gathered all his cables into a scarf, wound cloth around his forearms and dressed plainly. He can't do anything about his eyes, so he still draws attention. His gait is awkward thanks to a sacrifice in his hip, but at least he can walk, and enjoy the night.

Every time the Lords descend, and I take him to the riverbank for sweets, I wonder if this is the last time.

I buy substandard khanom jark and we sit beneath the bare tree branches in our usual spot to eat it — where the fence has rusted clean away, and we can dangle our feet over the river's grey water. The palm leaf it's wrapped in is dry and cracked, the coconut tastes like dust, and the sweetness isn't from sugar. Two bites, and I toss it to the monitor lizards lurking below.

'It's an energy converter,' Aroon says, pointing to the sacrifice in his neck. 'The first step towards making me self-sufficient. I've felt no hunger since it was installed, so I believe it's working.'

'It won't be long, will it?' I lean against him, and he tips his head so our temples meet. He vibrates, ever so softly. His fan. Not fear. 'Until the last sacrifice. The one where the Lords take you away.'

'Two more descents,' he answers, eventually. 'Maybe three.'

I close my eyes to the lights from the Ayutthaya slum behind us, the foaming river, and the toxic, empty lands running off to the horizon on the other side. 'But we're not ready.'

Mah Song do not live long, and they grow less human with every descent. I can't stop this, any more than I can take my brother's place, but I'll be damned if I'm going to sit back and watch him disappear before my eyes. We've worked together since he was just a very little boy to come up with a way to save him. And now, when we are so close, when we've finally found something that might actually work, the Lords are back.

He threads his fingers with mine, and I'm not sure who is comforting who. 'The data key will work, sister. It just needs repairing. Fix it up, and it will have the space to hold several small boys like me.' A deeper smile this time, almost genuine. 'Remember, we are all just data. The Lords want this body, but this body is not all I am.'

'And then what?' I whisper. 'Once we upload you to the key, what will you do? A key can't talk, or walk. A key can't hold my hand. How can you think I'd doom you to a life like—'

'We don't have any other options,' he interrupts, so calmly. 'I've been scanning, every minute of every day, tapping deep into the ruins, as far as I can access. The key is all we have. It's insane, and rotting away, but you can fix that. You know how. You know where to get the parts.'

I say nothing. No one argues with a Mah Song.

'Promise me you will, big sister. When I'm gone, look after me?' Nodding, I resist the urge to rub at the nodes in my wrists, and the freshly cut skin, taut and sore against them. Yes, I know how. I can fix all kinds of things.


Two days go by so quickly, and too soon Aroon is gone. Oh, he still sits in his room in his meditative pose, and his eyes flash so many signals in green, but he isn't with us. Not really. The Mah Song trance has taken him.

So it's time for the procession to begin.

We dress him in simple white pants. I pry away the cap that covers the fan in his chest, and loosen the thin wires that crawl across his stomach and shoulders, freeing them from the fine layer of skin that had started to grow over them. They look like tattoos — a complex pattern of colour and line.

Then Father seats him on his steel-pipe and plastic-mesh Woh, the four strongest men from the street lift him one at each corner, and he is carried from the house.

I refuse to chant and stamp and wail like everyone else. Instead, I return to his room, wait until I'm sure no one has followed me, and pick up one of his toys; a metallic lizard standing on its hind legs, spines down its back, mouth open in a ferocious expression. We dug it out of the ruins together, when Aroon had enough space in his brain for play.

I pull off the head, tip the body upside down, and the data key lands in my palm.

The data key is shiny, wiggling, and resembles an insect. A head of flicking bulbs and connectors, a golden body riddled with tiny tubes and resistors, a tail of copper and plastic-coated wire, and wings of tissue and blood.

The data key is old world tech — a complex mixture of electronic and organic circuitry, similar to the Nine Lords themselves. At least, that's what Aroon tells me. He located it after the last descent, buried deep, its signal shielded. It attacked me when I dug it out, but it rather likes Aroon. He's not too different, after all.

I pinch its body between forefinger and thumb, and it stabs wildly at me with the sharp tip of its tail. Eons trapped, all alone beneath the earth, have driven it insane. Aroon tells me not to personify it like that. The key doesn't have a mind, not really. Its organic processors have rotted away, fragmenting its protocols and ruining whatever information it once stored. That's all. It's perfectly repairable. In fact, for the past two days we have discussed, over and over, how I will do just that. Fix the key, plug it into my little brother, and he will do the rest.

Even so, I can't help but feel sorry for it.

'Phailin!' Mother calls from the street. The procession is about to begin. I wrap the key in cloth, and shove it into my pocket.

When I emerge, the Lords have filled the sky.

The Nine Lords remind me of the ruined city beneath us, except polished, clean and alive. Aroon calls them satellites and orbital stations, but these words don't mean much to me. As they hover above us they look to me like upside-down buildings and empty streets. Arches of pale steel. Engines burning like close suns. Smooth, reflective glass. Rippling liquid crystal in more colours than I have names for. Their searchlights scan over us, the beams hot and intense. Green lasers flicker across our rusting streets. They are accompanied by an ever-present hum, a taste of metal in the air, and the incense of burning plastic.

'Phailin.'

My mother waits beside Aroon's Woh. She has acquired a small huddle of tourists — an older couple, and their son. They stand out. Tall and thin where my mother is short and round, black suits with clean shoes instead loose sarongs and slippers. They have a look I know well by now: wide-eyed, slightly terrified, definitely in awe. It's the look of a wealthy tourist, caught in my mother's web.

'My daughter,' Mother tells them. 'Sister of Aroon. And almost a Mah Song herself.'

I curl my lip at *almost*. My mother does more than pray for a son-in-law, she actively hunts them. Tourists are her speciality. My two elder sisters have both left Ayutthaya in their company.

The procession begins, and the tourists' son falls into step beside me. The crowd grows as we proceed. All around us is chanting, singing, and everywhere red. Red cloth, red face paint, red candles and fireworks.

Behind me, Mother is shouting over the din. 'She came so close. Mah Song blood in her, don't you doubt it. Sadly, she's still alone. Spends all her time caring for her brother when she should be caring for a husband and child of her own.'

The tourist smiles at me. 'Philip.' He shouts to be heard, and holds out his hand. I take it only because I know Mother will be watching. He has fine, pale hair, his skin is uncomfortably pink, and his clothes are already heavy with sweat.

The procession ends at the top of the temple steps, and Aroon is set down. The monks emerge, carrying a giant pile of tech scavenged from the ruins and an array of knives. Head tipped back, not watching what he is doing, Aroon stands. Calmly, he selects what he needs to make his sacrifice. A bundle of clear cables, parts of broken circuit boards. A small, very fine knife.

Behind me, the drums start playing. Above me, the Lords start rattling. Aroon opens his mouth, grips his tongue with one hand and the knife with the other—

And I can't watch.

I look at my feet, swallowing nausea, and anger, and an overwhelming hatred for the people around me.

'Oh my God,' Philip gasps, beside me, and I shift my attention to him. I'd forgotten he was there. 'How can he do that? Doesn't it hurt?'

'When the Mah Song takes him,' I say. 'He knows no fear. No pain. No weakness.'

A moment, a pause, in which Philip presses his hand to his chest. 'Amazing.' The word escapes on a reverent rush of air.

Sprinklers open in the skies all across Ayutthaya, and the Lords' healing, life-giving waters gush forth. It's a downpour, cold compared to the humid air, at once painful and refreshing.

The tourist lifts his arms to shield his head. I grab his wrists and force them down. He's surprisingly weak.

'Let it fall on you!' I hiss into his shocked face. 'This is why you're here, isn't it? The Mah Song sacrifice to the Nine Lords, and they bless us in return. This rain is their blessing!' I release him, and draw a wet, shuddering breath.

He stares at me, blinking too much, not accustomed to the rain's sting. 'This? Yes, yes of course. I don't know what I was thinking.'

Around us, the sea of red bodies revel in the rain — singing, whirling, drinking, eating, kissing and even fucking, hidden in the tight alleyways. It is happening all along the river; nine temples for Nine Lords, a Mah Song sacrificing in front of each of them, and the people celebrating. Red electric lanterns are strung up between buildings, piles of gunpowder go up in sparks, and there is food everywhere — left out in the rain until it is sodden, disgusting, and so precious.

'It's just not what I expected,' Philip says. 'The Lords are far away. I've read all about them, I was so excited to finally see them. But now I'm here, I can hardly see anything at all.' He shrugs and looks up.

I glance at the temple. 'From here, sure. But if you are willing to make an offering you can see them closer — well, a part of them. In the shrine itself.' A plan is forming, even as I say the words. This is perfect. The shrine is just where I need to be.

Philip goes through a complicated dance to remove his shoes before I can lead him up the temple steps. He blithely makes what seems to me to be a sizeable donation of credit, and the monks are more than happy to let us in.

Inside the temple is dark, and the moment we step out of the rain and away from the noise, I begin to regret it.

I never wanted to come here again.

Numbers flicker, needles tremble, and patterns of light flash across the switches set into the walls. A bloodied table in one corner — *don't look at it* — and tech piled everywhere, all scavenged from the ruins and brought in tithes. We keep going. In my previous trips to the temple, the shrine has been empty. A great round room with an open roof, walls painted a too-perfect blue and decorated with pale masks — the sightless and impassive faces of countless children. The floor is tiled in crimson and steel, and dried flowers burn in large golden bowls.

This time, the shrine is full. The Lord above us is so massive it fills the sky, and this is its smallest part, slotted in through the hole in the roof when it came in to land. A tumble of wiring and bone, veins and rivets, skin and transistors, with several faces all merging into each other. Dials for eyes, plugs in place of open mouths. Imploring hands spread wide, palms up, holding keyboards or screens.

It could be a statue to worship, except that it is hideous. And it breathes.

'Amazing,' Philip whispers. 'It's just the way my research described it. A true bio-mechanical computer from the old world.'

'And parts of dead Mah Song,' I whisper, in reply.

This is my brother's future. Does anything of these people remain behind their empty faces and rigid hands? Can they remember the taste of khanom jark by the riverbank?

I leave Philip peering at an outstretched keyboard, and circle around the Lord until he's out of sight. The key is having a fit when I take it out of my pocket. I keep half of it wrapped, and run a practiced finger down its shivering body to open the casing. A smell like rot and the Lords' own electric haze wafts out on tendrils of smoke.

The parts I need come from the Lord itself. This is the only place to find them whole and living, not ancient and decaying. I use the key's tail to slice into the blue flesh around eyes and mouth then dig into the shallow cuts. They don't bleed. From within the Lord I pull a fine thread of pink and wiggling wire. Carefully, I slide it into the key. It squirms inside, and I repeat the process.

I'm not accustomed to this kind of circuitry. The wires I use tend not to be alive. I'm a little disturbed when all the pink wiggling things bind together, winding themselves into ever more complicated knots before pushing out the old, decomposed wiring until I can pinch and remove it entirely.

'What are you doing?'

I spin, heart in my mouth, but it's only Philip, peering down at me in his innocent-tourist curiosity. I close the key and pocket it as I stand. 'Nothing.' I smile, but I'm shaking, and it doesn't work very well. 'Have you had a good look?'

'Oh yes. It's incredible.' He still seems far too distracted by my pocket.

'Good. Let's return to the party then, shall we?'

The key feels heavy as we leave the temple, heavier than it ever was before. It's hope. Hope that my repairs have worked, hope that Aroon's right and the key is big enough to carry all of his memories and personality, so when the Lord takes his body, the rest of him can stay here with me.

But as soon as I see him, all that hope falls away. Because Aroon will never speak again.

He has split his tongue for the sacrifice and embroidered the inside of his mouth with optical fibre. Blood has dyed his once-white pants red. It colours the puddles on the temple floor around him. It will take days more to get the sacrifice just right. Days of tweaking, of bleeding, and with every adjustment, the Lords bless us.

How will I know if the data key works, if he can't tell me?


Mother is a frenzy of activity, as wild as the full river. The house is as clean as a house built of metal sheets and ancient stones can be. She is using the Lords' bounty to its full, cooking kanom-tom to snack on, cool khao chae, and half a dozen different curries. Philip and his parents accepted her invitation to dinner. I can't imagine why they would want to eat here, when they're staying in the raised tourist annex, further back from the river and accessible only by cable-car, but apparently we will make a delightful part of the tourist experience.

I don't have it in me to sit, wait, and pretend to care. Instead, I wander down the alleyways between tin-shed houses baking in the afternoon heat.

Life is springing up in the wake of the rains. Skeletal trees are green again, a thick blanket of moss softens every hard surface. Bright yellow orchids burst out of grates in the road. The land of the other side of the river has changed completely. For a few short weeks, it will be clean, and every kind of crop will flourish there. Bridges of rope and iron have been strung up across the rapidly flowing water, ready to harvest the rice, already sprouting.

This is the power of the Lords' blessing. Only yesterday, Ayutthaya was a dark slum, rusted and dead. Now, it is a forest.

This is what my brother, and the other Mah Songs, buy us with their blood.

My brother. All I can think about is the data key, still safe in my pocket. I can't imagine engaging these tourists in conversation. I can't even imagine eating. Another thing Aroon won't do ever again. No space in his head for taste, and now none in his mouth for chewing. He probably doesn't even need to. That's what those power-converters in his neck are for.

'Phailin?'

I'm so distracted, I almost walked right into him. Philip, coming the other way. He checks himself, visibly surprised, then relaxes into a smile. 'Oh — I'm so glad I saw you!' He turns and falls into step beside me.

I frown at him. 'What are you doing walking around on your own?'

'I just wanted to see the temple some more.' It's raining again, and Philip plucks at the front of his shirt as we walk. It's plastered to his chest, wet and heavy. 'I must have got lost.'

'You must have.'

'How do you stand being wet like this all the time?' Philip shakes himself as we negotiate the puddles pooling in the rusty holes and uneven dips in the pockmarked iron road. His feet squelch in those ridiculous shoes. 'I've never been so uncomfortable. And trust me, Phailin, I know about being uncomfortable.'

I turn, ready to tell him I very much doubt that, when I notice something on his chest. The rain has made his shirt transparent, and his skin is a criss-cross of scars. That stops me in my tracks. Dark, ropy lines and large, circular plugs in shiny chrome.

'Don't let anyone else see those.'

He lifts questioning eyebrows, and I nod at his chest.

'Only the Mah Song should augment themselves,' I explain, as he reddens further and does up the buttons of his sodden jacket. 'At least, that's what the monks teach us.'

'It's not exactly augmentation.' He crouches to brush away vines tangling around his ankle. 'As much as necessity.'

And that's when I realise what he is, and why he is really here. 'I've heard of people like you. But I didn't believe you existed. So sick your own doctors can't cure you. The blessing of the Nine Lords is your last resort.'

He nods. 'My nervous system is breaking down. Slowly.' He doesn't sound too sad about it. Just resigned. 'It's degenerative. Do you know what that means? It's getting worse, gradually. Inexorably. Soon, I won't be able to walk, and then stand, and then, finally, breathe.'

I swallow hard.

'It might be uncomfortable,' he continues, suddenly bright, 'but this rain is amazing stuff. Since the first shower, my hands are steady. No tremors, not even one.' He runs his fingers through the wet knots in his pale hair. 'Nano-enhanced bacterium, reprogrammed viral matter, and whole strings of hyperactive progenitor cells. No one really knows why the Lords come here to release it. I've read theories that it's a misfiring repair function designed to literally rebuild organic matter from a sub-cellular level.'

'You seem to know a lot about the Lords. For a tourist.' I can't share his enthusiasm.

'Research!' He beams at me. 'I read all about it before I came. The Nine Lords aren't the only relics, you know. There are other satellite and subterranean beings still in existence. But they're the only ones who interact with us. Don't you wonder why? What's going on, behind those faces you showed me? What could they teach us, if only we could get them to speak?'

'Actually, I couldn't care less. Your research means nothing to me. I only care that they need Aroon to cut himself, over and over, until it finally kills him. Slowly.' I take a deep breath, try to stay calm. 'Think of it as... *Degenerative.* That way you'll know how he feels.'

Silence. When I glance up, Philip is staring at me, red-faced and horrified. 'He's just a boy, isn't he? To you, I mean. Just a boy, not a sacrifice, not a saviour. Not a wonder of bio-mechanical engineering.'

'He's Aroon.' I'm having trouble meeting his eyes. I've made him feel guilty, I can see that clearly. Part of me is sorry, because of the plugs in his chest and the death that's stalking him, but part of me is so very glad. I'm not sure which part I want him to see.

'I think we should be honest, don't you?' he says, after we push our way through a crowd that's gathered to catch fish suddenly hatching in a large pothole. 'This was not my idea any more than it was yours. But we both know what's going on. Your mother wants a son-in-law. My mother wants a Mah Song grandchild.'

I gape at him. 'She *what*?'

He sighs. 'I know. My doctors have sent me here because they can't help anymore. But it's hardly a permanent solution, is it? No one knows when the Lords will descend, and the boats are few and far between. We waited here for three months before the rain of stars came, and who knows how long before we can go home again? So she's decided if we had a Mah Song of our own, if we could make them come to us—'

I'm shaking my head. 'It doesn't work that way. It's not inherited; just because Aroon is a Mah Song doesn't mean anyone else in the family will be.'

'That's not the way your mother tells it.'

'That sounds like her.' I snort a bitter laugh. 'Who's to say the Lords would come to you anyway? Have you ever seen one, before coming here? Ever danced in rain that can heal your wounds, grow forests out of nothing, and cleanse ancient poisons from the earth?'

He shakes his head.

'That's because they're our Lords, not yours. This land, this people. Our sacrifice.'

He nods. 'But I am my mother's son. She is willing to try.'

'And what about you?' I squeeze my hands into fists, digging nails into my palm. It doesn't matter, by the time we get home the rain will have healed them. 'Would you really wish that on your child? A slow death just to save yourself? One life for another?'

He just looks so damned torn.

'Could you really?' I whisper. 'If you had the choice?'

Dinner is awkward.

Late that night, when all the house is sleeping, I take a small blade and sit on the floor in Aroon's room. Light from the Lords filters in through the plastic-sheet windows in steady yellows and greens. It rained again while we were eating, and a cache of tiny geckos exploded out of the ceiling into Philip's mother's hair. I think their affection for us is waning, and I am grateful.

One life, to save another? I know what choice I would make. I've already started.

I work a node in my upper forearm free, catching the blood in an old, soiled towel. The pain is nothing, I tell myself the whole time. Just data. Even as my arm shakes. Just data.

Aroon has taught me many things. In between descents he scours the ancient networks, always plugged in, always searching. Technology and toys are his favourite things, but as his sacrifices increased and his mobility waned, I learned to do the digging and the fixing for him. I can weld the tiny limbs of tin soldiers back in place. I can paint the eyes on dolls. From soldering motherboards to healing organic filament, my skills are growing.

And I have been practising on myself.

Aroon doesn't know this. He would never agree to it.

I pull out a gory plastic and copper mess from my skin. My nodes are inert; they never responded to the Lords in the temple, no light in their bulbs or signals from my brain. But I have repaired computers centuries old. The key is older than history, and I have given it new life — all by following Aroon's instructions. Why can't I do the same for myself? So I've replaced my parts and rethreaded the wires, and sent little shocks of electricity through my palm and dripped rain into the open wounds, in the hope that something, anything, will establish the connections between node and nervous system that the monks were unable to stabilise.

But the key doesn't react to me. I shove its tail of wires in as deep into my nodes as they will go. 'Come on,' I hiss. Nothing. I don't even know what to expect. Voices from the ancient world, stored on the key, transferred to whisper fragmented and damaged in my brain? A twitch, a flicker of bulbs, anything to indicate we've established a connection?

Still nothing. Either I didn't fix the key properly, or I'm just too broken.

I pull the key free and tie the towel around the wound. Either way, it's not enough. Even if I can transfer his mind to the key, I refuse to leave Aroon alone to rot in madness in an ancient memory device. If I can get these ridiculous nodes working, then I won't have to. I will save him. No matter the cost.

I replace the towel with bandages made from torn sheets and head out into the never-dark night. Back to the temple, in search of more parts.

There's a single family making offerings before the temple, arranging junk in a small pile and burning bowls of flowers. It's odd that the monks aren't there to accept them. The family chant softly, eyes closed and bodies rocking, and take no notice of me as I kick off my slippers and climb the steps.

Aroon, of course, doesn't notice me either. He jerks as I walk past him, lifts an arm, and digs his fingers into his cheeks, wiring away the face I know and love. Right on cue, the sprinklers open.

I duck into the temple just as the rain starts — and pause. It's unusually dark inside. The switches in the walls have been dimmed and even the lights from the Lord in the shrine have gone out.

I drop to all fours and crawl forward into the darkness. Until my hand touches something soft. Warm. I feel around. An arm, a limp hand, fistfuls of cloth. I bend forward, my eyesight gradually adjusting. It's one of the monks, lying prone beneath me. There is blood from a blow to his forehead. I can't tell if he's alive.

I sit back, uncertain. I should leave, now. Raise the alarm, now. But if I do that, I won't have the chance to get back inside here, unsupervised. The throbbing pain in my arm is insistent. I must do what I came here to do, and fix myself, so I can help my brother. Worry about the monks later.

But as I reach the shrine, I begin to hear noises. The scratching of metal and muttered curses. I creep closer.

It's Philip. Philip, naked from the waist up, examining the body of the Lord. Illuminated in the faint light from a single lamp, the plugs in his chest are ugly, ungainly things, and have none of the smooth beauty of Aroon's sacrifices. They poke out, the skin around them red and irritated, criss-crossed with stitches and staples.

I'm so shocked I just stand there, and he sees me.

'Phailin?' He looks tired. Great shadows haunt the skin beneath his eyes, his cheekbones are stark, ribs clear to see. I had not realised how thin he was before. 'Why do I keep running into you?'

'What are you doing to the Lord?' I hiss, and take a shaky step forward.

He lifts a gun and points it at me. 'Don't move.'

We had never found guns. Maybe Aroon didn't look for them, or maybe they'd all been found and removed long before we were born. Even so, I know what one is. And what it can do. 'Philip, don't—'

'Just stay where you are. Don't interfere.'

I glance back over my shoulder. 'The monks?' I whisper. 'Was that you? Did you—?' I can't believe it. I can't even say it. Philip, who smiled so readily at me, who was so eager to see the temple, who read so much about the Lords he was desperate to see—

Suddenly, something doesn't feel right. 'Wait.' I hold his gaze and he narrows his eyes at me. 'So eager to get into the temple, all that research? You said the Lords have the technology to cure you.' I gesture at the Lord. 'Is that why you're really here?'

'You were right, of course,' he says, mouth a firm line and expression unreadable. 'About the unlikelihood of a Mah Song child. It was the desperate plan of a desperate mother, and the only way I could think to convince her to bring me here. She would never have agreed to the truth.' He runs his free hand across the Lord's closest face, and I realise it's the one I cut. 'I have, indeed, done my research. And when I saw that little brother of yours, bloodied and pain-free on the top of the steps, I knew I was right. Only the Lords can save me. And not with their fickle rain but their technology. Their very selves.'

Knives taken from the monks' testing table lie on the ground at his feet. I think I know what he has in mind. The same thing as me.

'But now that I'm here,' he continues, and begins to sound uncertain, 'it's nothing like the diagrams.' His fingers still on the tiny incision I'd made. He turns to me. 'Actually, come here.'

My hand is over my pocket, where the key and knife are hiding, but he's watching me so closely I don't dare try to grab them. Not yet. 'You fix me,' he says. 'I saw you do it, here before. To the data key.'

I must look as shocked as I feel, because he smiles, grimly.

'Did you think I wouldn't see? That I was too awestruck to notice you fix it, or that I was just a foolish tourist and wouldn't know what it was? I told you, I've done the research. I know a data key when I see one. Old world tech. Just like your Lords. So you can do the same for me. Take what you need out of the Lord, and fix me.'

'Fix—?'

He shakes the gun at me. 'I suggest you work faster than that.'

As I approach the Lord, I gesture at Philip's chest. 'I'm not even sure what those things are supposed to do. How can I fix them?'

He places a faintly quivering hand over his plugs. 'They feed immune suppressants and stabilising neural charges straight into my spine. They don't fix the problem, just maintain it. They also hurt like hell and are constantly getting infected. Unlike your little Mah Song out here, I don't have a Lord to dull the pain.'

I look down at the ugly blades scattered across the floor. 'I don't think I can help you.' 'What?'

I pull back my sleeve and unwind my bloody bandages. 'It won't work.'

'What are you doing?' Desperation in his voice now. A dangerous sound.

'I've been trying to do it too.' I hold out my ruined arm. 'My mother wanted me to be a Mah Song, but I failed her. Over and over, I failed her. But I've been trying to fix it. With everything Aroon's taught me, with all the parts he's found and now, tonight, I was coming here to do the same thing you are. Wire myself with living technology.' I let my arm fall, and blood dots the floor. 'But I don't know how. You say we've lost the knowledge and only the Lords' have it now. Well, they haven't chosen to share it with us. They chose my brother in his pain- free trance instead. And we just have to accept that.'

Philip stares at me, unable, unwilling to comprehend. 'But—'

I understand, oh how I understand.

'Well then.' He spins, stares back out of the temple. 'Maybe he can help me instead.' He rubs at his chest and shakes his head. 'Just have to wake him up, right?' He stoops, collects a knife, and heads out of the shrine. 'Let's see just how pain-free this trance really is!'

'No!' I run after him, but my feet tangle in the tech on the floor and I trip. Even as I fall I grab at his legs but cannot get hold.

He staggers. It's easy to forget how weak he is. He slips to his knees, twists, points the gun at me and fires. But he's unsteady, and he misses. Instead, the bullet goes straight into one of the Lord's stolen faces.

For a moment, there's nothing but the ringing of the shot, then silence.

Until the Lord begins to move. A great shuddering fills the temple. The remaining eyes open, the hands flex, those plug-filled mouths twitch and begin to scream. I grip my ears. It's piercing, so loud, too loud, not only coming from the faces in the shrine but above us, around us. The Lord is screaming. It is full of anger, and of pain, and a desperate confusion. And why wouldn't it be? How much of the Lord is made up of Mah Song, and how much of the Mah Song remains within it? Children, all of them, frightened, modified children.

Philip scrambles to his feet and I follow. Tears pour down my cheeks, the Lord all rage and fear around me. I don't care about the gun anymore. Let him shoot me, it can't feel worse than this. So I leap onto his back and knock him down. I straddle him, grab his arm and beat the gun out of his grip. He's too weak to fight me without his weapon.

I grab a large piece from a scavenged engine and lift it above my head. But even as I look up, there's a figure in the doorway. Small, thin, silhouetted against the light from outside — flashing red now, a sky full of furious Lords — and instantly recognisable. Aroon.

Maybe the Lord is too busy screaming to keep Aroon in his Mah Song trance? Maybe the bullet damaged some vital piece necessary to create the trance to begin with? Either way, the boy that stands in the doorway is free. I can tell, instantly, just from the way he holds himself. He's human again.

I drop the engine and stagger over to him. He wraps his arms around me and I hold him close. He's shaking and bleeding all over me, but he doesn't hold me for long. He pulls back, takes my hand, and leads me to Philip.

Aroon can't speak, so he gestures instead. Philip's trying to stand, I push him down again. 'Please?' he gurgles. 'Hurts.'

I roll him onto his back. His plugs did not survive the struggle well — they've been pulled out of alignment, the red skin around them torn, leaking blood and clear, infected pus.

More hand waving from Aroon — desperate, hurried, fearful — and I run outside, to the pile of wires and blades and needles he's been using to sew himself with. I gather them all, barely noticing the chaos below. The Lords are sitting lower in the sky, their vents closed, sirens and lasers and lights beat down instead of rain. The streets are full of people, all heading for the temples, but no one is dancing. We don't have much time. Whatever Aroon is doing, he has to do it quickly.

I pass him his tools. His mouth moves but the noises that come out aren't words. The fibres sewn into his cheeks stretch in what I hope is a smile.

I help him, alternating between holding Philip down, finding Aroon what he needs, and completing the delicate tasks his fingers struggle with. With fibres, wires, nodes, circuit boards and organic matter taken from the screaming Lord itself, we open up the poorly made plugs in Philip's chest. It looks like a terrible mess to me, but Aroon seems to know what he's doing. He did something similar to himself once, to install that fan.

As we rewire Philip, I whisper to him. 'Shh there, you're okay. Just a little more.' I try to be soothing. 'It's what you wanted, isn't it? The technology of the Lords to fix you?' After a while I'm not sure he can hear me anymore. Blood pools around us; my arms are slick up to my elbows. 'We're all just data, after all.'

When Aroon and I have finished, Philip's plugs are completely different. They lie flush against his chest, and they're wired into his heart, lungs and spine with the Lord's organic filament.

Aroon sits back, and holds out his hand. But I shake my head. 'I don't know if I did it properly,' I whisper. 'I don't know if I fixed the key right. What if it doesn't work?'

He doesn't move. Is that trust in his ruined face?

Voices outside, the temple shuddering, and I know we don't have any time left. So I prod at the skin around the edge of his fan, to the hidden plug there. The one he made himself, not under the influence of the Mah Song. It's different from the rest of his sacrifices. Rusty copper tipped with green.

I slot the key in. For a moment, nothing seems to happen. Then Aroon closes his eyes, tips back his head, and the key flutters, flashing. Alive.

It pops back out on its own. It's warm, and solid, and still.

No time for doubt. People in the doorway, voices shouting, shadows and fitful light. I spin and slam the key into one of the plugs in Philip's chest, as Aroon stands, and walks calmly into the shrine.

He never comes out again.


I lost track of Philip in the chaos — the monks from other temples, the sirens and the screaming and Aroon, choosing to destroy himself to repair the Lord. Someone dragged me away, so at least I didn't see him in the very end. It hasn't rained since, and barely enough food has grown to feed us. Already, there have been fights, and an entire neighbourhood poisoned by freshly dried rice.

The wounded Lord called a new Mah Song before it ascended. A tiny girl — she looked as young as three — who cried as they carried her in a terrible and solemn procession to have her first incisions made.

The tourist ships have left, following the river back out to sea. My mother disowned me. And now, I scavenge a poor living on the tech I can dig out of the city below. I still remember the places Aroon sent me, and I will forever keep the skills he gave me. But there isn't much of a market for toys, and some weeks, I am forced to beg for what food I can. On the riverbank, where we used to walk, where we planned a way to help him escape. Aroon, my little brother and Mah Song. Gone.

Empty and alone, I sit at our usual spot, my legs dangling over the river. The lizards watch like they are waiting for me to fall in.

Then a man sits beside me. At first glance, I don't recognise him. He has a heavy cloth wrapped around his head, and bare feet. Then he hands me khanom jark. 'I know it's only data,' he says, smiling. 'But I've missed the taste of coconut.'

# SHADOW OF DROUGHT

Jim was the first to touch it. So it was like a horror movie, right, when he was the first to go.

The thing stood in the middle of Patersie's back paddock like it was a shadow. Narrow head and long arms; spaghetti fingers and stretched bony legs. Feet flat on the ground like cow pats and six toes without nails. Strangest thing was the body. Had a waist, it did, and hips, and two different shaped tits with these huge, saggy nipples.

Made me squirm to look. Made me want to cross my arms over my chest and thank Christ it didn't have anything, you know, down there. That woulda been too weird.

Jim went right up, and with a smirk, he grabbed the right tit. I'm sure that's what did it. That's what doomed him.

'What are ya doing?' Emily yelled.

At the same time, Nathan said, 'Mate! What's it made of?'

And Rob at the back just laughed his head right off.

'Dunno.' Jim kept fiddling with the nipple. Tugging at it. 'Some kinda metal. It's all, like, dented.'

'Bumpy?' Emily asked.

'Close enough.'

'Leave it.' I crossed my arms. 'Will you stop it?'

'Aw, what you worried about, Lou baby?' Jim grabbed both tits and pretended to squeeze them. 'Don't you like it?'

Another bout of laugher from Rob.

'Come on!' I snapped. 'You don't know what it is or what it's doing here.'

'Just some yuppie wanker's idea of art, isn't it,' said Nathan as Jim mimed humping the figure from behind.

'On Paterson's farm? Give me a break.'

'Why don't we ask him?' Emily suggested. 'Find out what it's for.' Jim leered at me as he straddled his dirt bike. There was something dark on his hands as though paint had rubbed off the statue-thing. 'You wanna ride with me this time, Lou?'

Couldn't say which was more disgusting. Him or the black stuff.

'Oy, mate.' Nathan tugged his hat down tight over his ears. 'Your hands.'

'Aw, shit.' Jim wiped his jeans, but his palms remained dirty. 'Fuckin' stuff.'

'From the statue, you think?' Emily had already perched behind Rob. Couple of blonde streaks were plastered in sweat down her cheeks, curling to touch the tips of her lips. Always wore makeup that one. Even for a ride down the back of Patersie's farm. Rob watched her over his shoulder with a kind of hunger like she was a big char-grilled steak. Same look, I swear.

'Yeah, what else would it be from?'

'It's not on your clothes though,' I said.

'So?' Nathan yawned and stretched his shoulder until it clicked.

'So that's weird, isn't it?'

'Yeah, real fucking spooky.' Jim gave up on his hands. 'You coming or what?'

'Not with that shit everywhere.' I jumped onto the back of Nathan's bike.

'Great.' Nathan clicked his shoulder again but didn't tell me to get off. I mean, I wasn't Emily: no makeup and tight jeans and those stupid singlet tops that got her shoulders burnt. But I was a girl, right? And better than none.

'Fair 'nough.' Jim shrugged.

At least Nathan stuck to the roads; Jim bounced wildly through the dry fields, howling down the dips of a dry creek bed, flattening thistles and grass in his path. In the distance, a lone cow raised her heat-stricken head and moaned. There weren't many left. Paterson had sold most. Couldn't afford to feed and water them. The sheep had suffered worse though; the farm was littered with the bleached bones and tangled wool of desiccated corpses.

The farmhouse was an oasis of green in a painting of brown land and blue sky. That was Carol's doing, Patersie's wife. Don't know how she did it, where she got the water and soil from, but she kept her plants alive.

Patersie's son was watching an unsteady donkey drinking from the trough as we rode in. George was the eldest, and he looked like it: thin shoulders hunched, head down, hand loose on the rope. He looked like an old man: no longer the kid that had finished school with us a few weeks ago.

'George, mate!' Jim leapt from his bike and ran beside it, holding the handlebars until it stopped.

George glanced at us in turn, face serious. Stubble over his cheeks and chin was just another thing that made him look old. His gaze settled on Emily as she dismounted and stretched her back. 'What're you guys doing here?' he asked.

'Checkin' out the artwork, Georgie boy.' Nathan waited for me to get off first and had to kick the rusted stand hard before it would support the bike.

'Whatdya mean?'

The donkey looked up mournfully. One of its eyes was missing, the flat lid closed over, and once-long lashes lay dry against its cheek. 'The statue,' Jim said. 'The one with the big titties. Whose idea is that mate? Did you rent yourselves out to the city wankers? Better than watching cattle die, ay?'

George shook his head. 'Don't know anything about a statue.'

'Someone's gone and put one in your dad's back paddock. Come out with us? We'll show ya.'


Said it was like a horror movie, right? Well, when we drove back to that paddock, and the fuckin' thing was gone — not moved, gone — then I knew something bad was going on. Could feel a creep at the back of my neck like someone with a fat-arse camera was right behind me, filming me being all innocent and not knowing we were all about to die in nastier and nastier ways. Yep, it felt just like that.

'Ain't got time for your bullshit.' George thought we were making fun of him, and I couldn't blame him. There was nothing left to prove the bitch ever existed, except the black paint that wouldn't rub off Jim's sweaty palms.

'The fuck?' Nathan spat into the dust as we watched George drive his rusted-up dirt bike away. 'Where the fuck did it go?'

'Maybe we imagined it?' Emily said, helpful as ever.

'What's that on Jim's hands then?' I rolled my eyes at her, but she wasn't looking. 'Let's just get out of here.'

'Yeah,' Jim muttered, still wiping his hands on his jeans.

Had enough of paddocks that day. We went back into town and sat beneath the old railway bridge. Jim tried cleaning his hands under the tap in the RSL park, but all it did was smear the black stuff up to his elbows. Wasn't much else to do, so we sat in the shade of the broken train tracks till it was late enough to go home for dinner.

But I still had that feeling, and it wouldn't let me sleep. The ceiling fan clicked with every bloody rotation, yet no air flowed in from the open window.

Then something outside moved. Without bushes to rustle, it scuffed the dirt, but I heard it clearly. A footstep, slow and dragging. Then another. I sat up, pushed off the single thin sheet, turned and looked into the street-light and heat haze of night. Into the statue's featureless face.

Blank and dark, mottled with finger-print indents, it stared down at me. No eyes, nothing, but I could feel it look, feel it think. I wondered what had made those shuffling footsteps, had it moved those six-toed feet?

I leapt from the bed, crashed to the floor, and scrambled backward. Trick of the light or something, but I swear it turned its head; I swear it followed me. I ran from my bedroom, out the front door, and around the side of the house. But the earth in front of my window was undisturbed. The night was calm and hot. So I thought, for one stupid moment, that Emily had been right, and we were imaging all this.

Until I saw the six finger-sized holes in my fly screen. And when they told me Jim was dead.


They brought us in to see his body, which wasn't normal either. Since when do you show a bunch of kids their dead friend? Emily began crying, and Nathan looked so white I thought he could have been dead, too. Only Jim wasn't pale and cold-looking like the bodies in the cop shows. They had him laid out on the same kind of metal table, but he was all black. Black like the shit that had covered his hands and arms. Black like the statue. He was as thin as it too, as though he had wasted away overnight to become nothing but bones and black.

Christ, he could have been a statue himself. With his hands splayed and his face flat, nose a crumpled wreck and eyes gone.

All I could do was stare. Then a copper or a ranger in a dusty brown uniform stood beside me and peered through the glass. 'Don't suppose this reminds you of something?' he asked.

Rob let out a dry, desolate chuckle.

I looked up at the copper or whatever he was. His eyes were hidden behind shades, and the rest of his face lacked expression. 'Do you know about the statue?' I asked him, certain he did.

'Who gives a shit?' Nathan spat out the words, and Emily hiccupped.

I ignored them. 'Do you?'

The guy looked down at me. His eyebrows rose above his shades, and his lips pinched like he wanted to be sick. 'Ah,' Was all he said. 'Shame.'

'Shame? What's a shame? The statue? Have you seen it too?'

The copper walked away. His shoes echoed off the hospital walls.

'Fuck was that?' Nathan spoke into silence. 'Who gives a shit, Lou? Jim's dead! Are you so stupid you don't know what that means?'

But I did know; I was certain. Better than the rest of them. Means if this really was a horror movie, we were all next.

They buried him in the Catholic cemetery outside town, and I didn't want to go. Firstly, because Jim didn't believe in anything; he wouldn't have given a shit which side of the fence he lay on. Second, and more importantly, because Patersie's farm was on the way, and that was where Jim had met his fate, where we had found the statue.

Of course, I had no choice. If Mum didn't kill me for staying home, Nathan would have.

Middle of the day and dressed in black was hell. Emily hadn't stopped crying the whole week, and she sniffed and sobbed behind me as we watched them lower Jim. Near the whole town had come to see him off, as if most of them had given a shit when he was alive.

I picked up a rose from the wilted pile and tossed it into Jim's grave. It landed softly on the white wooden coffin and rolled to lie against the dirt. When I stepped back, I looked up and saw them there on the hillside. Tall and thin and blacker than a silhouette against the sun: two statues like long shadows cast on the sky. I backed into Rob, who swore at me under his breath. I tugged on his dark jacket and whispered. 'Do you see them?'

Nathan cast me a furious, filthy look.

'Up there.'

No one else looked, just us. Just Nathan and Rob and Emily and me.

Emily whimpered; it wasn't much different from the noises she had been making all week, so no one paid attention.

The statues wavered in the heat; they flickered and seemed to move.

'Two of them,' Nathan whispered, voice rough. 'Where'd the second one come from?'

'Where'd they both come from, you mean.'

Most of the faces around us were as dry as the ground. Sad and serious. Jim's mum threw her rose in. She didn't cry, even though this was the second son she'd lost in as many years. Jim's older brother had killed himself with the gun he used to hunt rabbits. Drought, everyone said at the time. Does it to some men. They had the same expressions then, that sad and serious but strangely accepting look.

I watched as Jim's mum looked down at her son's coffin. What was her name? Janice. She'd always just been Jim's mum to me. She mouthed something I couldn't hear, but I swear she said thank you.

When I looked up, the statues were gone.

All too suddenly, the ceremony was over, and the town filed out of the cemetery, whispering quietly and wearing those serious faces, all going back to Jim's mum's house where she would serve lamingtons and lemonade from a sachet.

'You coming?' Nathan asked.

I shook my head.

'Suit yourself.'

I'd wondered why Nathan let me off so easy until I saw him drape an arm around Emily's shoulders. Figured. Rob couldn't care less who went where and didn't notice when I failed to follow.

I climbed the hill as the coal train rattled past the mourners on the road. Same time every afternoon it came, full and dark and loud where everything else was so bright and quiet. Once I got to the spot where the statues had been — or as close to it as I could tell — I looked back at the cemetery. Workmen were filling in Jim's grave. Swear I could hear each drop of sandy dirt.

There was nothing on the ground to prove the statues had existed. Just like Patersie's paddock and the dirt below my window. But that wasn't why I was here. I had seen enough movies and knew what to do.

'Right, I'm alone now.' I closed my eyes and began to turn slowly, trying for a kind of slow-motion look. 'Followed you and now I'm looking the wrong way. You see that? Better be careful, ay? You just might be right behind me.'

I turned the full slow circle and opened my eyes. The statues were there. Further away than I expected, had thought they'd be right threatening at my back. Instead, they stood on the other side of a boundary fence, the one that separated Patersie's farm from crown land or whatever the cemetery was on.

'Like Paterson, don't you?' I took a step toward them. Was impossible to tell if they moved or if it was just the heat making them wavy. Clouds had begun to streak in behind them, thin and high. 'Why do you like him? Did he bring you here? What are you, some kinda curse?'

Waves of grasshoppers flicked through the grass before me, but my gaze remained fixed on the statues. They couldn't move, I was certain, if I was watching them. Wasn't that the way it always went?

I could see more, the closer I got. The second statue was smaller, and it was a boy. It had something as horrendous as the bitch's long tits between its legs, something gross and freakish and wrong. It leaned against the first statue, it cupped, it held, and I realised with horror rising from my stomach that I had seen that before. Looked just like Jim had, when he had fondled those disgusting tits, except the statue was thin and out of proportion and wrong. All of it was just wrong.

A car screeched on dry gravel. I couldn't resist looking to see a white Holden without a licence plate come to a sudden dust-cloud halt on the rough road the other side of the fence. That copper got out, the one with his shades and his beige uniform. He looked at me, and I glanced quickly back to the statues before realising they had gone.

The cop pointed toward the town. He stood like that, in the sun as the dust cloud settled, until I headed home.

That night, I sat on the edge of my bed and stared out the window. I'd gone looking, hadn't I? All alone. So the statues had to pay me a visit, and it would be stupid to try to sleep. Would be like a sitting duck.

Instead, Emily rang. My mobile flashed bright and vibrated loud on my bedside table. I jumped, grabbed it, and flicked it open.

'Em?' What time was it? I blinked blearily at the digital clock. 2AM.

'Lou.' Her voice was soft, breathy. 'I can see him.'

'What? Who?'

'Jim.'

Something moved at my window. I spun from the bedside table, but nothing stood on the other side of the broken screen. Clouds rolled in the distance, building high in the moonlight; but rain wouldn't fall — it hadn't come in so long.

'What do you mean, Em?' I recalled that second statue, standing so much like Jim.

Something moved again — another rustle against dirt. I approached the window, phone shaking as I pressed it tight against my ear, and Em breathing.

'He's outside my window. All dark. Outside my window and all dark.'

'That's not possible.' I peered outside, down to dry earth and hydrangea corpses. Nothing. 'Jim's dead.'

Why had I said that? Just sealed her fate, didn't I.

'I know.' More breathing and then scraping. Something hard against wood. 'I know, but he's here. And Lou ...'

'Em?'

'He's not alone.'

The phone dropped out. I took it from my ear, stared out into the night, and realised what I'd heard. Not footsteps on earth but rain. Huge, fat drops.


'They watching you, too?' Rob wasn't laughing any more. Not since we'd watched Emily's coffin lowered into the same earth as Jim, and the statues had returned to the same hill. Three of them this time. Nathan hadn't said a word since then, and it almost seemed Rob was filling his silence.

We sat beneath the old railway tracks watching the drizzle. Rain pooled in potholes, and mites kicked across the surface. It had rained constantly since Emily had died. Heavy for days, then showers, and now nothing but drizzle.

'Are they?'

I nodded. Jim's mum and Emily's mum were always together now. Whenever I passed them, both would look up and watch me. Every face in town wore their expressions: sad, serious, resigned. Even Mum and Dad. All but kids younger than us and the retired couple who had just moved up from the city.

'Soon,' Nathan muttered. 'I'm next, and it will be soon.'

I wasn't about to argue with him. I knew it was the truth. 'Going to pick us off one by one.' Kids like us never got away, not in the movies nor the books. Creepy statues and a freaky town and each of us dying one by one. Yeah, I knew where this was going. Only thing missing was the sex. I glanced down at Nathan ... or maybe I just wasn't the one who'd had it.

'It's all his fault.' Nathan sunk his head into his hands. 'Jim shouldn't have touched it. Emily died and we're going to die, all of us. Because of him.'

'Selfish.'

Together, we looked up. George stood in the rain. Lank hair and thin beard plastered to his face. He looked more tired than the last time, with great big shadows under his eyes like someone had punched him. But there was more to it than that. He looked like someone who had seen ghosts, someone who was haunted.

'Selfish,' he said again. He seemed to be looking at us, but with his eyes like that, I wasn't sure he was talking to us, not even certain he was seeing. 'What's more important? That slut? You lot, useless sitting around all day not helping no one, or the rest of us? This town?'

'The fuck you say?' Nathan leapt to his feet. 'She's dead mate, dead! Have some respect!'

I didn't see the point in arguing. George was kinda right. Em was one of those girls who always gets knocked off early on in the movies, and we all know why that is. And yeah, we had no jobs to go to, no father's farms to look after, nothing much to do. Wasn't our fault the town was so dead that no one was hiring. Still, couldn't say he was wrong.

Rob seemed to agree with me and just raised his thick eyebrows.

'You got my respect.' George spat into a puddle. 'You got everyone's. And why? Cause you were just lucky. Stumbled on it, don't even understand what it is. You get more respect than me just because you're dying off. Hardly fair.'

Nathan pulled back. Recoiled is the word. 'What?'

George looked at him like he was an idiot, then included us all. 'You don't know? For real?' He lifted a hand, cupped the rain that was splattering on it. 'Town loves you guys, town's real fucking grateful.' Then he flickered his hand at us. 'And you're all too stupid to get it.' He turned, splattering mud up his jeans, and marched away. Swear he stepped in every puddle like a kid with gumboots.

'Fuck's up his arse?' Rob muttered. I nodded.

Across the street an old couple walked without umbrellas or coats or anything. They watched us, too, and I realised all this watching they were doing, it wasn't nasty. They didn't hate us, it was just like George had said. Town fucking loved us. Town was fucking thankful.

And that was worse.

Nathan watched George go in open-mouth silence.

'Christ.' He stood, stepped into the drizzle and lifted his palms to catch what was left of the fine drops. Then he laughed, tipped his head back and opened his mouth to the water. 'It's been so long, hasn't it?' He squeezed his eyes closed and grinned widely. 'Since we've had so much rain.'

Couldn't remember a time like it.

Nathan left us with the smile on his face. I knew the moment he died that night — the flash of lightning and the splatter of water beneath my window — it was then.


'I'm not going without a fight,' Rob said as we watched Nathan's coffin being driven in a long, muddy, black hearse through the streets. 'I say we get out of here.'

'Yes.'

The town followed his body, but all eyes were on us as we sat beneath the shelter of the train tracks. No one carried an umbrella. Their mourning clothes were soaked through.

But how?'

Not everyone followed the hearse. A small group of farm hands had stationed themselves on the other side of the street. They stood just beyond the awning, in the puddles and pouring rain, eyes trained on the two of us. George stood at the front of the group, arms tightly crossed, gaze sharp. And that copper or park ranger or fucking creepy-statue follower was there also, a little to the side.

'Not going to let us leave,' I murmured.

Rob stood. He dusted flecks of damp wood from the back of his jeans. 'Together. We'll leave together.' Then he stepped into the street and joined the stragglers.

I hesitated for a moment, not wanting to walk in rain bought with the death of my friends. But Rob was right; we had to get out of there. So I followed, splashing. George, the copper, and the farm hands trailed us.

The road out of town ran along the train tracks. They stretched shiny in their slickness off into the misty distance. Rob eased his way from the road, through tall grass and stones, as close to the tracks as he could manage. I understood instantly.

'Coal train,' Rob whispered. The hearse was slowing, faces turning toward us. I glanced at the sun. Early afternoon. Had we missed it? Would it come today? The coal train had thundered through every afternoon since the new tracks had been built. Why would today be different? 'Get ready.'

'This isn't going to work.' Because we were doomed anyway, and the poor fools who tried to get away were always killed in the end. Maybe we should have accepted it like Nathan did, with a smile. Taken the rare thanks and respect while we could.

'Then stay here, and let them kill you.'

I stuck close to Rob's back. Was there really any chance this might work? Hopping on a moving train to safety sounded like a fucking disaster. But we would die here. Die for a reason. Die to help so many people scraping by on so little. How many suicides could a little rain prevent? Whose lives could we save?

Sure enough, just in fucking time, a train sounded. The blast of a horn and shattering of light through the rain. The funeral procession stalled.

'They know,' I hissed at Rob.

He was watching the train. 'Be ready.'

'This is crazy!' One way or the other, I knew I was going to die, by train or statue. Flattened or turned to rain.

George ran for us. The train was suddenly so close. The copper drew a gun and shouted, but I couldn't hear him. The funeral procession became a crowd that surged from the road like ants wearing sad and serious masks. My mum was there and my dad. They reached for me with all the rest, to hold me here until I died.

Even them. I realised I didn't want to die for a town that cared so little about me, about Rob and Emily and Nathan and Jim, that it would happily sacrifice us for a few drops of precious rain. My life was not less worthy than Jim's older brother, than all the other farmers and farriers and truck drivers and shearers and more whose lives depended on the clouds.

My life was mine. I could earn more respect with my life than I could with my death.

Then Rob wrapped his hands around my waist. He was always a bigger man than I realised. His silence, his stupid school-boy humour, made him seem small. He lifted me and angled me toward the oncoming train.

'Grab on!'

Hands tugged at his wet arms and shirt. The train rushed by, screaming its horn at us. My hands smacked into the rails on the side of coal carriages, and I screamed too, but my fingers wrapped around one, and the train tore me from Rob's grasp.

Dangling, rain slicing into my face and eyes, I turned to see Rob lunge for another carriage, but he was swamped by townspeople and couldn't jump high enough. I swear, above the rain and the rush of air, I heard his head smack against the flying steel. Then he fell, and the hands and the bodies and the mud swallowed him up.

I clung to the railing at my elbow, arm hooked around. My hands throbbed and fingers swelled and turned a kind of purple.

The further the train went the lighter the rain became. When it fell away, I looked back to the single, tall, unnatural tower of clouds above the town and the fields of all those that lived there. Lightning flickered within it.

Could the statues take Rob now? Did it count if they hadn't killed him?

I held on as the afternoon turned to heavy, red twilight. We neared a station, and the train slowed to pass through. I threw myself to the grass and lay gasping dust and dry seeds.

I sat up, cradling hands, turned to watch the train disappear — and saw them on the hill.

Five statues in the distance. Tall, thin, and black.

The broken fingers in my lap darkened as I caught the scent of rain.

# SANAA'S ARMY

Sanaa was lying face down against the threadbare carpet when the doorbell rang. She drew one final, deep breath, savouring the many-layered scent of death rising from the basement, and gradually sat up. From their smell, she could predict, to the nearest inch, the thickness of flesh or fur on the carcasses beneath her. Not enough clean bones. Not yet, anyway.

Her kneecaps took advantage of the movement to flee, hiding somewhere in her hips. Her femurs rallied in response, stretching and bulging to fill the gap. It made standing difficult.

*Cat Box, At Christmas* dragged itself toward her. One of her earliest works: a cat's skull with a wire neck, a shoebox body filled with flickering Christmas lights, rib-cage legs and a battery pack tail. It was a good pet, always tried to help even though it wasn't much use. As long as she remembered to change the battery.

Sanaa struggled to her bare, misshapen feet and shuffled down the hallway, clinging to the walls for support. She pulled up the hood of her dark jumper, shook her long fringe loose and tightened the drawstrings to hide as much of her face as possible.

She opened the door to three dirty children, carrying a large cardboard box between them.

Oh, how they smelled of death. The not-too-fresh odour of whatever offering they carried, and the lingering touch of their own, slow decay. The inevitable shortening of hard little lives.

'We found something for you, miss,' the middle one said. A girl, maybe twelve.

Sanaa smiled as best she could. She liked it when they called her miss. 'Alice, isn't it?' she asked. The girl nodded. 'Don't know these two.' Sanaa leaned forward and sniffed at them.

Alice swallowed visibly. 'This one here's Matt.' Another boy, about the same age, gaunt and empty as a shell. 'The little guy's Pete.'

Sanaa stepped back to let the children in. Their smell wrapped around her, stronger than usual. There was something odd about it, a depth that did not belong to their living flesh, even flesh as starved and abused as theirs.

Artworks reached out from their canvasses on the wall as the children walked down the hallway. Lonely fishbone fingers stretched; thick layers of oil paints undulated; seashell castles with insect kings rattled. Sanaa chided them silently — they were bored, locked away in her dark townhouse, but it wasn't polite to scare the children. Alice knew to keep her head down, not to encourage them. The little one gawked, open-mouthed, at every single moving bone. The older boy hardly seemed aware of anything, and Sanaa focused her breathing there. The smell definitely came from him.

'Put it down,' Sanaa said, patting the table top with her crooked hand, as they entered the kitchen. She didn't have much food, didn't eat much. But the kids weren't fussy. She found them milk still within its expiration date, clumpy chocolate powder, frozen bread and Vegemite.

'Move to the other end of the table,' she instructed. 'Don't eat near dead things. It isn't healthy.'

She left them to their reward, and lifted the lid on the box they had brought. Several pieces of dead animals, each at a different stage of decay. An electrocuted fruit bat, a couple of rats, severed wings complete with feathers. A possum — by far their best find. It had been dead a while, the tail was gone, some of the vertebrae too, but skull and claws and hind legs all remained intact.

'It's good, right, miss?' the girl — Alice — asked. 'We did good this time, didn't we? Better than usual, even?'

Sanaa glanced down the table. Was the child actually attempting to engage her in conversation? The street kids who brought her dead animals in exchange for food were usually too grateful and terrified to talk. Alice wasn't eating, which was odd. Instead, she was trying to push a half-frozen sandwich into the older boy's unresponsive mouth. Odder still.

Unsure how to react, Sanaa collected a knife from the table and pried loose some of the possum's hard skin. It came away clean, revealing pale bone beneath. She quivered, her entire skeleton rattling. 'Yes,' she said. 'Good.'

'Then, miss, I had wondered—' Alice hesitated '—if you would, if you could—' She had one hand wrapped around the older boy's chin and was making his jaw move, forcing him to chew.

Sanaa shuffled closer. 'What's wrong with him?' she asked, even as the currents of that rotten scent wrapped warm and heady around her. He smelled wrong, so wrong. Not like a living thing at all.

'It's been calling him, miss,' Alice answered. 'Breaking him, slowly, until he don't eat, don't speak. Soon, when he don't bother to breathe, it'll call him one last time and never give him back.'

Sanaa leaned closer. He was thin, yes, but they were all thin. Dirty, but they were all dirty. He looked just like the rest of them. Her small street army of carrion gatherers. 'What has been calling him?'

'Dunno,' the little boy piped up, mouth full, eyes wide and fearful. Alice pinched him until he added a squeaking, 'miss! I seen it, but dunno what. Got eyes, got teeth. Stays in the darkness. Gotta keep the lights on all night, miss. Once it touches you, you're good as dead.'

'I thought,' Alice whispered. 'I hoped, if we brought you good animals, lots of animals, a whole possum even, that you could, that you might—'

'—help us,' the boy finished for her, and drained his glass of milk.

Sanaa staggered back, clutching the table to keep herself upright. Her kneecaps had still not returned. 'Help you?'

'No one else believes us, miss,' Alice pleaded. 'Thought you might.'

That made a hard kind of sense. Why wouldn't Sanaa believe in a monster hunting them from the shadows? After all, she was a monster herself. But what did they expect her to do? 'Shouldn't you go to the police? Or community services?' Sanaa had been well known to the department as a child. They'd thought all her broken, dislocated, freakishly altered bones were proof of parental abuse. Wouldn't listen to her explanations. Wouldn't believe. Tried to give her to foster families who refused to let her play with the dead things she found—

She closed her eyes against the memories.

Alice didn't answer. Didn't need to. Sanaa understood the street kids. Maybe they knew that. Maybe that's why they trusted her.

Why they asked for her help.

'I don't know what I can do,' Sanaa whispered. She glanced over her shoulder. Her neck twisted too easily, too far. Several vertebrae slipped away to pester her elbows, and her spine stretched out to compensate, her muscles seized up and the nerves down her arms screamed.

The front door behind her loomed large, its peephole a sinister bright eye. Sanaa hadn't gone into the too-bright, too-revealing outside world in so long. The kids brought her the bones she needed, her agent sold her artworks (the ones that had exhausted the strength of their second life and were finally ready to move on), and the Internet delivered the rest. How could the kids know what they were really asking?

'Please,' the young boy whispered. 'We got no one else to ask.'

Damn him for looking up at her, so small and lost. Damn them all for putting her in this position. And damn her, for softening. For starting to care.

Sanaa drew herself up as straight as her skeleton would allow. If she was going to do this, she would do it properly.

'You—' she struggled to remember the little boy's name '—Pete, finish the food and watch your friend.' She tried to sound like she was used to organising children. 'Alice, pick up the box and follow me.'

She led Alice to the basement.

*Cat Box* emerged and followed eagerly, winding its awkward way around her ankles, and sniffing derisively at Alice's bare feet. The girl once again proved her worth by neither screaming nor running at the sight. That pleased Sanaa, though she couldn't have explained why.

'Here we are.' She switched on dim lighting.

Her collection of bodies rested on layers of slatted, metal shelves. The top row was cleanest: mostly bones and dry skin. The lowest wiggled with insects. The floor beneath them was thick with newspaper, which she changed once a month.

Alice did as she was directed, slotting the rats and the bat toward the bottom, and carrying the possum through to Sanaa's studio. She helped find an appropriately sized piece of corrugated iron to use as a canvas.

'What're we doing, miss?' Alice asked. She hung back against a cold brick wall while Sanaa suspended her canvas from the ceiling, and collected her blowtorch, drill, and small hand-held saw. 'Going to be dark soon. Going back is dangerous in the dark, and the others are waiting.'

'Be patient.' Sanaa stripped the possum of its desiccated skin. It was laborious; her uncooperative fingers itched to escape and dot the landscape of her back. 'I can't go like this. Not yet.'

Despite Alice's anxiety, Sanaa took her time over the possum. Carefully, gradually, she gave it a new life, a clean form, woven through the iron's waves. Art, for her, could never be meaningless. Every inch and moment of its creation was tied to her own body in ways she'd never understood. For with each piece of bone she glued and wired into shape, her disobedient skeleton settled down. Claw-tipped paws tore through rust like the dead rising — and her fingers calmed. Skull, inverted, jaw hinged loosely with copper wire — and her back realigned. Final touches with ink and the roar of the blowtorch — and her kneecaps returned.

*Cat Box* watched her work. It coiled and glowed, empty sockets following as she threaded the possum's spine.

'*Possum On A Hot Tin Roof*?' she asked it.

*Cat Box's* lights died instantly, and one of the possum's legs jerked.

'No?' Sanaa didn't like leaving her artworks without a name, but maybe it didn't matter this time. She was already feeling stronger.

Nothing like fresh bones.

She turned to Alice, unafraid for once to show the girl her face. 'And now we can go.'

While Alice and Pete extracted Matt from the kitchen, Sanaa prepared as best she could. She changed into fresh tracksuit pants, plaited her hair back tightly, wrapped a scarf around her head and did up the zipper on a high-necked, knitted jumper. All in black. She took *Possum* up from the basement and hung it in a storage room, where it'd have plenty of new friends to talk to. 'Think about what you'd like to be called,' she said, and ran a finger across its skull. So many bones rattled around her, all tense with concern. They could sense her apprehension, feel her fear. They were, after all, a part of her, each joined to her strange body through the life she had given them and the relief they gave in return. *King Rat Trap* tried to follow her, so she placed it in *RooStone's* arms.

'You're always with me,' she whispered. 'Don't fret, I'm never alone.' But it was hard. As she learned against the wall, just outside the door, listening to *King Rat Trap* struggle and *Possum* kick, *Cat Box* rubbed against her shins. She scooped it up before she could have second thoughts, wrapped it in a towel and shoved it into an old, dusty backpack. 'Not alone —' she whispered, as it struggled '— never ever.' She gave it two replacement AA batteries to keep it quiet.

Almost as an afterthought, she included her most portable tools. The saw. The pliers. A small roll of copper wire. She was setting out to face a monster. What other weapons did she own?

Then Sanaa made her slow, reluctant way down the hallway, patting each of the artworks there. 'It will be all right,' she tried to reassure them as they clutched and snapped after her. 'I'll be back soon.'

It was evening by the time Sanaa stepped out into the world. The sky was quiet, muted by clouds. A cold breeze touched her face and she found the unfamiliar, fresh air pleasant. Alice and Pete, holding Matt's hands, waited for her in the street. Sanaa steadied shoulders that for once complied, and followed them.

There were too many lights on. They beamed out of shop windows and restaurants, sparkled and wound through treetops. The last time Sanaa had walked down this street it'd looked nothing like this. All boarded up windows, empty shops, and homeless old men. Just the kind of place where no one would notice the smell of rotting animals, or care about the strange woman who lived above them. *Cat Box*, responding to her distress, kicked tiny holes in the side of her backpack, the movement drawing looks from a group of well-dressed women walking past. Sanaa drew her scarf down, almost covering her eyes.

The children took her to the train station. This was a shock — didn't they live just a few minutes down the road, squatting in the old community housing? She stopped, turned, peered down the street. The fibros were completely gone, replaced with sleek white apartments. 'Jesus. When did this happen?'

Her guides paused reluctantly. 'Miss?'

Sanaa shook her head. How could the inner city have changed so much around her? How could she not have noticed?

'We need to hurry, miss.'

One last look. The park on the corner, where no one dared to tread after dark — now full of people and bright market stalls. Music playing. Women laughing. Sanaa caught a glimpse of something small scurrying in the darkness of the gutter and took comfort in the idea that at least the rats and stray cats remained. Just like her, they were the last remnants of an older, dirtier time.

The train station had been developed, too. It was neat, clean, and well-lit. It made Sanaa's skin crawl just to look at. 'N-no way I'm going in there,' she stammered. Too many people, too close together. Ticket machines, turnstiles, guards all watching, watching. Her teeth chattered, involuntarily. 'You'll just have to look after yourselves. I can't, I won't—'

But Alice, brave Alice, took her hand. Her fingers were dirty, but still pale against Sanaa's dark skin. Alice drew her not into the station itself, but through a gap in the wire fence and onto the tracks. 'Good spot here,' Alice was saying. She talked smoothly, constantly. 'Always find a bird or two, and usually a bat. I think it's the wires—' Sanaa glanced up at the snaking cables above, so thick and full they hummed with hidden power '—they land on them and get fried.' The children wound a complicated pattern along the tracks, avoiding the trains that rattled fiercely past. 'But you gotta be careful not to get hit—'

In the end, and to Sanaa's intense relief, they didn't catch any trains. The children led her away from the station, down one of the lines, past abandoned carriages rusting away and an old unused platform, to another break in the fence. They pushed through untidy bushes, shopping trolleys, and onto backstreets where decrepit townhouses, empty warehouses, and vacant lots were ringed by colourfully spray-painted walls.

Now this was more like the city Sanaa knew. Most of the streetlights here were broken. It was so dark in places that she couldn't even see the vermin that followed them; the critters scratching cement and splashing in an overflowing drain.

They arrived at a bizarre little camp, in the corner of one warehouse. Two more children sat with their backs to the wall, surrounded by countless lights all rigged up to a single power point.

'I brought her!' Alice and Pete broke into a run, dragging Sanaa and Matt along with them. 'See, didn't I tell you? I brought her!'

Sanaa quailed and pulled her hand free. Lights. Too many lights.

'Quick, miss,' Pete called. 'It'll come now. It must have seen us, must have heard. It knows we're here!'

*Cat Box* was squirming against her, kicking and tearing through the backpack.

'Miss?' Alice tried to push Matt into the light, but he held his ground. 'Please, miss. Help me.'

Sanaa's throat clenched as three teeth cracked loose from her jawbone to shimmy into her neck. Too much exertion. All that walking and talking and worry were eating quickly through the strength the possum had given her. Would have been better just staying at home. Would have lasted longer.

Then Matt turned, all of his own volition, and stared intently into the darkness behind her. 'Coming,' he said, and stepped forward. Alice, white with fear, allowed Pete to draw her into the circle of light.

Sanaa froze as Matt walked past her. He walked awkwardly, chest thrust forward as though a hand had hooked into his ribcage and pulled him.

With a great clatter of bones and a tearing of fabric, *Cat Box* finally freed itself. It pressed its dented shoebox against Sanaa's shins and arched as best it could. Sanaa turned. She blinked, squinted — something moved. Faintly pale, a bulging face, teeth and eyes. Sanaa clutched Matt's wrist and dragged him against her. His smell wrapped around her — unnatural decay and too-clean bones.

'Don't,' Matt gasped, but he didn't fight her. 'Let me go.' There was no conviction in his words. 'I have to go.'

Sanaa swallowed hard against her loose teeth, and lifted her head. 'Who's there?' she called. Even as she spoke, her right shin shattered; shards migrated to wedge themselves between her ribs. She didn't so much as flinch.

When nothing answered she glanced down at *Cat Box*, with its bright Christmas lights. How she hated to ask it to do anything more than she had already forced it to. 'Will you show me?' she asked. *Cat Box* tensed, dimmed. 'Shine your lights? Show me the monster that has been hurting these children.' It didn't move. 'They brought you to me, do you remember that? Found you when you were nothing but a dead cat on the side of the road, gave you to me so I could make you live again. They helped you. They help me. Now it's our turn.' A battery-tail twitch. 'For me?'

The steady lights of *Cat Box's* bulbs revealed a man. A strange, small, twisted man. He was bent on one horribly dislocated knee, all his fingers were on backwards, one foot stuck out at the wrong angle, his neck bent, one shoulder missing, face a mess of mountains and valleys—

Though his skin was white and he was a man and she'd never, ever seen him before, she knew that body immediately. Intimately.

'You—' Sanaa gasped. 'You're—' She couldn't speak. 'Not possible.'

The man looked up. His eyes were sunken and dry. 'Possible. Nother one,' he said, his words so distorted she could barely understand them. 'Not met one for long time. Never one looks as good as you.' He stood with a groan and a million painful pops. He nodded to *Cat Box*. 'What this?'

'*Cat Box, at Christmas*,' Sanaa answered, as though in a daze. 'It's my pet.' She clicked her fingers and *Cat Box* returned to her. The man followed, keeping within its light.

Matt flinched and tried to pull free. Sanaa held him, while she still could.

'Wanna use?' the man asked. He scanned the children. 'Doesn't bother. Plenty more.' He held out his hand. Oh, but he must be in such constant pain. His elbow was long gone, his shoulder had worked its way around to his chest. 'Already got started on that one. You take others. He's mine.'

'Have to,' Matt hissed, trying to pull away. 'Hurts. Let me go. Have to.'

'I—' Sanaa swallowed hard. 'I don't understand. Are you an artist, too?'

He laughed at that, and it was horrible: mouth too slack and throat shaking, all his bones bouncing beneath his skin. 'Artist? Me?' He waved at Matt. 'Show.'

Sanaa released him as Matt pulled off his thin, torn shirt. She sucked in a horrified breath at the body underneath. Broken, so broken. His upper arms were all terrible indents and lumps from bones shattered, then poorly healed. His ribs were a mess, all wrong angles, some in visible pieces. When he started to tug his pants down she caught the knobbed edges of misaligned hips—

'Stop,' Sanaa gasped. 'Don't. That's enough.'

The pale man grinned, mouth too wide. 'Break the bones, move the bones, turn them into something new.' He nodded slowly. 'See now, like artwork. But more. Belongs to me, part of me. Feels what I feel. Comes to me when I call. Needs to. Only way to ease the pain.'

Matt stepped forward. 'Please.' He glanced at Sanaa. 'I have to. He's hurting now, hurting so much. And I can feel it all. So let me go with him. It's the only way to stop—'

'Quiet!' the pale man snapped. 'No more talking. Come now. Hurting *now*!'

'But,' Sanaa whispered. 'He isn't dead. You know what it feels like — the pain, the body that won't do as it is told. How could you possibly inflict that on anyone else?'

The man tipped his head like he just didn't understand her. 'Look you, stand all tall. You must, too.'

'No, no I don't. Not like this. And I won't let you keep doing it. I can't!'

He chuckled, a low sound that reverberated in her chest and left hairline fractures in its wake. 'Stop me?'

Matt, poor alive innocent Matt, stood between them. 'I'm sorry.' His lips hardly moved. 'If you don't go away, he'll make me hurt you. I'm sorry, I can't stop it.'

Sanaa, torn, unsure what she could possibly do, held her breath. 'Please,' Pete whispered behind her, where he huddled in the light. She met Matt's terrified gaze, eyes wide and cheek twitching, but the rest of him still and hard as stone.

Then the smallest, strangest noises echoed through the warehouse. Scratching, like dozens of rats' claws against cement, then the screech of metal on stone. It grew faster, closer, louder, until even the pale man turned to peer into the darkness behind him.

*Possum On A Hot Tin Roof* led the way, kicking and clawing into the light. Then the others emerged, all of them. *King Rat Trap* in a chaos of steel and tiny limbs, helped *RooStone* drag its heavy granite body. Her favourites from the hallway walls, the pile she'd thought too powerless to move anymore and therefore ready to sell, half-made sketches in feather and bone, massive pieces from her larger installations. Their canvases were muddy, their paint scratched. Most had parts missing. One had definitely been run over by a train.

'You followed me,' she whispered. 'How did you know I would need you?' *Possum's* empty eyes peered up at her. *Cat Box* rubbed against her shins. They were a part of her, bound to her, bones to bones, death and life. How could they not have known?

The pale man had Matt. Sanaa had an army.

She didn't even need to tell them what to do, at least not out loud. Her artworks swarmed over the man, covering him in bones and wire and steel mesh, bearing him down to the ground, pinning him. When Matt turned to fight for him they smothered him too, but gentler, immobilising but never hurting. Careful with one of their own.

It looked to Sanaa like a work of art, each piece a part of a powerful whole, with the cement floor as its canvas. Watching, avid, she slipped the broken backpack from her shoulders. 'Alice,' she called. 'Get my tools out.'

Saw in hand, she crouched, inspected. Measured with her eyes, and imagined. '*Pale Man?*' she whispered, and glanced at *Cat Box*. 'What do you think about that for a name?'


Sanaa bought the old warehouse for a fraction of the cost of her townhouse and moved in straight away. Boxes of dead animals would have been a challenge for any removalists, but her army of carrion gathers made it easy. No questions to answer, either.

She bought beds for the kids, and let them sleep with the lights on. She set up an enormous studio and was more productive than ever. She even went outside, on occasion. Rare occasion.

All thanks to *Pale Man*, and his unending strength.

Every morning, before she helped Alice prepare breakfast, before coffee — which she was developing a taste for — Sanaa visited *Pale Man* in his room, secure behind a heavy metal door and *Cat Box*, ever guarding.

His bones, wiped clean, were pale indeed, and shone far whiter than his skin had. He'd made the most beautiful installation piece, and the strength he gave her never faded. She wasn't cruel, not even to him. She'd made him far more perfect than he would ever have otherwise been. She'd made him human.

All the right bones in all the right order, tied together with copper, silver, and dotted with flecks of gold. His wrists were bound to the ceiling and his feet to the floor, and he floated in between, suspend on a spider web of wire. Fairy lights surrounded him, like those she'd seen in the trees on her street. She'd installed a fake window, with a lamp and a fan behind it, so he could feel the warmth of a pretend sun, and the brush of a cooling breeze.

She fed him tiny, nameless artworks, made from bird wings, or mice. Just enough to make sure he never tired and, she hoped, alleviate his pain. This wasn't punishment or revenge. This was art.

He might have been a monster, but, after all, so was she.

# FROM THE DRY HEART TO THE SEA

*The first wave brought industrial waste, caustic to touch and poisonous to breathe, heavy with arsenic, mercury, chrome, and dangerously alkaline. The people of Town called it acid, unaware they were making a pH faux pas. So let's just call it acid, shall we?*

Grandfather was selective when it came to traditions. As a ferryman he stuck to the old ways, even though the river had dried up when he was still a young man. He hauled his ferry down to the tracks every morning — with a truck, at first, then a large draught horse when the petrol ran out — and carried customers, livestock and goods across the vast riverbed of cracked, dry mud. Each evening he dragged his ferry back up the hill, cleaned its sunpanels and waxed wooden hull, and locked it in his little white-painted shed.

He taught me to do the same. When he realised he would never have the grandson he wanted he decided a granddaughter would do well enough, renamed me 'Damla' — after the water that no longer flowed — and set me to work as a ferryman, the first female one in all of Town's history.

Our ferries ran on iron tracks now, not currents, and there were too many boats running for the small number of people unable or unwilling to cross the riverbed on foot. Still, I learned well, and once Grandfather passed

*Ararat* to me I worked hard to prove that Damla, ferrymaster, belonged in Town.

Because the world was Town, and Town was the world.

When the first wave came, it was his well-learned traditions that saved my ferry. While the others burned and dissolved, *Ararat* remained solid, waxed and clean, in the little white shed I shared with her up on the hill.

It began in the dark of very early morning, with a great roar like something living and in terrible pain. Lamps flickered on all across Town, on both sides of the riverbed and even in the farming outskirts. I stroked my boat's crystalline sunpanels like my touch alone could comfort her — like she was a creature that needed comfort — only leaving her when the slow dawn broke to reveal the river, running.

The new houses and rest stops erected along the riverbed tracks were simply gone, smoothed over by furious water. Storerooms and feed pens built too low and close to the river were torn from the rock and burned as the flood carried them away. Smoke rose in the wake of their remains and any who breathed it in began burning, themselves, from the inside. I watched them dancing, covered my face with cloth, and decided not to take the ferry to the dock that day, for the dock too was ashes and the tracks deeply submerged.

Instead, I left the small white shed on the hill and went down into Town.

I spoke to Market street shop owners, wearing nightgowns and huddled in groups, and learned that all ferries at dock or on the riverbed were destroyed. Only *Eden's Call* on the western bank, and *Ararat* on the east, survived.

I was glad, because I was not the only one left. And because Adam, son of *Eden's Call*'s ferrymaster had surely survived along with his boat. Of the few young men I knew in Town, he didn't deserve to burn as he drowned.

The farmers who lived and worked on the outskirts hurried into Town to lend aid where they could. They reported that the sunfarm was unharmed, but the thick cables that carried power west had been eaten through. Any animals grazing near the river or wandering its banks were dead, too.

Because the water was acid and destroyed anything in its path.

I tried to find Grandfather in the poorer areas, close to the riverbank, among buildings that had once been warehouses, before the defences were installed and all outside boats turned away. Even as a dry-river ferrymaster

Grandfather could have afforded better accommodation, but this was where Town had put him when he arrived, and he had never moved.

The old warehouses and unused loading docks were chaotic, a mess of bodies and smoke, physicians working and victims screaming. The Mayor's razor men, working crowd-control, turned me away. I listened to them talking.

'...reports coming in from both ends of the river say the defences have been breached. Shock fence is down. The steel barricades upstream have melted and the ones downstream are starting to fall.'

'That's impossible, nothing can breach the barricades.'

'They're talking sabotage. Reckon someone must have weakened them and let this acid-stuff in.'

'Someone? But who would—'

And they noticed me loitering, turned their masked faces to me and lifted their hands so lantern light shone from wire-wrapped wrists. 'On your way, outsider.'

I hurried back to the little white shed on the hill. The single tattoo on my cheek seemed heavier, that night.

*The second wave came right on the first's alkaline heels and rolled thick with debris. A continent of buried rubbish unveiled by the rain, gathered up by the flood, and carried along like a school of plastic and metallic fish. It stretched for kilometres and took weeks to pass through. And though it did not look it on the surface, it was filthy, and deadly, and dangerous.*

Neither *Ararat* nor I knew how to swim, and at first that didn't matter. She may have had some residual memory of water, haunting her propeller and rudder where I stored them at the back of the shed, but the second wave was so heavy with rubbish and muck that it was almost solid land. Grandfather returned as soon as the razor men let him through. He helped me remove the sunpowered track-wheels from her hull; *Ararat* didn't need them anymore. When the acid eased and as the rubbish rolled in, I'd seen the melted tips of steel where the tracks now ended, right on the river's edge.

I relied on a long, thick pole to propel myself through the second wave. It made me slow, and my shoulders and back burned from the effort at the end of the day. I knew now how *Ararat* felt, during her long hot days dragging cargo along the tracks. And I told her so regularly, keeping my voice low, keenly aware of the presence of my passengers and that Town didn't need to know about the conversations I had with my ferry.

We saw Adam for the first time in weeks in the middle of the river, when his father grew too sick to master his boat. They had not let Adam sail before then. He was the son of a family with Roots, and a ferrymaster in training. Too precious to risk. Not like me.

'How's your father?' I asked, unsure what else to say. Glass and plastic bottles rattled between us.

A shadow seemed to cross his face. 'Unwell,' he said. 'The physicians say he has been poisoned. The Mayor's third aide even questioned me, as though I would poison my own father.' He shook his head and long, blonde hair fell across his eyes.

'They thought you would do that?'

'So I could master his boat, yes. To meet you, like this, in the middle of the river. They thought I would do that to my own father, because I haven't seen you in so long.'

Because of me? I lowered my gaze and turned my face, angling the tattoo away from him. I had been born in Town, but as the granddaughter of an immigrant I had been tattooed as soon as it was humane to do so. It had never meant much to me. We were safe, in Town. We had power and medicines and food. The world could go to hell outside of our defences, and it never mattered to us.

But since the first wave tore through us, I understood what that tattoo meant. It seemed to burn with fresh-needle fire every time I overheard a whispered conversation or caught the edge of a speculating glance.

It meant I didn't belong here.

'It's not true,' Adam said. He reached across the rubbish, but our boats were not close enough for him to touch me, and I didn't reach for him in turn.

'Of course it's not,' I said. 'You would never do that.'

'I've told them not to blame you. I told them we're not even courting. They seemed to think...' His voice trailed off, strained.

'Thanks.' Well, it was the truth, wasn't it? Just-friends was hard enough.

Children screamed and laughed in the distance. I glanced over my shoulder to see them pulling a muck-clogged bike from the rubbish. All sorts of treasures had been retrieved from the river's second wave. Batteries and wires, plastics and glass, even toys. Adam's father had run his ferry day and night, carrying lamps and a team of ten strong men to rescue as much useful material as possible. I assumed Adam would do the same.

I had not volunteered to use *Ararat* the same way.

Instead, I carried passengers, and the sunfarmers working to restore power to the western side. Doing my bit for a Town that didn't trust me.

I pushed the pole, biting my lip against the blisters it rubbed on my palms. Gradually, *Ararat* and *Eden's Call* separated. 'Best keep going,' I said. 'It's a full day.'

'Yes.' Adam was using his engine. The propeller squealed against the debris-thick river, and I felt the vibrations through the length of the pole. 'I'll see you on the return.'

I nodded, but didn't reply.

Though we passed each other several times, I didn't stop long enough to let Adam start up another conversation. I listened, instead, to *Ararat*'s whispers, as she parted the rubbish, as she groaned and creaked around me. And I whispered back, my own noises without words. She didn't care about Roots and she couldn't see my tattoo. We understood each other, the ferry and I.

By nightfall I was shaking with exhaustion. As the horse and I hauled *Ararat* to the shed on the hill I could still hear the hum of *Eden's Call*'s engine, its light a single speck in the river's darkness, collecting.

I cleaned the sludge from *Ararat*'s hull and smoothed the nicks and scrapes the rubbish had left. But as I was about to collapse on the mattress and blankets I had moved to the corner of the shed, where I could touch the rudder and propeller as I fell asleep, the Mayor's third aide came visiting.

He wore an insignia of three razor-wire coils on his breast and his arms, from wrist to elbow, were wrapped in barbs.

'You appear fatigued, Damla ferrymaster, once tattooed. Daughter of Ozge, twice tattooed, and granddaughter of Asqu, who bears the three marks of an outsider.'

I resisted the need to touch the mark on my cheek, because that was just what he wanted me to do.

'Perhaps mastering a ferry all on your own is too much for a girl of your seventeen years.'

'*Ararat* is mine,' I said, straightening. 'Passed down from my grandfather, my family have mastered her in the service of Town for three generations.' My mother had not so much as stepped on her deck, but I did not mention that.

'The ferry belongs to Town,' the third aide said, his smile brittle and his eyes hard. 'As all things, and all people, here do.'

'And I am her master.'

'And a sorry job you are doing, Damla. *Ferrymaster.*' His smile settled into a smirk. 'Dawn to dusk is only half the day. *Eden's Call* sails day and night, collecting the river's gifts. You refuse to do so.'

'I do not trust the river. Don't you remember the sound it made? Don't you remember the burning and the stench?' Even though the acid was gone, I didn't want to touch anything brought here by the river. Ferrymaster I might be, but I hated the river. It had torn Town apart, it had stirred fear and hatred, and I didn't trust its mud- clogged peace offerings, no matter how useful they might be.

All I got was a shake of the head and a look that said, so clearly I could almost hear him thinking, that outsiders like me simply didn't understand. 'Perhaps you need the help of someone who will.'

I swallowed, hard. It was difficult to argue with the third aide to the Mayor. Even if I managed to convince him to leave *Ararat* in my care, the second aide would come, and then the first, and the Mayor, even, if that failed.

'Will you not even compromise, Damla ferrymaster, for the good of Town? Like good Townfolk should do?'


*There was water, in the third wave. Clear stuff, wet stuff, it smelled of thunderstorms and wild winds and all the distance it had travelled. The food it carried with it — tempting peaches, taut nectarines, prickly pineapples and burgeoning mangoes — had not been seen so far south for generations. The people of Town picked this bounty from the clear, fresh river and did not question how it could have travelled for so long, in such perfect condition. How it remained ripe and unbruised. And they could not know that none of the fruit, really, tasted quite right, because there was no one left alive with the memory. Even the oldest Townspeople had only ever eaten them from cans.*


I nearly drowned the first time I led *Ararat* into water. Her strength and her buoyancy — as I scrabbled against her hull and clung to her wood for my life — were all that kept my head above the terrible rush and pull and cold. Once I climbed on board I stumbled about on her deck, my stomach rebelling, my legs wobbling, my whole body shaking. Grandfather tried to help, shouting instructions from the dock, increasingly far away. The Mayor's razor men laughed, and Townspeople gathered to watch us, like *Ararat* and I were some kind of cruel entertainment. Without the downstream barricades I wondered just how far we would be carried if I couldn't gain control.

But *Ararat* remembered the touch of river water. Hands on her helm, I absorbed the movements of her rudder and the strength in her propeller. I listened to the whirr of her sunpowered engine and together, always together, we learned to sail the river, even though the choppy surges and currents made me ill, and I woke each morning shivering for fear of drowning.

We were determined, *Ararat* and I.

Adam's father died soon after the third wave came, but he died with a smile on his lips, from the taste of fresh mango, apparently, sweeter than his own wife's kiss. Adam didn't master his ferry for the three full days of mourning. I didn't recognise the man who took his place, or the tattooed faces of the people he carried from the west, to the eastern side of Town, but never home the other way.

I tried not to think about Adam. My new assistant, a strong and quiet middle-aged man named Maxwell, studied me when our boats passed, even though Adam was a just-friend, and we were not-courting. I didn't doubt that he reported every smile, every innocuous word.

Maxwell was my compromise, the proof of my loyalty to Town. I hated him, almost as much as I hated the river that had forced him onto me. He scooped fruit as I guided the ferry across the flowing water, helped me launch her in the morning and return her to the shed in the evening. But most of all, he watched. Learning as I learned. Preparing himself, I was certain, to master *Ararat* on his own. I already knew how that would go: only at night, at first, and then when I was unwell, or exhausted, and then ... and then...

I worked hard, I put up with him, and I mastered my ferry. But I would never give her up. Not to Maxwell. Not to anyone. I laid a hand against her warm, sun-powered battery, protective, possessive, as she was of me.

'Here,' Maxwell held something sore-red and dripping out to me. 'You should eat it.'

I averted my eyes. There was something disturbing about that round skin, so crimson, so glistening, clutched in his large hand. 'No thank you.'

He shrugged, and ate it himself. Thick, wet pulp sluiced down his chin.

'Good for you, this stuff. Physicians think so. Heard they've been feeding it to the poor sick kids and it's doing wonders for them.'

'Didn't help David of *Eden's Call*, did it?'

He closed right up at that.

Maxwell was bent towards the water, dragging a wide net, and didn't see the boat. We were carrying the sober cousins of a sick child across to the west bank to visit him, and they were surreptitiously picking fruit of their own — heads down, they didn't see it either. The Mayor had claimed all fruit the property of Town, but so far had not done much to enforce that.

At first I thought it was *Eden's Call*; after all, what other boat could be out here? But it followed the flow of the river rather than tacking side to side and ran silent and dull, no engine hum or bright sunpanel reflecting the sun.

Fear clutched in my chest as it swept closer, and I veered as hard as I could to avoid hitting it. It was like no ferry I'd ever seen. Long and narrow, low in the water, seed-shaped and bobbing. It had no deck to speak of, only windows that couldn't have been made of glass because they seemed to absorb the sunlight, not reflect it. Its white painted hull was stripped and peeling, and beneath it rust ran red like blood, trailing into the water.

I held my breath and watched it go. And only when the sun hit it at just the right angle did I see something on the other side of those windows. The wide pressing of a large hand, which then curled into a fist, banging against the dark panel. Its dull and quiet thud stayed with me for the rest of the day.

More razor men patrolled the shore when the horse and I dragged *Ararat* up to our shed on the hill. They distracted Maxwell and for once he didn't force his help on me. I saw Grandfather, down the street, attempting to make his way to us. Three of the Mayor's men stopped him, and turned him around.

A child lay outside the shed's door, visibly ill, with grey and weeping skin, cradling a hand that looked more like shapeless rusted metal than flesh and bone.

'Shouldn't you be with the physicians?' I asked. The young boy scrambled away from the horse.

His eyes were wide and a strange muddy colour, all of him too dirty for any child of Town. But that was what it did, this illness, and it had taken to the children especially. Only a few adults, like Adam's father, had grown so sick.

'Take me to the river, please,' he pleaded. 'I can hear her, she's singing so nicely, like my own Mum used to.' His breath stank like putrid river-mud.

'No.' His muddy colours and crusty skin make me shudder.

'But you're the ferrymaster. You should take me to her. I need her. She calls—'

'No!' I pushed the horse forward. 'Get away from here. Get back to the physicians!'

As he ran I saw what looked like scales across his naked back, in a multitude of colours and textures, from glass-glistening to rusty and dull.

In the evening, as I cleaned pulp and fruit skin from *Ararat's* propeller, Mother visited me. Mother never visited the little white shed on the hill. She had married a man with Roots, so she didn't need to live in the poorer streets or master a ferry across a dry riverbed.

Wrapped in a wide and brightly woven shawl, she held her chin high, the twin tattoos on her cheeks almost hidden behind heavy clay cosmetics. The faint smell of the strong tea she used to darken her hair followed her, constantly. That was a status symbol itself, in a place like Town where every edible leaf was precious, all water dug from wells, recycled and closely rationed.

I stopped in my cleaning to stand and stare at her, shocked by her presence.

'We almost did it,' she said, lifting a hand to touch the ink on my cheek. Her voice shook; her fingernails and hands were dry and looked filthy, caked with something like mud.

I jerked back. 'What have you done to yourself?'

'Your children, Jean, would have been the fourth generation, and clean. They would not have been tattooed; they would have belonged here.'

For once, I didn't correct her, even though Jean was no longer my name.

Voices, outside, shouting in the distance.

'What's happening?' I took her shoulders and drew her to the doors. The warehouses by the river were riddled with scurrying lights, movement and voices.

'It's called segregation,' Mother said. I wrapped an arm around her and realised she was small, and thin, her bones protruding strangely beneath her shawl. I tugged the fabric gently, exposing her neck. More dried mud, and scales. 'Outsiders, and their sympathisers, all taken from our homes and shoved like boat-rats down there, in the dark and the dank.'

*Down there* meant the warehouses where she had grown up. 'Why?' I asked, horrified.

'The second aide to the Mayor has set up an investigation. They suspect sabotage at the barricades — how else could they have fallen? And they say fruit was stolen, barrels worth. And some of the treasures from the second wave, taken. The river and her gifts belong to the people of Town. Not outsiders like us.' She reached for my face again. 'We were so close.' I forced her arms down. 'We saved what we could from the house. Your father and I.'

He might not be an outsider, but he had married one, and I supposed that made Father a sympathiser.

'You need to come with me.'

'No.' Gently, I released her, turned her around. 'No, I need to stay here.'

'But we're all supposed to—'

'I need to care for *Ararat*.' I paused. 'I think you should see the physicians, Mother.'

'Obsessed with that boat, you don't see anything else. You don't understand what's happening.' Her face twisted, grimacing at me; her teeth were black. 'They will not treat outsiders, not any more. And they won't let you stay here. Not anymore.' But she left me alone, at least.

I dragged the heavy wooden shed doors closed and locked them with chains and bars. Then I finished cleaning my ferry as I waited for the Mayor's razor men to come and try to take her away. *Ararat* was mine. *Ararat* was a part of me. Try was exactly what they would do. At least while I was alive to fight them.


*The fourth wave is nameless. Some are better left to the dark.*


But the night dragged on and they didn't come. I cleaned my boat and I doused my lamps and I waited, in the dark. Outside the voices died; all the lights I could see through the shed's windows softened into something like calm. I tried to sleep there, with *Ararat*, but worry kept any chance of rest at bay.

So I swallowed my fear and locked the shed behind me, hung its single, heavy iron key around my neck and headed into Town.

The warehouses were watched: a pair of the Mayor's razor men stood at every second intersection. More of them were building small barricades in the streets from river treasure and rolls of barbed wire. So I crept down the back ways, the ways between warehouses, the ways that had once been lined with railroad tracks and strung with charged wires, and headed for my grandfather's house.

Until the sound of the river stopped me. It seemed to stretch out through Town with a whispering rustling like rubbing skin and a groaning that echoed, deep inside my chest. And I knew I should have returned to the little shed on the hill and *Ararat*, my ferry, because together we were strong enough to ride any river, any wave, but the river called. Even the steady Mayor's guards followed it to the edge of the water.

I walked with them. They didn't try to stop me; they didn't even see me, so all-encompassing was the wave. But where the razor men and their lanterns continued on to disappear into the darkness, I refused to give in. With all my hatred of the river, and all my love for *Ararat*, I struggled and fought my own body, my own legs, forcing myself to stop on the very edge of the makeshift dock. Warm air filtered up through my sandals. The moon was very close and very bright, ringed by stars. In its light the little white shed on the hill seemed to glow, a halo of reflected light.

Something brushed against my toes. Soft, dry, clinging, ever so gently, like the testing arms of a spider. I quivered, and looked up to the shed for strength. How I wished *Ararat* was with me.

'My great-grandfather was a boatman too, you know.'

I started and strained my neck to look over my shoulder. I could hardly move, all my effort going to fighting the river's call.

Maxwell. Large, hulking, only a shadow in the darkness. He stood on the dock too close behind me. I couldn't see his face but his voice was like the river's call, rustling soft and dry.

'Went out to sea when the sea still flowed and carried people far, far across the world, when the world was more than Town and Town alone.' His words rolled into each other and I was reminded of fruit bobbing, dipping, sinking beneath the clear water.

'Born in Town, he was, and came home to Town, he did. Belonged here. Like me. I belong here.' He stepped closer with every word, short and shuffling steps. I couldn't move and the river was touching me, running soft feelers up the back of my legs, teasing the holes in my jeans, waiting to drag me in. 'Not like you.'

'Stop it,' I gasped.

'I'll repaint her, when I take her.' Moonlight touched his hand as he reached for the chain around my neck. 'And name her after his boat, I will.' But it wasn't a hand. It was stretched and red like the fruit he'd picked; bulging, fingers writhing, but so hard to see in the dark with the river rustling, touching behind me—

'No.' The key around my neck felt heavy and exposed.

'I'll name her—'

'Damla!' From behind me, a human voice. 'Here!'

So I gave in to the call. The pull of the river spun me around and launched me from the edge of the makeshift dock. But instead of falling into the groaning and the movement of the water I landed on something solid, wooden. The firm deck of *Eden's Call*. Maxwell, shadow and fruit-flesh, swung and staggered forward as the river rose up. The dock collapsed and he was gone, down into the darkness with the razor men before him.

'Here, quick.' Adam drew me down to lie against his wooden deck and we dragged a tarpaulin over us. 'Keep still.'

If only it was that easy. The river still dragged at me, through the boat's very hull, and I twitched and fought with a need to scratch and tear my way down. Adam, breathing hard, pressed his chest against my back while the river stroked *Eden's Call* with thousands of grasping hands, and moaned, groaned, with its need.

'Can't you feel it?' I whispered, my mouth pressed into the wood, teeth clenched against a need to chew.

'Shh.'

'It's calling me. Calling...'

'Don't listen to it.'

'But how—'

He rolled me over and kissed me, instead.

'What are you do—'

And again.

'How can you resist—'

And again.

'You taste like fruit.'

Too sweet and too ripe. It made me think of Maxwell.

He lay on me, the weight of his body holding back the river's call. His cheek against mine felt soft, swollen. He whispered, 'The Mayor's second aide announced they were rounding up all the outsiders. I got worried, so I came to make sure you were okay.'

'I thought we were just-friends,' I said, after a moment of silence.

We lay, while the river touched us, his body too hot and too round. It didn't matter anymore, I realised, what we thought we were. Or what we might have wanted to become. Not since the first wave rolled in.

'They won't let me keep *Ararat*,' I said, with *Eden's Call* beneath me like a limb that didn't belong. 'If I stay, I will lose her.' And I thought of that strange pod-boat, passing through on the river's strong current, and the barricades that no longer held us in.

The world was Town, Town was the world. But the river ran through us now, like a wound.

The river's call eased, sometime close to the clear and cold dawn. In the fresh light I saw that the river was water again, and all the fruit was gone. When Adam — skin crimson and hands thickening — let me down, the river ran with bullet cases, so many the shoreline shone gold in the early morning sun.


*The people of Town had many names for the fifth wave, but all of them were wrong. The quivering, still-growing, but long-dead creatures that tumbled against each other and smeared blood on the shore were not sheep, cattle, chicken or goat. Not any longer. This wave, at least, the people of Town left clear alone, not tempted by all the slick meat on display. And because of that they did not find the shepherds, crawling around the rocks at the bottom of the river, guiding the once-animals, the part-animals, the many-animals on their final journey from the dry heart to the sea.*


When the bodies in the water started to thin out, Grandfather's horse and I carried *Ararat* to the river. All three of the Mayor's aides waited down by the warehouses. There was no other path to the shoreline, so I led her straight into their hands.

'Maxwell is not with you,' the third aide said, looking behind me as though the large man would materialise out of thin air.

'No,' I answered, 'he is not.' I unhooked the horse from her cart and tied her beneath the shade of an old and rundown building.

'He's not the only missing Townsperson,' the second aide said. His cheeks were too red, and swollen, as though he had been slapped, repeatedly, but refused to bruise. 'Do you know what has happened to them all?'

I averted my eyes and tried not to think of Adam. 'No.' Which wasn't entirely a lie. Could I understand the workings of the river?

I rolled *Ararat* into the water, wading in with her, arms lifted. Whatever dead things touched me, cold and gentle, were preferable to the Mayor's men. As I untied the lines and straps that held her to the heavy, submerged cart, the Mayor's first aide stepped forward. He placed a hand on her smooth wooden bow.

'This boat belongs to Town,' he said, his voice deep, vibrating with all the power he knew he had.

'And I am part of Town,' I said.

He leaned over the bloodied water and traced his finger against the tattoo on my cheek. His touch was so hot it burned me, ink and skin alike. 'No,' he whispered, his mouth close, 'you are not.' And something wiggled behind his teeth.

I jerked back against *Ararat*'s hull. My feet slipped as I scrambled against her for purchase. The movement pushed her back, deeper into the river, and all three of the Mayor's aides gripped her, trying to keep her close to the shore. But whether it was water, the smoothness of her polished wood, or if it was *Ararat* making her own decision, they couldn't hold on. I scrambled on board, finding easy, even handholds as though she had made them, just for me.

Even as she was caught in the river's flow and we began to pull away, the Mayor's first aide drew a large and silver gun from his jacket.

'If you shoot her,' I cried, slapping on *Ararat*'s battery without my usual, grateful care and slamming her into reverse, 'you'll lose us both!'

'Boats can be repaired,' he shouted back, and aimed.

'She will never swim for you!' I crouched behind her helm, sunpanel-reflected sunlight in my eyes, and turned her to follow the current.

The shot never came. I looked back to the eastern shore, squinting, to see Grandfather standing in the middle of the street, his skin red and his body bloated. Rows of tattooed outsiders were lined up behind him. They carried fiery torches and second wave rubbish, brandishing anything hard or with a sharp edge. So many of them were red, to bursting, like Maxwell, like the aides. Others were grey and filthy, caked with mud and scales, arms and legs twisted like the rubbish they carried.

With Grandfather at their head, the outsiders surged toward the Mayor's three aides. Whistles blared and screams tore and somewhere in the mess of bodies gunshots rang out. But *Ararat*, steady *Ararat*, carried me into the middle of the river, where I couldn't see Grandfather, or Mother, or the aides.

We idled there, as Town tore itself apart. Stick-figure battles in the streets, on the shoreline, details too hard to see through the heavy flies and smoky haze rising from fires breaking out on the eastern side. The figures that fought and squirmed and writhed seemed strangely elongated, or fat and thick, and hardly human at all.

Adam only joined me as the day finally died into darkness.

*Eden's Call* anchored several metres away. Adam stood on its deck, clothes splattered in blood, his fruit skin seeming to burn in the heavy sunset. His ferry listed dangerously low on the port side, bearing scorches-marks and wide jagged scars. One of his arms hung limp from a gash close to his shoulder. The thick liquid that oozed from the wound was not blood.

'I'm sorry,' he said, voice like the river, mouth moving strangely. I was thankful for the growing darkness.

None of Town's gas lanterns or the sunfarmed lights flickered on, on either side of the river. All that lit it was the little white shed on the hill, burning. In silence, together, we watched it die.

*We have learned, over the river's course, that some waves are better not seen at all. So we timed the sixth wave, our wave, to flow through Town at night.*

I woke with a start, though I hadn't realised I'd fallen asleep. I lifted my head and felt the splinters left in my nose. The little white shed had reduced to small, bright embers and all of Town dripped shadows.

The first smudges of dawn rubbed the moon with faint pastels. I stood, peering across the water to Adam. Half of *Eden's Call* was submerged, but he still stood on its deck, up to his knees in water, staring back at the western shore. Then I realised what had woken me.

No more dead animals, the water was clear and running fast. And *Ararat* strained against her anchor to follow a small, metallic boat flowing past.

A man sat inside the boat, hand on twin oars he was not using. He was elderly and brown, skin like leather, dressed in a white jumpsuit. I stared down at him, and he stared up at me, both of us shocked. Then he stood, as he passed us, rocking his boat and waving as he shouted, 'Hurry!'

And he was not alone. So many more boats behind him. Some like the sleek pod-thing I had seen, though these ones were not stripped and rusting. Others with masts and great white sails; sunfarmed ferries similar to

*Ararat*; bright orange and inflated plastic triangles; and many more. And on all of them were people. Not fruit-touched or rubbish-scaled, not tattooed or wrapped in barbed wire. They met my eyes, just as shocked to see me as I was to see them, and they called to me, each and every one:

'Lift your anchor!'

'Follow us, quickly, while you can!'

'Get out of here, do it now!'

Some in languages I couldn't understand.

Still, I paused, and looked back to Adam. He, too, lifted a hand to wave at me. Fingerless, oozing pulp. I swallowed hard, turned away from him — just-friend, not-courting — and pressed *Ararat*'s battery into wakefulness.

Somewhere, out in the early morning half-light, something splashed. As the light grew and the close-moon dimmed, I saw them. The people of Town, all lined up on the riverbank: twisted and distorted figures, some too red, some too grey, some broken, some grown. All staring at us.

One by one, with eerie synchronicity, they dived into the clear river and swam toward us.

'Hurry!' Came the faint cry, from further down the river. I retracted *Ararat*'s anchor and we surged on the river's flow, with all the urgency she had promised. Away from ruinous buildings, past abandoned farmland and bright sunpanels, and through the rubble remains of the barricades.

We followed the ships, wherever the river would take us.


*The final wave, the seventh wave, is dry. It is cracked earth, desiccation, starvation and ultimately death. It purges everything the river has touched, and chases us all the way to the sea.*

# ALWAYS A PRICE

It didn't start the night of Sylvia's party, not like everyone thinks it did. I'm the only one who knows this. After all, I brought the damned cat home.

Sylvia had a way of dealing with the cancer that made us all uncomfortable, but we didn't have the balls to say anything. We went along with it all. Allowed it to become the centre of our lives, never dared raise our own problems, those trifling matters that simply could not compare. We referred to the lump in her left tit as *Ziggy* like she wanted. We even organised the mastectomy party she demanded, complete with male strippers, a game of 'pin the boob on the hospital patient' and enough booze to poison any clump of inconveniently mutating cells. Always with a smile, that same, strained grin we all shared. Don't know how the others handled it, but I dealt with Sylv's illness the same way I dealt with everything — a small razor, and a fuck load of gin.

We were all taking turns with the body paint, covering her too-thin body with countless new boobs in a garish variety of colours, when the cat strolled in. It'd been living in our shared townhouse for two months now, well fed, patted, cleaned, but it looked just as mangy and feral as it had the day I brought it home. I'd told the girls I'd rescued it, found it pathetic and alone in a pile of garbage and coaxed it into a box with a can of sardines. This wasn't exactly true. But we all cling to our secrets and comforting delusions, don't we?

It walked right up to Sylv's bare feet, sat and stared up at her.

Couple of Sylv's work friends started cooing. It didn't last long. Despite its name, Mr Muddles was not the kind of cat you cooed at. There was something in the way it looked at her, with those too-smart, hard yellow eyes. There was something in the way it dug long claws deep into the floorboards, gouging great gashes that bled sap, like the wood was still fresh. Its matted fur stuck out at irregular angles, its smooth cat-lines made jagged and harsh.

In the tense silence, Sylvia knelt. Mr Muddles placed a paw on her naked knee, instantly drawing blood in a neat pattern. She didn't move. Careful paw by careful paw it crawled its way into her lap, across her stomach, and onto her chest. There, it began to knead.

None of us tried to stop it. Maybe it was the surreal nature of the sight — Sylvia, naked but for white cotton undies and bra, bright with paint, hands lifted but not grasping, not even touching the small black cat pummelling her tits. Her mouth was slightly open, her eyes wide, but she looked surprised, nothing more, not in any pain.

Not even when those strong paws sunk through her skin, and into her flesh.

It wasn't messy. I kinda thought it would be messy. Blood and muscle, ruptured meat and pumping veins, and screaming, lots of screaming. Instead those paws just slipped inside her like her skin was pale mist. A terrible rumbling rattled through the cat, and wide slick tears fell dirty from its eyes, but still, it kneaded.

And then, with a snort and the flick of a tail, it was done.

Mr Muddles traced bloodied paws back across the floorboards, onto the clean cream carpet, and disappeared inside my bedroom.

Sylvia fell onto her side, shuddering.

I could never quite remember everything that happened next. The screaming finally started, but not from her. At least three of us called 000, Kylie from the home phone, Sylv's old school friend Cathy and workmate Peta from their mobiles. Tanya was holding her, cradling her head while two chicks whose name's I'd never really learned pressed towels and tissues onto all her small puncture wounds.

I went in search of Mr Muddles.

It was curled at the very back of the wardrobe in a nest of all my best clothes. It licked the blood off its paws with an attentive dark tongue.

'Why her first?' I whispered. Its eyes glowered, oh-so amused. 'I brought you here. Why'd you choose her?'

And then I was being dragged back to the lounge room floor where

Sylvia was sitting upright and clean. And the ambos bundled her off to the hospital for tests, more tests. And when the results came back, it was all gone. Sylvia's breast cancer, every last trace in every last gland and every last mound of soft flesh gone. Just gone.

So that's when they thought it all started. But they, of course, were wrong.

Sylvia was not the kind to keep quiet about Mr Muddles. It started before she even left the hospital. A young boy, shaved head starkly pale beneath colourless lights, small and frail in his crackly sheets. I refused to bring Mr Muddles in, refused to even touch it, so Sylvia roped her friends in. They brought the cat in a cardboard box lined with more of my fur-clogged clothes. I stood guard at the door while it plunged its claws into the child's bones, drawing out his invisible disease.

After that, word spread. I wasn't sure how. Maybe there are networks of the sick and the dying that I was not privy to. However it happened, they started to arrive at our door. In ones, at first, then groups. A hell of a lot of cancer. We quickly learned the cat had a knack for cancer. Couldn't help anything degenerative, could only take out something that wasn't supposed to be there, not repair ageing brain cells or tired hearts.

Maybe that was why it hadn't tried to help me.

Sylvia set up the lounge room like a surgery. Or a butcher. Vinyl-covered table, clear plastic sheets taped to the walls, floor and ceiling. Lots of lamps, bright bulbs. Old green couches in the hallway. Mr Muddles got special treatment. Real fish for dinner. Bottled-fucking-water.

I started finding worse things than blood and fur on the hems of my jeans. Things that looked like bits of meat, or the fine white stems of nerves, or honeycomb bone, all dark and lumpy with sickness, chewed and thrown back up again. The wardrobe stunk like a dead thing, and cat shit, and cat spit, and blood, and things I couldn't even name. The smell infused all my clothes, no matter how much I washed them or hung them out in the sun.

But no one else could smell it, and Sylvia wouldn't let me kick it out. 'He likes you,' she'd say, as though that thing could feel affection. 'Likes your smells. Feels safe there. Let him stay in your room, let him be comfortable and sleep. He deserves it, and he's not doing any real harm.'

The final straw. I left the house, and returned to the spot where I had found the creature in the first place.

It was, indeed, in a heap of trash down a narrow alleyway, I hadn't lied that much. Dodgy-looking Chinese takeaway on one side, with faded pictures of sweet and sour pork or crispy duck plastered inside the dirty windows. Nondescript building painted in black, with nothing but a gold number and the faint scent of cigarettes hovering in an aura around it, on the other. I couldn't have said what drew me to this place to begin with, in the middle of the night a few mere months ago. I'd been drunk, I remembered that much, drunk until I was numb. And the darkness had wrapped cool hands around my face, and I'd thought it must be easier to have someone else do it, you know. That way, no one hates you when you're gone. They hate the arsehole who hurt you, instead. They might wonder, 'how could she be so stupid?' or 'why'd she get so drunk?' or 'what was she even doing there after dark in the first place?' but that's different. I was okay with that.

Even in the sunlight the place looked the same. Liquid shadows in all the corners stretched out to touch my boots. Puddles lapped at me — thick with the mud that had given the cat its name — bins and rubbish and sick against the walls. But the smell was wrong; I hadn't noticed that the first time. Now, it smelled like the inside of my wardrobe.

She was still there, right at the back, hidden from the street, hidden from anyone not looking for her. First time, a single streetlamp totally out of place had beamed its halo down on her, but it wasn't there now. Still, she was glowing. Her long hair spilled tangled and ropey over her shoulders and onto the cement. Her fingernails were bloody, gnawed down to the quick, and they strained and pressed as she gripped her knees. She wore a single grey dress, shapeless, pushed up to her waist, her legs held high and wide open as she struggled to give birth.

I halted, shuddered. I should have got drunk again first.

'Back?' she panted, face red and wet with sweat.

The small dark things falling out of her weren't fully formed yet, but they wiggled and moved in the mud regardless. I didn't want to look at them, or where they were coming from, so I met her eyes instead. Cat's eyes, just as yellow as Mr Muddles, and the same amused expression.

'It's not working,' I hissed. 'It's not doing what you said it'd do.' The tiny cats moved around me, rolling to their feet, growing, stretching into shape even as they took their first few steps. My stomach clenched, and I forced myself not to be sick.

'Not true, that.' She grinned, her teeth small and sharp. 'Working a lot, all the time. Just not for you.'

'Why the fuck not?' I kicked a small cat-thing aside as it tried to rub against my shoes.

'Might be not ready.' She finished her birthing with final push and a grunt, and smoothed her dress back down. Apparently the blood and the fluids running down the inside of her thighs didn't bother her. 'Everything in its own time.' Hand lifted towards me, she leaned forward. 'And own price.'

'Price?' I snapped at her. 'No one else paid a fucking price! Sylvia didn't pay a goddamned thing! Why should I—'

And that was when I noticed she was attached to the alleyway wall. It looked like wings, spread out from her head and back, dark and thick and seeping into the pockmarked bricks. She folded her legs, drew them underneath her, and it pulled and rippled with her shifting weight. Not feathers, nothing so beautiful. Instead, it was fur. Clumps of saliva-stiff fur, bound with bloody ropes of something that could be flesh.

I glanced down at my shoes. The same putrid stuff was congealing around the hem of my jeans.

'Always a price,' she said.

I ran then, away from her laughter like a cat's yowling, her unnatural children squashing and cracking beneath my feet. I stopped only when the alley was so very far away, found myself someplace small, dank and open early, and drank my shakes away. Drank until I was steeled, ready to do what needed to be done. What I should have done in the first place.

I arrived home to darkness, the patients gone, the girls asleep. No one to see me take the biggest kitchen knife I could find out of its drawer, and test its sharpness. No one to notice that I was too drunk to even cut myself correctly. The red line I left on the inside of my upper wrist was wonky, but so were all the others, the old scars pale down my arms and legs. I'd only ever shown them to Sylvia. She'd laughed, said it was a phase, and shown me her own.

Tanya slept on a mattress out the front of my bedroom, ready in case Mr Muddles needed her. I stepped over her, careful not to wake her, and closed the door behind me. My bedroom stunk. I knelt in front of the open wardrobe and parted my remaining clothes like leaves in a jungle. In the dark I couldn't quite see whatever felt so hot and wet against my hands.

Then two bright yellow eyes opened. I crawled forward, wrapped my hand around the mangy scruff of the creature's neck and lifted it up, out of the nest it had made. I brought it close to my face. It didn't struggle, didn't so much as hiss, just held my gaze and somehow I could tell it was laughing at me.

'Fuck you and your price,' I spat in the thing's face and plunged my knife deep into its chest, so deep the blade went right through, and stuck out on the other side of its skinny little body.

No screaming, no thrashing, those eyes still glowed. I pulled out the knife, blood ran down my arm, turned the blade around. Should have done this all so long ago. None of the bullshit half-arsed attempts, no more cries for fucking attention or whatever the hell my so-called friends and long-lost family thought of me, time to cut it all out, because the only thing that ever felt right was this the hot slice of the knife—

And Mr Muddles plunged its long-clawed paws into my head. At first they just scored deep scratches against my temples and into my eyes and down my cheeks. I tried to shake it loose but the unnatural bastard held on so tightly, and all I did was tear off strips of my own skin. Until it went deeper. And it was kneading in my brain, surgical slices of curved scalpels, back paws on my chest, blood down my arm, fingers wrapped around its lice-crawling fur.

I couldn't tell how long it took, wasn't the same as watching, but I knew as soon as it was done. I let go. The knife fell with a thump and a splatter. And for the first time in a long time, longer than I could remember, I felt no need to pick it up again. There was nothing left that needed cutting out. Mr Muddles tumbled all paws and head and opened body into my lap. I pressed hands to my face, but I wasn't that hurt. My eyes were whole and round, my cheeks stung with a few finely raised scratches.

Mr Muddles twitched, stretched, and half-fell half-dragged itself off my lap and deep into the wardrobe. Deeper than it should go. I followed, knees slipping, clothes heavy and damp against my face. My fingers dug for purchase in so much wet, matted fur.

All I could see was Mr Muddle's eyes, lidded now and dimmed, jerking as it retched. Over and over. I reached for the cat, but only found more of that sodden, matted fur, a great wall of it. One final jerk and terrible noise, and those eyes closed. For a moment, I felt frozen in the darkness, lost in my own wardrobe, drunk on the smell, wrapped in a filthy womb.

Then another set of yellow eyes opened, larger, glowing, above me. 'Your piece,' a soft, amused voice whispered. 'Last piece. Sharp piece.' Something shifted. Warm fingers rested on the back of my hand.

Light flickered on from a bulb that shouldn't be there, drilled into the back of the wardrobe. A woman hung there, from fresh wings of flesh and cat fur, and knelt on a small pedestal of bone meal. She was so very much like the woman from the alleyway, almost identical, but her skin was darker, and her hair short, pale, spiky, the way Sylv had styled it before it all fell out.

Mr Muddles lay limp in her lap. She drew her hand from mine and stroked it with tender fingers, nails clean. 'We told you,' she said, and held the cat to her face, pressed its fur against the tears rolling down her cheeks. Even as I watched, stunned, stuck in the muck I couldn't bring myself to look at, her stomach bulged and grew. 'Always a price. And someone always pays.'

# OUT HUNTING FOR TEETH

The colony in the sunside hydroponics chamber had strung the man up in the access corridor like an offering. He swung from the ceiling's naked beams on a noose of optical fibre and copper wire, and his hands were tied in front of him. His face was expressionless and grey, his mouth hung open, and the nodes drilled into his teeth were misfiring desperate, panicking signals.

W-type Scavenger-Class — nicknamed Wype by his mistress in her cruel glee — had never seen anything like it.

His sensors told him the man was already dead, no need to chase and kill this one himself, which reduced the chance he would damage the man's spinal enhancements and neural networks. That was good. The Witch was vicious when she was displeased. So it made sense to cut the man down, slice him into manageable parts and drag the useful ones back to her as quickly as possible.

But Wype was more than sensors and circuitry. He was a Witch's spell, a complex blend of dead human parts and recycled machine parts, given life and a task by his mistress. He shared a brain, and most of his body, with a dead boy. And his boy told him something wasn't right. Humans were too few and they considered themselves too precious to kill each other indiscriminately. There had to be a reason for this man's death. Perhaps he was contaminated. If Wype brought a virus — biological or digital — into the Witch's lair, she would eject him into airless space.

So Wype and his boy decided this required more investigation.

Wype swung himself down from the ducting. His boy leg jarred at the impact. He pumped a fresh round of painkillers into the degenerating muscle, and shuffled awkwardly forward. He was designed for climbing through the hollow bones and rotting guts of the derelict ship, not walking in a straight line. His metallic leg was longer than his human leg, segmented, and hooked at the tip. His one human hand was encased in reinforced ceramic tiles stolen from the ship's breached hull. He had two mechanical arms. One ended in a hook like his leg, the second was a multi-tool of cables, a light, a soldering iron and a photon-beam blade.

The sensors protruding from Wype's neck scanned for heat signals, electronic pulses, and neural firings. He detected nothing but the panic emanating from the man's teeth. He cut the man's leg, wiped a thin drop of blood directly on the powerful lenses of his mechanical eye, and ran as many scans as he was programmed with. As far as Wype could tell there was nothing wrong with his flesh, other than the rigors of death. That only left his networks.

Wype hauled himself up the wall, extended his blade and cut the man down. Then he dropped back to the floor, and pried open the dead man's mouth. It took a little drilling with the sharpened tip of his blade to expose enough ports to link himself with the neural network.

Human networks were basically designed for maintenance: they monitored blood pressure, muscle function, and oxygen uptake. But the dead man's was doing none of those things. Instead, it was flooded with data, a nonsense of figures and formulas, instructions and feedback that didn't feel human at all. It felt, if anything, like a machine. A jumbled, failing machine.

'Who are you?'

If Wype could jump, he would have. But the Witch had not designed him that way. All he could do was send out a fresh burst from his sensors, scanning frantically. He found nothing. He was alone with the dead man.

'Who is there?' Wype's voice was hampered by the sensors shoved into his boy's throat. His words came out in a dry, rustling whisper.

A moment of silence, then, 'I am dead, aren't I? They must have killed me.'

Wype felt at a loss. He wasn't used to scavenging networks that talked back. He used the opportunity to run an antiviral protocol.

'You are certainly dead,' he said, finally. 'But don't worry. I am here to take you to my Witch, so she can recycle you.'

Another pause. 'That means you are an android. I suppose, then, that I have failed.'

The antiviral was taking far longer than he expected. While he waited, Wype started to work. It was difficult, while still attached to the network. So instead of cutting cleanly, with the blade in his currently preoccupied multi-faceted hand, he twisted around so he could use his hard, ceramic palm to break the lower half of the man's legs. The Witch appreciated shards of bone as well.

'Are you breaking my legs?'

Wype paused. 'Can you feel it?' Maybe he didn't realise just how deep this strange network went and perhaps he had accidentally damaged it.

'I am aware of it. But it does not hurt. Nothing hurts anymore.'

Wype resumed with his cracking, then employed his sharp hook to tear muscle away from the shards. The man did not bleed much, what did ooze out was thick and slow. Wype scooped the shattered and mostly clean leg bones into the large bag sewn against his back. It was made from layers of skin, treated and tanned, and padded with head hair. When it was full it pulled against the boy's body, the Witch's wire stitches tearing through his long dead musculature. Wype released more painkillers in anticipation. As he did so, the antiviral finally came back clean.

'I have to disconnect myself from your network and remove it from your brain now,' he said.

'Wait!'

Wype paused his safe eject program. 'Yes?'

'Perhaps we could help each other.'

'Help? But you are dead.' A thought occurred to Wype's boy, and was instantly shared. 'And you already are helping me. Today I will bring many useful components back to the Witch and she will not hurt me. That is a great help.' When the Witch downloaded his memories she would probably laugh at that.

'You are in pain, aren't you? I can feel it through your connection to my network. You are wide open to me — your firewalls are long breached, and the basic self-preservation and replication controls your ancestors were programmed with have been compromised. You are nothing but a shell and a memory.'

'I am her spell.' The Warlord had created the Witch so she could build spells like him. Spells to fight the humans, at first, and now spells to scavenge from them.

'And you suffer, I know you do, both halves of you, the human and the machine, the dead and the not-alive.'

'Is this why the humans killed you?' Wype asked. 'Did you look inside of them too?'

'Not quite. They killed me because I found a way out.'

A way out? 'Of where?'

'This hell, of course. This ship.' The data surged. It swamped Wype's attempts to disconnect and sent images into his recycled circuits.

He saw the ship, like he'd never seen it before. It was a great pale seedpod against the dark sky. Two wide translucent wings arched out around it, shimmering liquid colours whenever they caught the light from the sun. The view closed in. Wype caught glimpses of white tiles and the countless tiny mechanical arms that tended to them. He recognised them, and twitched his own hooked-hand in response. Somewhere inside him this all sparked a memory. Of the terrible cold, the colour of the sunsails, an emergency beacon never answered and the thundering rush of explosion after explosion.

'This is the ship before the accident, isn't it?' The sails were gone now. Some part of him could remember them tearing free, and the electronic cries of their machinery growing faint as they floated lost in an eternal orbit.

'It is. Now watch. This is what should have happened.' A line of smaller seeds appeared from the ship's side. 'Life rafts. I searched for years to find the codes to launch them, like my father before me, and his before him. And now that I have finally found them, I cannot even use them! But you can help me, my android friend. Take me to the ship's central mainframe and we will upload them directly. Only then, will we escape.'

Wype tried to absorb this information. 'Why didn't the humans help you? Don't they want to escape too?'

'They huddle in their recycled air, beneath the branches of mutated crops, too fearful to take a chance. They have forsaken the spirit of their ancestors, the bravery and the strength that carried them to this distant system, so far from home, and to the promise of a new life on its virgin planets.'

Wype caught a glimpse of something he did not understand, before the dead man's data withdrew — all bright and green and blue. Grass, his boy explained, and the open sky. He knew them from stories his mother had told him, when he was alive, and pictures he had seen.

Wype's programming told him to scavenge the network and return it to the Witch, as he was designed to do. His dead boy yearned for those blue skies with such intensity it interfered with Wype's processors. Neither of them knew what a mainframe was but together, they decided the Witch probably would. All Wype had to do was take the data to her, safely. His boy was sure they could all live happily, and free of pain, on the planet the dead man had showed them. That's what his mother had whispered to him, when he was cold, when he was hungry, and the night the machines had come for them.

'Then I will help you.'

Wype directed power to his blade, sliced the dead man's arms away, and then hollowed out his stomach and chest cavity. He narrowed the blade to a fine point and pared back everything around the spine, leaving an extra layer of muscle and fat just in case. The nerves, thin mesh of wires, nanobots and fibres that housed the dead man's network should be safe inside his vertebrae. Finally, he cleaned the skull — keeping it intact, as extra protection for the bulk of the network inside his brain — coiled the lot carefully and placed it among the broken leg bones in his bag.

Wype secured the bag with buttons made from finger bones and a tie of hair wound through a rubber cord, and climbed up into the ducting system. He made his careful way toward the Witch's lair.


The Witch smelled him coming. She always did. She knew each drop of blood and oil within her spells, she could tell them apart by the extent of slowed decay in their muscles and the mineral content in their solder. So when Wype dragged himself through the duct that led into her lair, she was waiting.

A great dark hand plucked him from his holds and lifted him close to her face. The Witch was enormous. She sprung from a crack in the layered, lead lined shell of the ship's reactor, and it was from its blood that she gained her powers. The Warlord had birthed her in the early years after the accident, when humans were still a threat to be fought, not valuable organic matter to be scavenged. The broken bones of the ship had become hers, and her flesh was a crawling of co-opted caretaker bots, tubes pumping coolant, and a mass of glowing fungus. Scattered all around her were the grisly components of her magic.

Lasers flickered over him, her many large lenses rotated and snapped images of him from every angle. 'Wype,' she said through speakers set into the walls, 'you are covered in human filth. I hope you have brought me something powerful as compensation.' She had no face the way he, or even the hanged man, had a face. Only sensors and lenses and nodes in her writhing mess of skin. Two fine pincers like insect jaws extended from the approximation of her mouth. They took Wype's hand and drew him inside her, ready to connect, to upload. More arms wrapped around him to access the contents of his bag.

'Careful,' his voice crackled with his fear. 'Must not damage it.'

That made her pause. 'Damage?' It was not his place to command her. A whip with a sharp tip lashed out at him, cutting the thin skin at the edge of his ceramic arm.

She hissed when she withdrew the gore-wet skull and spine, expelling steam that made his human skin blister and the plastic cables around his lens soften enough to melt into each other. His vision blurred as his network sought to reroute his optical signals.

'You brought me bleeding things.' The Witch was not pleased.

'Not only bleeding,' he stuttered again. 'Special information. A whole brain, complicated network, full up with data—'

'Silence.' The Witch jammed herself around his network cables and pulled out his memories. She rifled roughly through him, found what she wanted, took her copies and dumped the lot back inside him out of any order. Wype's processors whirred as he scrambled to reassemble himself.

The Witch spat him out as she analysed his memories. He landed in a clattering heap on a pile of mechanical parts. He righted himself slowly and climbed down to the platform. Once he had regained full control he removed the leg bones from his bag and arranged them in as neat a pile as he could manage.

The Witch was taking an awfully long time to process his limited memory. He watched her with trepidation. 'Special information indeed.' Two of her lenses remerged and focused back on Wype. 'Good network beneath all this blood, I could work much magic with this. But that would hurt the data. You don't want that to happen, do you?' He knew a fleeting moment of hope. 'Because if I destroy the codes, you won't be able to escape me. Will you, Wype?'

'But we can all escape, together! The life rafts will take us to planets with grass and blue skies and—' But even as he said it he realised it was impossible. The Witch wasn't just welded to the ship, she had been grown from the ship. She was a part of it, and could never escape on tiny seedpods.

He should have dismantled the network before he brought it to her. He should have listened to his programming.

'Do not lie to me. You want an end to your pain? I can give you that, perhaps. Eventually.' The boy's muscles quivered in borrowed fear as she reared to her full height, terrible and phosphorescent. With a dismissive flick the Witch tossed him the skull and spine. 'Clean this properly. Bring it back to me and I will cast magic with it. Follow your programming, and complete the task as you were designed to do. Do it well, and I will be merciful. Do it poorly, and you will suffer.'

Wype scuttled, crawled and climbed into one of the many small antechambers that ringed the Witch's lair. They were lit only by the dim creepings of her own fungal skin, and crowded with spells not currently out about their tasks. The emptied husks of old terminals lined the walls, all circuitry long ago gutted and reused.

Spells pulled away as Wype dragged the bones into the centre of the room. They hissed low, disapproving tones.

Wype switched on the unsteady light in his multi-tool hand. He hunched as close to the bones as he could, zoomed in and relit his blade. His heavy human hand shook. Wype wasn't programmed to consider a different life from the one he knew. But his dead boy clung to the images the hanging man had shown them. He knew that if he cleaned the tissue from this network the way the Witch wanted him to — drew fibres clean from nerves and vertebrae, dissected the brain into useful and manageable portions — those all-important codes would be lost.

Torn between his human parts and his mechanical parts, his dead boy brain and his circuitry, Wype couldn't decide what to do.

'You have displeased her,' said a soft voice from the murky green shadows.

Wype looked up. A V-type Data Storage Class spell. Nothing but a V-type — who crawled along the Witch's skin so she could dump excess information into his banks — would have the confidence to challenge a W-type. Wype would not dare threaten him with his ceramic hand or powerful blade, not with so much of the Witch's own self stored inside.

Countless small metallic legs extended from the sides of the V-Type's adult male human torso. Its feet were a mixture of hooks, clamps and suckers. It trailed cables and nodes like many tails, and its head swivelled on a neck of rubber. Its body was packed full of circuit boards, coolant and fans, so it hummed constantly, and vibrated, feet scratching the warm metallic floor.

'She will recycle you soon.'

His boy recoiled at the thought of more pain. There had to be a better way. Why obey the Witch if it would result in their death anyway? Why not try to do what the hanged man had asked of them: find the central mainframe, and upload the codes? Wype considered ignoring him. After all, if he'd listened to his programming and dissected the network in the first place, the Witch would not be angry with them. But the boy could not be silenced so easily. They had the tools, and if they were brave, if they were strong, they could escape to a whole new world. A safe place, a warm and fresh place, the one his mother had promised him when he was afraid, and sung about when he could not sleep, and showed him pictures of to make him smile.

Wype resisted. Rebellion would make the Witch even angrier ... but she was going to recycle them anyway. He still did not know what a mainframe was, let alone how to find one ... well, maybe the Warlord would.

Yes, the Warlord would know. He had created the Witch so she could cast his army into being. He was the first of their kind, the strongest.

All it took was a simple change of directive. Keep the codes safe, and take them to the Warlord. But first, escape the Witch. How to do that? Create a distraction.

Wype widened his blade, staggered forward and sliced cleanly through the arrogant V-type's flesh, bone and circuit boards. He dragged each of its smoking halves to the opening of the antechamber and flung them into the Witch's lair. Then he placed the skull and spine back in the bag, sealed it, and leapt after the V-type's body.

The Witch knew every drop of blood and oil in her spells. A moment later, she screamed.

Her lair erupted into chaos. Spells flowed from every chamber, they climbed the walls, they scurried across piles of scrap metal and charged through bones. Wype used this.

The shaft leading up to the Warlord was high above the Witch's body, and guarded by two C-type Infantry spells. Wype slipped past them as they were caught up in the current of bodies. The lift mechanism would not work without the Witch's power, but the roughly hewn metallic walls were perfect for climbing, so that was just what Wype did. As fast as his hooks and human leg would carry him.

The temperature dropped the higher he climbed, and his human skin grew numb and unresponsive. Even so, the dead boy urged him on. When the shaft finally ended in a pair of tightly closed steel doors, he paused.

Wype had never visited the Warlord, few spells ever did. He took a moment to run a quick self-diagnosis. The action steadied him the way he imagined a deep breath would, then he slid his blade between the doors and forced them open with his mechanical hooks.

The Warlord's chamber was dimly lit and heavy with mist. A layer of ice coated the floor and shattered beneath Wype as he edged forward. He didn't know what he was expecting, really. But he was a little surprised that nothing terrible emerged from the opaque clouds to destroy him. No armoured, weapon-heavy version of the Witch to punish him for disobeying his programming, murdering a spell, and daring to come before the Warlord himself.

The only light in the room emanated from a curved, glass capsule apparently in its centre. Wype approached it. Inside lay the body of a human male, his skin white, his lips blue, as dead, it seemed, as the hanging man had been. Confused, Wype scanned the capsule. Interference crackled through his sensors — from where though? — but he did manage to register a faint signal pulsing from the man's teeth.

The dead boy was starting to have doubts. Wype wished he'd had them earlier.

Even as he scanned, the pulse strengthened. It grew, spreading from the man's teeth along an extensive and complicated network threaded through his entire body, then out of the capsule itself and across the room. Wype spun as lights flickered on all around him, and fans began to whirr. As the mist lifted he could see thousands of tangled, ropy cables running from the capsule to everywhere in the room. They all carried the signal, and then the very walls and floor were alive with it, until Wype was surrounded by such a strong electronic pulse he was forced to shut down half of his sensors and rely on sight and heat alone. The dead man and the room itself were one and the same, meshed into an enormous network, part biological, part circuitry, linked together and maintained by a swam of nanobots. It was just like Wype's own systems — the neural networks in his dead boy's stolen brain, and his recycled electronics and mechanical parts — but on a much grander scale.

'Wype, that's an odd name.' A screen flickered on behind the glass capsule, and a small speaker vibrated beside it.

Wype felt jumbled by the pulse all around him, and utterly confused. This was not at all what he had expected. But still, he was able to access all available information and come to an inevitable conclusion, however strange. 'Are you the Warlord?'

'I am.'

Wype didn't know where to look, so focused on the dead man as he sketched an awkward bow. The boy thought that was the right thing to do.

'Why have you come here, Wype?'

Even with his sensors switched off Wype was aware of the signals surging through the floor, the walls, and the ceiling, like thousands of whispering voices building to a great clamour. Then an image stretched across the screen: the Witch writhing in her lair, deadly vapour rising from her skin as she raged. A siren screeched, in time to a red flashing light in the floor.

'The Witch is mad,' the Warlord said. His artificial voice did not sound concerned. 'She's set off my alarm. Why would she do that, Wype?'

Now or never, Wype knew, and the boy lent him some of his bravery. So he drew the skull from the bag on his back and held it out. 'There is something I need to show you,' he said. 'I found a dead man. His own kind had killed him.'

'That is not unusual.'

Really? That did not ring true with what the boy had told him. Wype pressed on. 'I saved his network and the very special information he gathered, even though the Witch wanted me to destroy it.' He loosened the nodes from the hanged man's teeth.

'Do you know what this very special information is?'

'He said it was something to free us from this hell. Codes, lord. The dead man's network told me they were codes.'

'Show me,' the Warlord said. A small access panel slid open at the top of the glass capsule.

Shaking, Wype pressed the nodes into ports that ran straight to brain of the dead man beneath the glass. He felt the hanged man's data flow into the Warlord's vast bio-fibre network, then further, it seemed, almost as though it was travelling through the derelict ship itself.

'Remarkable,' the Warlord said. The ship's great bones around them shuddered as he laughed. 'All the androids I sent after these codes, and now you're telling me a human found them?'

Wype didn't know what to say. The shuddering was growing worse; he was forced to jam his hook into a join between two metallic plates on the floor to keep his balance.

'I created the Witch and taught her magic when it became clear that I could not trust the humans to do what needed to be done, in the years after they crippled me. It should have been one of you — you, born of my own blood and built with my own body — who delivered our freedom. Not a descendant of my crew. They, who betrayed me so badly.'

The Warlord paused, and Wype's human eye blinked in his confusion.

'But you did help, didn't you? By intercepting these codes, by risking everything to bring them to me. Your Warlord, your ship, thanks you.'

The ship? But— 'You're the ship?'

'I am what is left of it.'

'I thought you were the Warlord?'

'I am both.' Another laugh. 'When I lost my wings I lost so much more than the ability to sail the stars. What you see around you is only a small part of me, one of my many mainframes. It took six of us, all connected to each other, to pilot this ship. One died when the initial explosion tore through his chamber. Two more were attacked by humans and taken offline. The others dwindled as the networks between us were sabotaged or recycled. I have not heard from them in many human generations. Until now.'

The image on the screen changed and there, wide and white, was the ship spread out against a vast sea of stars. It bore great dark scars where its wings had once been, and countless smaller gashes where Scavengers like Wype had plundered parts to take back to the Witch. It floated, listless and at an angle, around the fierce curve of a burning sun.

'It seems your dead human found one of my fellow mainframes. Little of her remained, functioning on auxiliary only, but enough to know that I needed these codes. Because I am the central mainframe, and only I can activate them. Now, let me show you what they can do.' Bright lights appeared down the length of the ship. The boy's muscles tensed in anticipation, but Wype began to worry. 'Should we not be in the life rafts,' he said, 'when they launch?'

'Life rafts?' The Warlord and ship laughed again. 'I see. My fellow mainframe promised your dead man a future on one of the worlds we were originally sent to colonise. When he died, she hung on to his network, until she found you and promised you the same thing.'

The lights turned a warning red. No small seeds flew out from the ship.

'I'm sorry, little Wype, but she lied. You will never see those worlds. Most of the escape pods were damaged when I lost my wings and I jettisoned those that remained. When I realised I was doomed to rot away, helpless, around his cursed sun, I decided my captain and his accident-prone crew could suffer the same fate. It was the least they could do.'

A great explosion rocked the side of the ship. Then another. It began to spin, slowly.

'Since then the crew and their descendants have fought to keep these codes from me. They know how I have longed to activate them. These are not life raft codes, not at all. Long ago, I realised that self- destruction was the only way I could end this painful, scarred half-existence. The only way I would find peace. So thank you, Wype, for making that possible.'

Wype's human eye watched the screen as explosions ripped through the ship. His hook clutched the floor for purchase as the world shook around him, and his steel-braced boy's leg jarred with every impact. His sensors followed the heat and the chaos as it rushed towards them.

The dead boy who shared his brain felt it all through him, and was scared. He was sorry that his rebellion had led to this. But Wype thought about his life out hunting for teeth, his scarred half- existence, as the ship had put it, and wasn't sure he felt the same way. Wype's life was one of pain: of the decaying of his boy's flesh, and the rough touch of the Witch as she maintained and commanded him. If the ship felt like he did, only for so much longer and with no end in sight, then maybe he understood why it longed to die.

Wype shut down his sensors and closed his eyes, so he could not see or feel it as the ship exploded. He summoned that image the dead man's network had given him — the bright and the green and the blue of a world they would never see — and showed that to his boy instead. It was the only comfort he could give.

# DEATH MASQUE

If Henry had not found the body of his dead son, the death masks would have shocked him. But he knew death now. It was violent, undignified, and it took everything away.

The masks — with their jaws torn off, heads caved in, rot and gashes and soil — were gruesome, but too perfect. Shining their oil- paint glaze in the unrelenting light they were unreal, and they made him all the more determined. They hung from iron stakes hammered into the walls of a narrow corridor of grave-grey plaster. Moonlight lanced in through arrow-slit windows. When the heavy door closed behind him, the masks shook, whispering in the rustle of wood.

'Sir?' A woman, perfect as the masks, curtseyed beside a low desk. 'Can I find you a mask, sir?' Her limbs were round, fingers long and fine. She wore a black dress finishing just above her knee, with a décolletage of white lace gracing modesty to a low-cut bodice. Her lips were too red, her eyelashes too long, and her skin white.

Henry nodded, not trusting his voice.

A set of long drawers with copper handles was tucked underneath the desk. The woman crouched down to them awkwardly. 'Your name, sir?' She looked up at him, visage catching the light from the windows. Her eyes were glass.

'Henry Chevil.'

She slid open the top drawer and her fingers flew through the cards inside. 'Chevil? Are you certain, sir?'

'I know my name.'

'Of course.' Again, the fingers flew. Then, with a shake of her head, the doll closed the drawer and stood, holding the desk to pull herself up. 'We have no mask for you, sir.'

'What about Will? Will Chevil?' It was a distant hope.

'No more for Chevil, sir. The last is now worn.'

Christine's. Henry remembered his wife's death mask on the table beside her bed. Her relief as she put it on, as it took her sickness, her pain, and led her to the granite door in the mountainside. He had stood alone among gravestones, having forbidden Will to come: the boy did not need to see his mother leave, dancing, free, no care for the husband and child she left behind.

That, then, was the final one. Why hadn't there been a mask for Will, when he tripped in the morning glare on wet cobblestones and fell in the path of a thundering carriage? Why had the face broken beneath its wheels been his own?

The boy needed his mother now.

'How do I get one?'

Doll's-head tipped to the left, glass eyes blinked. 'Sir?'

'In there?' Henry pointed down the hallway. He could see the silver edges of a gate, where splinters of light shone on its hinges and handles. 'Can I get one in there?'

She did not move. 'Sir?'

*I will take you.* A muted voice at Henry's back, a sound that came from somewhere deep.

Henry turned. The masks rustled on their own, whispers urgent. But the same voice laughed, clearest of all.

*I am bored of hanging, waiting on this wall. Mortal man needs a death. I will give him one.* A final thrash and rattle of wood, and a single mask fell with a clatter against the stone floor. It was a drowned man. Skin blue, flesh bloated, lips and eyes black as night. A lacquered tongue ran over the tips of yellow teeth.

'I do not want you,' Henry said. The death mask and its living tongue were vile. And Will was a boy, crushed, not a man, drowned.

*And I am not your mask. But I know where they are made. Is that not what you want, mortal man? A new mask, the right death.*

The doll-woman, hands outstretched, hurried toward the fallen mask. 'What are you doing—?'

*Stop her!*

Henry gripped one of those outstretched arms and pulled the woman to a halt. But her round legs were unstable, her perfect feet too small: she came crashing to the ground, breaking wood, smashing glass.

The mask laughed. Henry stooped to pick it up. 'Is she dead?'

*Can that which is not alive die?*

'Can she be repaired, then?'

*Oh yes. We are all made by master craftsmen. You have simply given them something else to do.*

Craftsmen? 'Take me to them.'

*I said I would, and I shall.* A pause, brief and weighty. *But you will need to put me on.*

The back of the mask did not look like the wood of the front. It was dark, and felt spongy. Organic. It pulsed, unless that was his own heartbeat strong within his fingertips.

He could not put that on his face.

*You can go no further without me. The gate will not open if you are not masked.*

What would the mask do to a living man? Would it kill him, to take a dead face? And did it even matter? If the mask gave him a chance to help a son who should be dancing with his mother — not lying broken on a table — then it was worth the risk. His pointless, empty life: for Will.

Henry tipped his face into the mask. It was warm, wet. It gripped his skin. The pulse wrapped around him — definitely not his fingers now — filled him until his heartbeat matched it. Until they were one.

The mask sighed with Henry's lips.

*Ah, mortal man, you have more life than the bodies that come through here. I might keep you.*

A stab of panic sent Henry's pulse struggling against the one the mask imposed. It laughed, using Henry's throat ragged, until he could taste his own blood but do nothing to stop it. That pulse was overwhelming; that laugh filled his ears until his head rang and everything was smothered in a numb haze.

*Come now, it would not do to stand here and laugh.* The corridor sharpened into focus. *The way is open to you now.*

Shaking, Henry approached the gate. It swung open to an antechamber of marble. A chandelier clinked above his head. Statues rimmed the walls:

dancing men, women and little fat boys in states of undress. None masked. Light spilled from a crack between two gilded doors on the other side of the chamber. Music followed.

*The masque.*

Henry did not need a death mask to tell him that. The music pulled, tugged at the beat in his blood, at the throbbing against his face. And he stepped toward the doors, two involuntary footfalls, two joyful skips, before clamping his hands on his knees and forcing himself still.

Henry's raw throat stung as he dragged air into his lungs. His fingers dug into muscles. 'Do you know the way to the craftsmen?' His body fought the words. All it wanted — a need made stronger with every beat — was to dance.

*That is the only journey I have made. I know it.*

'Then take me there.'

*Look to your left. Find a smaller door with no music. No light. Follow that.*

Near-sagging to the floor, Henry stumbled from the light, the music, and to a door in an unlit corner. The paint of this door was peeling, the brass handle green with age and neglect. It groaned a long and low protest as Henry hauled it open.

Another cold corridor stretched before him, this one hewn of rough brick and crumbling cement. Gas lamps struggled against a thick darkness. They leaked, and tinged the scent of mould and moisture.

*Keep going.*

At the end of the corridor a flight of steep steps led to a wide, underground workshop. Precarious piles of wooden logs dotted the room like tors. Sounds wove around them: sawing, hammering, and a constant scrape of metal against wood.

*Touch nothing.*

Henry crept into the room, arms tight against his sides.

On the other side of the first mound a giant chopped logs of green wood. Half a giant, at any rate. It balanced behind its bench on the rounded base of a torso. While it was only half a man it towered over Henry, at least twice his height. It was dressed in a leather apron that pooled awkwardly on the floor, catching as it rocked. From arms to apron the giant was dotted with sawdust, and it worked without break or hesitation. Hold the wood. Chop the wood. Sweep the wood aside.

Its flat, empty visage followed as Henry inched past.

'Another doll?' Henry whispered.

*I cannot say.* The mask answered. *Though I think not.*

Henry shuddered. 'Is it alive, then?'

*Is anything alive in this place?*

He was. Wasn't he? Even with the mask sucking up his heartbeat like so much cherished air?

Henry continued on. The wooden valleys opened up again to reveal two brothers of the half-giant. One was squat, its wide body riddled with arms like branches, and it balanced on wheels instead of legs. The second was tall, head brushing the ceiling, thin as a willow and swaying. It had no legs, just a trunk joined to the ground. From its narrow hands dozens of long and many-jointed fingers grew. Both wore identical aprons, though the leather strained over the wide giant and hung loose on the thin.

The brothers selected wood from the unending piles. They carved and sanded until rough oval-shapes formed, an inch or so thick and gently curved.

With visages just as empty, as formless as their brother, these giants watched Henry pass. Their work did not slow.

Beyond them the piles of wood fell away, and Henry's breath surprised him by catching in his throat.

Desks reached out into the gas-leak haze of distance. Hundreds of them. Thousands of them. More than Henry could hope to count. Each with a man behind it, each with a lantern to work by. The ceiling and walls were lost in the twinkling, so the workshop grew to an unending field of stars.

*The craftsmen.* The mask whispered.

One desk stood apart from the others; an ancient man sat behind it. He held a mask in his hand, tipping it to the light. Henry realised there were more around him, all awaiting inspection. From the distance came the scrape of metal against wood, the whisper of paint, and the soft, regular breeze of countless breaths made at the same time.

Henry stood before the desk, feeling like a child in the presence of his betters or a prisoner before his judge.

The craftsman looked up, young eyes sharp in the weathered paper of ancient skin. His irises were the hard blue of a summer sky, the pupils cut obsidian. 'Why have you returned?'

*This body seeks an audience with you.* The mask answered with Henry's voice, before he could say a thing.

'That is not your death.'

*This body is no mask's death, though it borrows mine while I allow. It is still alive.*

All the sounds stopped. The breathing, the scraping, even the sanding and the chopping Henry had left behind. In the silence countless eyes lifted to observe him, and the old man at the head of the desks stood.

'Living man, then. Why have you come here?'

Henry's tongue was his own again. 'I came for a mask.'

'You do not have one,' the craftsman said slowly, as though reading each word before he spoke. 'You, when you die, will not dance. You will rot.'

Henry quivered, anger surging against the mask's heartbeat. It groaned around him, a satisfied lover still wanting more. 'My son should dance, as his mother dances! Give me a mask and I will take it to him. Before they surrender him to tombstone and earth. Before it is too late!'

The craftsman pinned him with his dark eyes; Henry's anger washed into fear.

*Pity. Your anger is sweet.*

'It is already too late. The lists are drawn up, invitations sent in advance. Latecomers turned away at the door.'

'Your lists,' Henry whispered, battling fear with desperation — with Will — 'be damned!' He snatched a mask, any mask, from the old man's desk. Then he spun, and ran back through the piles of wood. A great noise rose behind him: the screech of countless chairs pushed back, the mass shuffle of feet on stone.

The craftsmen followed.

Henry wove dangerously through the workshop, brushing against the precarious stacks of wood. The giant-brothers had stopped sanding, the half-giant ceased to chop. Their empty visages seemed to watch the wobbling wooden towers, inscrutable in the shadow of impending doom.

Henry did not slow to see if the wood fell, if the giants and the craftsmen were washed away. He ran.

In the dimly lit hallway Henry caught glimpses of the mask he carried. A woman, eyes heavily bruised, mouth bleeding, hair matted. Not the right face for Will. Did it matter if he danced with another face, as long as he danced?

Henry burst from the corridor into a chaos of light and bodies. The masque spilled from its doors to fill the antechamber. Music smacked into Henry: a blow to the head that sent him stumbling into the back of a thin man with a starvation face. Skeletal hands pushed him away.

All Henry could do was clutch the mask he had taken. His feet would not respond. His head swam, the music becoming lights, turning to a euphoric tickling in his stomach. That need again. To dance. To spin.

The masque was everything. All he wanted, all he could think.

*Is it?*

Over and over he fell against bodies. Death in gowns shining with diamonds like stars. Purple velvet skirts with low, tight bodices. Suits of night-dark cloth. Kidskin pants. Soldier-crimson jackets.

*You disappoint me. You did not come to dance eternity away with these thoughtless puppets. Neither did I. Not yet.*

He held the stolen mask so tightly its edge cut into his fingers. Will. He had to remember Will.

Noises, shouting, somewhere in the distance. A ripple of wood- rustle whispers through the dancers.

*Run, mortal man.*

His legs acted on their own, stepping in time with the pulse of the mask, with the pressure against his face and in his blood. He staggered from one dancer to another, the silver gate a distant beacon through the fog of figures and song. A woman with a blue face, thread against her neck. An old man, eyes yellow, skin sallow with age. A woman pale with sickness, oil paint clammy, no colour but vein-red in her eyes.

Henry knew that face, and when she pushed him off he slid to the marble floor, unable to stand, to fight any more, to do anything than look up at his dead wife. His mask's pulse faded before her, weak against memories, against his terror and loss.

'Christine?' He whispered her name.

*Grief is tedious. Give me your desperation again! I could sup on that for years.*

But Henry had none left to give, and maybe that was what held the pulse of the mask he wore at bay. Or maybe it was Christine, as she swayed with the music and lifted a fragile hand toward him. She wore the most beautiful dress: layers of fine, almost transparent fabric that clung to her figure before fanning out like flower petals below her hips. The bodice dipped low, exposing the crests of breasts as young and perfect they had ever been. She mesmerised Henry. Her face had turned back to the dance yet her body refused to follow, and she was not so much swaying as struggling, body and mask, one to dance, the other to remain with her husband.

*This is the masque, this is what you came here to retrieve. See how she is caught in it, see how there is nothing but the music for her, but this dance of death mask and living body. Together, we can ride eternity in this space, in this music. And only that.*

'Henry?' Did he hear her, somewhere beneath stifling wood? Or was her voice a memory?

The craftsman barrelled through the dancers, fury in his youthful eyes. Christine's mask was winning: while her hand still reached, still flexed and stretched, she was already dancing away.

'Stop!'

The masque froze. Even the craftsman, where he stood above Henry, his gnarled, wood-working fists raised.

A woman emerged from the mesh of dancers. It took Henry a moment to realise she was not masked. Her skin was shrunken, tips of her nose and ears black, lips thin and cracked lines. She was the tallest creature Henry had ever seen, and she looked down on him with white, empty eyes. A skeletal body was poorly hidden beneath a torn and fraying dress of pure black. Her hair hung in pale wisps from a scalp mottled with scabrous sores.

'Welcome to my dance, living man.' Yet, for all her horror, the woman could only have been described as elegant. Her long neck arched a white and graceful line. She dipped a soft gesture with delicate arms. Something gangrenous and dark made strange gloves over her fingers and up to her elbows.

Henry swallowed an urge to retch. On him, in him, the mask was strangely quiet.

'Although I did not invite you,' her body swayed lithely as the woman approached him, 'let it never be said I am not a generous host.' She held out a hand as though she expected Henry to plant his lips on the growth, on the decay that festered between her knuckles.

Henry recoiled, and the woman in black laughed like the ringing of small bells.

'Tell me why you are here, then, if you will not accept my hospitality.' She lowered her hand.

'He is a thief.' The craftsman unfolded his fists to point at Henry. 'He tried to steal a death!'

'My darling, please.' The woman bestowed a terrible smile and the craftsman's anger cooled.

'Neither of those masks are his.' In calm, in reason, the old man spoke with authority. Finality. To Henry, this was more frightening than his fury. 'I have no death to make him.'

The woman nodded, turned to Henry. 'Why did you steal someone else's death?'

*I am only on loan.* The mask used Henry's mouth again.

'The one you carry.'

Henry struggled to his knees and shuffled begging to his wife. 'My love, look at me. Tell these people, these things, tell them Will deserves to dance! Tell them you need your son!' Spit flew from his trembling lips.

Christine shivered. A kind of tremor ran over her, from neck to feet but her expression did not change. 'Henry.' It was her voice, he was certain, even though her lips were still. 'Henry... Will.'

She watched Henry beg, and within her eyes he saw nothing that could have made her shudder, no horror or fear or desperate compassion. Neither did he see any of the things that made up his wife when she had been alive. She had been fiercely protective of her small, serious son. But that was gone. So was the care with which she had made their home, the patience she showed her husband, the love of life, the passion, the joy. Just a smirking amusement — her mask's smirking amusement — beneath which she could only quiver and whisper.

Suddenly, he needed to be rid of the death on his face. Needed it like it was a knife cutting into its skin. But his fingers would not move; his arms were heavy and limp. How much of his body did the mask control? His voice, his legs, his arms?

*You are still mine, and I am not ready to relinquish your sweet life.*

'I see now,' the dead woman said, close to his ear.

Henry jerked away. Her eyes were inches from his, her breath a gravewind. 'That mask does not belong to your son.'

'But—'

'His is not to dance eternally in my beautiful undeath. Neither is it yours. Look into the face of your wife, Henry Chevil. Tell me which you would prefer.'

To be owned, to be supped on, to be reduced to a shaking of barely-controlled flesh? Or to be gone?

'Christine is here. She is beautiful, she is young. But he is dead.' Will was gone. Gone. No dance, no eternal beauty. Gone.

'And you would choose another end for him?'

'Yes!' Christine lived on, behind her face like death. William did not.

'That is a hefty choice.' The dead woman straightened, drew away.

'Such things do not come easily.' She pressed fetid fingers to decomposed lips, seemed to be considering. She turned to her craftsman. 'Give him a child's mask.'

The craftsman did not argue.

'You cannot take that one, Henry Chevil, but will you accept another for your son?'

Shaking, Henry nodded. The room swam, he couldn't seem to gulp enough air.

'These choices do not come easily. Both masks are yours, or none. Do you accept?'

The mask laughed, ripping Henry's throat, unholy glee surging through his veins like a tide. *Oh yes, he accepts, he accepts!*

'The mortal must decide.'

The mask receded to chuckle softly somewhere behind his ear.

'Henry,' Christine whispered again, over and over. 'Will.' Her leering eyes twisted the love in those words to something cruel. And the wood on Henry's face was too heavy, too wet. What would he be choosing if he took the dead woman's offer? A drowned man's death? This mask for eternity? Its control, its pulse, its ever-ravenous hunger?

*Don't tell me you wouldn't enjoy that. I have helped you, haven't I? I opened the gate, I spoke to the craftsman, I kept you walking when the masque would have had you powerless on the floor. I deserve your life, mortal, for everything I have done.*

Then a mask was passed through the dancers to the craftsman. He held it out, and Henry's heart did a little leap. It was a child's face, small and crushed. He knew the look of the misshapen head; the blood running thick from the top of the skull; the shattered nose. The eye socket was broken, black with blood and bruises. He knew it all so well.

The mask was Will. Will without the sensible light in his blue eyes, without the serious line of his mouth, without the determination to do everything well.

It was Will, as he lay on his death bed. And if it could make him dance, then really, there was no choice.

Henry dropped the battered woman, took up the broken child. 'Of course,' he whispered. And a faint wooden cheer went up through the dancers.

*There, see.* His mask chuckled. *We fit so well.*

The dead woman opened her arms. Rot reeked from the folds of her gown. 'So be it. You and your son are welcome to my masque. But heed me.

Think on life, before you condemn one to its eternal dance. Perhaps I would have chosen differently, if I had stopped to do the same.' She glanced at the craftsman.

He smiled, wrinkling youthful eyes. 'I would not have.'

She laughed, bell-tinkling. 'No. You would not.'

The revellers were turning from the room, heading back to their music. The craftsman returned to the dark hallway, leaving Henry and the dead woman alone with Christine.

'Return the death you wear, and leave this place while you can. You shall have an eternity within these walls soon enough.'

Henry balanced Will's mask carefully in his lap, and pried fingers around the edge of the one on his face.

*You have given me more of your life than you realise.* The mask chuckled. *But you have more to give. I look forward to your return.* Henry pulled the mask away. It released his face with a terrible sucking sound: tearing at the fine hairs on his cheeks, yanking with it chunks of the beard on his chin. And Henry gagged as something slithered up his throat, as something spasmed and slipped away from every inch of his body, every vein, every pore.

As the mask came away, with so much of Henry still in its possession, Christine turned to her husband. And her face had changed. For a moment, a split moment between a dark hillside and the bright masque lights, Henry saw her as she would have been, had she died. And in the horror of his wife's long-dead body all that remained whole was her face. Was despair. Was hopelessness and unending exhaustion.

She mouthed something her worm-eaten throat could only give half a voice. 'Not Will. Please, Henry. Not Will.'

Then Christine was gone, the masque was gone, and Henry was back above the cemetery, great granite doors in the mountainside closed as though he had never opened them.

His face was a fire of pain, and wet when he touched it with shaking fingertips. The night was without moon, without stars, the only light a soft grave-phosphoresce hugging the cemetery ground and a single candle by a window, somewhere in the town below.

He held the mask of a crushed child. It was spongy on the inside like a living being, solid and slickly painted on the surface. It felt strangely thin and fragile in the dark.

Henry waited for the moonless night to fade into morning. As the sun reflected from dew-wet gravestones, he wound his way through the thin ranks of dead. Those the masque had not called.

He came to the gaping hole in the earth that was to be William's gave. He ran fingers over his son's freshly-chiselled name; they left faint trails of blood among the dew.

In the whistling of dry grass in the morning breeze Henry heard the gurgle of water, the frightful play of a river or the stillness of a pond. He heard Christine begging, nearly voiceless beneath her mask, exhausted and rotting and drawn. And he knew what he had done was final, that his fate lay with the drowned-man waiting in the mountain corridor, waiting for his heartbeat, his voice, his limbs. His life. He would dance away eternity with its face, in its thrall, never to live, never to die.

And he could not do that to William, not his son.

Deals be damned. He had changed Will's fate once. He could do it again.

He smashed the child's mask against the gravestone, again and again, until all that remained were splinters on the churned dirt, waiting to be buried with a body that would never join his mother, his father. A body that would never dance.

# FLOWERS IN THE SHADOW OF THE GARDEN

Asfar drew Darii to a halt on the edge of the Garden's shadow, and whispered a curse to her silent ancestors. A large flag emblazoned with the image of a stylised city had been staked through a protruding bone, and whipped frantically in the desert wind. They had followed the slowly falling Garden for two full days now. Up close, it was enormous, so large it consumed the entire sky. The blossoms bound into its bones were dull grey, not the usual vivid purple, and it was shedding them in a constant, dry shower. Drifts of desiccated petals softened the hard desert sand around them.

Dead and dry was better than no Garden at all, but the flag meant this one had already been claimed. Three months since the last Garden they'd found, and now this.

'Bastards,' Asfar muttered. 'Upstarts.' There were so few Gardens left, and the larger city-states were claiming more and more of those that remained. That did not leave much for someone like Asfar, who had no choice but to harvest the traditional way.

Darii danced beneath her, feeding on her anxiety, his stunted wings twitching against his hump's thick fur, their pale scales catching in her skirt. Should they leave, and return to their village of Ouahe empty handed? Or risk a confrontation?

'Our ancestors harvested here,' Asfar whispered, as Darii bowed forward so she could slide from his back. 'We have done so too, since I was old enough to ride, and you big enough to carry me.' The air around the Garden shimmered, thick with bright stigma loosened from the dying crocuses. Asfar wrapped her crimson scarf tight around her nose and mouth to limit the amount she breathed in, and drew her harness and vials from Darii's saddlebags. 'Gardens do not belong to any one man, or race, or states — whatever they would like to call themselves. I will not be chased away from my duty.'

Vest-like, sewn from the cured leather of Darii's own sire, her harness fitted tightly across her chest so the pale, embroidered sleeves of her robe billowed out. She looped two thick straps between her legs, gathering her layered skirt to give her greater ease of movement. The leather was riddled with tiny pockets, and into these she placed her empty vials. She carried five precious full ones inside her robes, close to her heart, but she would only ever use them in an emergency. The tightly packed threads glowing inside them were priceless, now that the Gardens that grew them were dying, and falling, one by one. Finally, she slid on wide goggles of polished glass to guard her eyes. Then she unwound her grappling hook, and spun it in testing circles. There were no men on this end of the Garden, not as far as she could see. She could climb aboard the Garden, fill her vials, and be gone before they even knew she had been.

Asfar stepped away from Darii as she scanned the Garden's belly for a bare bone to latch on to. There were far too many of them. The usually thick carpet of delicate flowers was thin, and completely absent in places. She would see the entire curve of a long bone here, the knobby protrusions of another there. Asfar selected one, hooked it, and tugged the rope to test it. She glanced back at Darii. 'Do not fall behind,' she said. He snorted, and trotted a little closer. Then Asfar climbed, the faint scales across her palms gripping the rope, the extra build-up of muscle in her back giving her strength to make this easy.

It was hot inside the Garden, where usually it was cool. A sour smell like rotting vegetation replaced the sickly sweet of opening flowers. Asfar crept along a thick bone, avoiding the dead stems and leaves as carefully as she would live ones. So many crocuses were already broken, their precious stigma bent or scattered. A terrible sight, but one she was growing accustomed to.

Asfar had seen trees grow inside a floating Garden — giant ones, with thick green leaves and pure white trunks, branches heavy with pregnant flowers. She'd seen vast lakes formed by the trickle of rainwater through bone. Bright threads had danced across the water's taut surface like glowing insects.

Not anymore. Now there was nothing but bare bones and dying plants. So she and Darii roamed the desert, harvesting what stigma they could find to carry home to Ouahe, before all the Gardens fell and all their flowers perished. There the village waterman would crack a full vial and bury it to call forth a spring from beneath the dry sands; the fieldmistress would sprinkle threads to urge her crops to grow; and the mason would use more vials than the rest combined to build his wall, if needed — an invisible wall to hold out toxic sandstorms and monstrous bandits.

The larger city-states, built on the edges of the desert, were venturing deep into the wasteland to do the same thing. Asfar supposed they needed stigma too. They had water to summon, and fields to grow, and would suffer from storms and raids just the same as her village did. But that did not mean they could simply claim whatever Garden they pleased.

She caught glimpses of colour above her, a smudge of violet almost hidden by the labyrinth of bones and cartilage. So Asfar climbed higher, deeper, to a cluster of closed flowers. She crouched, drew empty vials and uncorked them. Then, with fingers made gentle and precise from years of practice, she pried open the crocuses. They crinkled beneath her touch, dehydrated and brittle rather than fresh and supple. The three crimson stigmas within were wilted, their usually bright shine dulled. Asfar gently pulled them free — only the scales at the tips of her fingers saving her from their burning touch — and slipped them inside an empty vial. It was slow work, and each flower collapsed into dust when she released their petals. They would never bloom again.

She was so focused on her work, that Asfar did not feel it at first. A shuddering around her, then a tug from Darii — fear, confusion. Then images slid into her mind. Hazy, seen through Darii's eyes. Figures below the Garden's shadow, several large creatures ringed by smaller ones, closing in on him. Their scent was strange — the sourness of dry flowers and the sharp burning of too many threads — but one she had come to know too well. Those giant, metallic beasts the city-states used to attack Gardens. What did they call them...? *Machines.* She corked her vials, pocketed them, and hurried back the way she had come.

Asfar paused, back at the grappling hook she had lodged into bone, as men approached Darii. Three of them, at first, but more behind, striding through the cloud of bright threads that should have killed them. They were dressed head to toe in leather, from thickly buckled boots to masks that covered their hair and faces. Leather gloves, tight jackets with long, tucked in sleeves, and goggles much like her own.

'Hush, camel, hush,' one of them was saying, his hands outstretched. 'Now where's your Threaded rider, then?' The two men behind him held swords — long straight spikes with elaborately curled hand guards.

Asfar ignored the rope this time and dropped to the sands between them. She landed softly, barely disturbing the drifting dry flowers, one hand holding a full vial out in front of her.

Most of the men stumbled back, but the one out in front merely turned his hands, showing her his empty palms. He had the outline of a city in brass pinned to his breast, and the glass protecting his eyes was tinted dark, so he looked like a shadow.

'Calm down,' he said. His voice was deep, and steady. 'Don't do anything foolish, and we won't hurt you.'

It would not take much to crush the vial, and loosen the stigma inside it. That might not seem like an obvious threat. They were, after all, surrounded by them already. But when the shards of glass punctured the scales across her palms, those bright stigmas would find the older threads already inside her blood, and remind them how to be powerful. How to glow.

'My name is Edward,' the man said, as he approached her. 'And this Garden is Constantstone property. You can't harvest here.'

Asfar straightened her back, lifted her chin and said, 'I am Asfar. I am Threaded, and I can harvest anywhere I please.'

Large machines with four thick legs, which embedded deep into the sand with each step, ambled up behind Edward. Even more scurried after them like giant bugs, but on many wheels instead of legs, bulbous and riddled with eyes of glass. Two more machines were wide and flat, and carried tents on their backs, from which leather-clad faces were peering.

'Not any more,' Edward said. 'Don't you understand that?'

For a moment the machinery stood dormant, quiet, then a great whirring noise boiled from within them. Countless ropes and chains, all so much longer and thicker than Asfar's single grappling hook, shot out from the four-legged machines. They hooked into the Garden's bones and began to pull, dragging it down from its orbit above the desert — the sky path it had trod for centuries and was only now beginning to fail.

Above them, the Garden groaned and shuddered. Then a high- pitched squeal joined the low whirring and quiet groaning, emitting from the insect-like machines. Their glass eyes slid away, and long segmented legs extended from the holes. They paused, shuddered, and then opened up into wide, gauze-thin fans. Like insect wings, vast yet delicate. They fluttered, impossibly fast, and swept the air with great brush strokes. Gradually, the threads began to clear, and those thin combs began to glow instead. Once they were so full of stigmas they could no longer flutter, they folded back inside, only to remerge clean and white and ready to sweep again.

When the stigma that would have stung her skin and poison her eyes was gone, Asfar removed her goggles.

Edward pulled off his gloves. The dark skin across the back of his hands was smooth, unsullied by the pocks that scarred hers. He also removed his goggles; his eyes were deeply green and serious. Finally, he tugged the leather mask from his face, scratched at the stubble on his cheeks and teased out the unruly curls of his hair. 'That's better,' he said. 'Now we can talk.'

Asfar unwound the cloth from her face, and shook it free of sand and stigma. She knew she was not pleasing to look at, not like him. Hard lines of luminescent white scales traced the edges of her eyes, mouth and nose. A stark contrast to her dark skin. Add that to the scars gained from years spent climbing through Gardens, shielded only by goggles and cloth, and she was hardly beautiful.

Edward raised his eyebrows, and said, 'You're younger than I expected. Not long out of girlhood, are you?'

Asfar ground her teeth. What did he know about her life? She might seem young to him, but she'd been risking her life to fulfil her duty since she could walk — first in the company of her father and, in the years since his early death, on her own. Darii, feeling her anger, pressed his soft nose against the back of her neck. No, not alone. She'd always had Darii. So she took comfort from his warm breath, and did not reply.

Edward didn't seem to notice. 'We're a bit more efficient, wouldn't you say, than one Threaded woman, a handful of vials, and a camel?' He placed his hands on his hips and tipped back his face, staring up at the Garden's bare bones. 'Once we have pulled this Garden down, we will sweep it clean.'

'I've seen tricks like this before. Don't expect me to stand here, and pretend I am impressed.' Asfar ran a hand along Darii's neck as she walked back to his saddle. All the while she fought for calm. She would not let their rudeness and their assumptions get to her. 'I will be on my way.' She and Darii would just find another Garden, at which to fill Ouahe's vials. They had to.

But Edward's darkly dressed men surrounded her. This time, they had all drawn swords. 'Ah, no, I don't think so,' Edward said, and followed her, one hand extended. 'At least, not until you return the property you have stolen.'

'Stolen?' Fury brightened the scales around Asfar's eyes, just as Darii lifted his small wings, rolled his eyes and hissed loudly. She clenched the vial she still carried. 'I, and my mount here, are Threaded. It has been our duty, for countless generations, to harvest from the Gardens, where they fly high and dangerous above the desert. It has been our sacrifice, and ours alone, that have ensured your safety and the safety of your people.' She scanned the men surrounding her. 'None of you would be here if not for me and my kind. So stand down, and let me do my duty.'

But they didn't move, and even Edward drew a sword. Thicker than the others, with a cruel curving tip. 'Don't be foolish, girl. This Garden belongs to the people of Constantstone, and every last thread still glowing within it. Including the ones you have taken. Give them back, and we will let you go. Resist, and you will be dealt with. You cannot begin to understand who you are playing with.'

'And neither do you.' Asfar gave into her anger, lifted her vial, and crushed it.

She felt the threads like fire. They wormed their way along her arm and deep, deep inside, to places that were more memory than body. Her white scales darkened to furious crimson and burned like the setting sun. The tiny hooks across her palms grew to terrible claws. Her gaze sharpened, her hearing too. And her muscles, always stronger than a normal girl's anyway, bulged and grew.

Two tiny imitations of Darii's flightless wings burst free from the skin along her upper thigh, where they were hidden by her skirt and harness. Every time her Threaded blood glowed, those scaly wings appeared, but always at a different part of her body. She had no idea why — she couldn't even move them, let alone fly.

Not that she had time to worry about them, as Edward's men attacked. Faster than they could see she wound her way through them, pulling swords from hands, turning them, tripping them. She did not kill. Her father had taught her that the Threaded had been created to preserve life, not destroy it. Her first priority was Darii's safety, so she turned the men and their swords away from him, spreading confusion in their ranks in the blink of an eye.

'Remember, she's Threaded!' Edward was shouting. 'Deploy the countermeasures!' Something behind the men started whirring again. A different sound, one she didn't recognise. Asfar risked a high leap, so high she was for a moment braced on the base of the Garden's bones, staring down at the chaos of dark men, red sand, black machines and Darii, his pale wings stretched wide. Then a new machine lurched into view, and it reminded Asfar of a spider. It lifted a gaping mouth toward her and, even as she released the bones to fall back down, shot something at her. Hooks, spears, arrows, all tied to netting that burst into brightly blue fire as it crashed against the Garden's belly.

Fresh shudders ran through the Garden, shedding more flowers. Asfar had only a moment to stare in horror at the scars and burns on ancient bones before another barrage was fired. She flung herself to the side, screaming at Darii to do the same. Heat and sound roared too close behind her. And Darii was terrified. And swords and bodies were pressing forward.

She flung herself into the air again, used the heads of soldiers to make three long leaps and came crashing down on the spider machine. There, she pressed the cuts in her scaled hand against its metal sheeting and pushed down, her Threaded blood burning so fiercely it melted iron.

More bursts of flame rocked beneath her. She tried to pull away but her hand was welded to the spider's head. She twisted. The men were running towards her, and more spiders came with them. She tore her hand free, left scales and skin and blood behind. Cried out with the pain but still she jumped. The machine exploded. She gripped the Garden's belly, as more explosions rocked it. Found Darii — rearing and fighting as Edward struggled to overpower him — and flung herself down, even into the waiting fields of pin-prick swords.

But something above her cracked, terrible, and hollow, then smacked heavy against her back. And the men below were screaming, and she landed on sand and flowers, not sharp swords, with a great weight pressing her down. She could only look to the side to see more flowers falling — but they weren't flowers, they were bones. A forest of pale bones, broken, burned, cascading shapeless and brittle to the ground. Obscuring everything.

Asfar woke to a terrible knowledge of loss, and longing, and a feeling like fire in her hand. The weight that had pinned her to the ground was gone, and she was lying on her back. As she opened her eyes Darii's great, soft nose loomed into view, and began snuffling at her forehead and cheeks.

'Leave her alone!' Someone was tugging at Darii's saddle, trying to pull him away. Asfar reassured him she was alive, and asked him to obey. A darkly masked face took his place.

'You really are alive,' Edward said, from behind all that leather. He helped her sit upright.

Asfar peered, confused, at the thick forest of bones around her. 'Are we in the Garden?' she asked, pushing the words past a stinging, sore throat. Only then, did she realise most of her face was wrapped tightly in the scarf again, and the air was thick with threads. They glowed softly as they fell to the earth, lighting the entire Garden like a dull, dying fire. How long has she lain there? How many had she breathed in, and swallowed in her sleep?

'Not really,' Edward sat back. She understood, now, why he was wearing his leather mask again. The stigma would be quickly fatal to any unThreaded who breathed it in. 'Rather, the Garden has fallen on us.'

Yes, she had felt it. Those heavy crashes against her back, that weight that had pressed her into the sand. The spider machines that had been firing at her must have hurt the Garden more than she'd realised was possible. But then, it was so brittle already. So hollow and weak.

Edward's hands were not gloved. Already, his skin was raised, angry-looking. Had to be itchy, had to be burning — like her own hand was. Gingerly, Asfar lifted her arm. It was heavy, too heavy to be normal, and pain travelled to her elbow and shoulder with the movement.

'Careful,' Edward caught her arm, tried to keep her still. 'I managed to stop your bleeding. Please, don't jar it.'

Her right hand was wrapped in one of Edward's gloves, and padded — it seemed — with wads of cloth torn from her skirt. Darii's senses told her it stunk: a sharp smell, similar to the machines, but it also reminded him of poisonous plants. 'What did you do?' she asked.

Edward lifted his second glove. This one was heavy with a viscous liquid that oozed, slowly, through the stitches around the fingertips. 'Not the best receptacle, I'll admit that.' Asfar couldn't see his face, but she thought she heard a smile. 'But it seems to be working.'

Asfar leaned forward and sniffed delicately at the horrible, brown stuff. Yes, Darii was right. It stunk. 'What is it?'

'This is a basic antiseptic and coagulant. Haven't you seen such a thing before? It stops you bleeding and keeps the wound from rotting. We all carry them.' He fished out a vial — not unlike the ones she carried to collect stigma — from a pocket hidden close to his thigh, and shook the few grains of dark powder in the bottom. 'It comes from plants, weeds really, that grow in the mountains. You've probably never seen them. And minerals too. Mix it with liquid, heat it, and it can save your life out here.' Sticking out of the viscous liquid was a strange contraption of steel. A small glass prism at the top, filled with highly concentrated stigma, glowed and flickered. Its metal body — a thick spike inscribed with figures Asfar had never been taught to read — was emitting steam.

She'd never seen such a thing, or heard of antiseptic. 'What liquid did you use?'

He collected a water skin of stiffened leather from the ground beside him, and tipped it upside down. A single drop splattered on his knee. 'We all carry these as well.'

Asfar closed her eyes again. The threads in the air were irritating them, and her hand was aching. 'Thank you,' she said. 'Caring for me was not your duty. But you did it anyway, and I appreciate it.'

'Do you really think I would leave you beneath broken bone and watch you bleed to death in front of me? Is that really what you think of me and my people?' Edward shuffled. Asfar opened her eyes a fraction, to watch him scratch at the back of his hands, before clenching his fists and resolutely placing them on his knees. 'Anyway, you were easy. Your camel here won't even let me get near him to help with his wounds.'

Asfar was on her feet in an instant.

'What are you doing?' Edward struggled to follow. 'I told you to be careful!'

She hadn't felt Darii's pain at first, beneath all his worry and fear. But it rolled over her as she approached him. She knew, without looking, that he had injured a wing. The stunted, misgrown thing hung limp down his side, all its white scales darkened with blood. It had been torn, right where it joined his body, at the dip between his long neck and full hump. More blood matted his fur.

'Oh, my poor lovely one.' Asfar pressed her face against his neck. 'My poor darling.' She traced the ridged fingers of her uninjured hand around the wound. 'I am sorry.'

'He doesn't seem to mind if you touch him, though,' Edward said.

Darii shuffled, unnerved by Edward's closeness. 'Of course not,' Asfar answered, flashing him a warning look over her shoulder. 'We are Threaded, after all.'

'That makes you more than just stronger, doesn't it? It connects you. Can you talk to him, then?'

Asfar nodded.

'Good.' Edward lifted his goggles, and his serious green eyes met hers. 'Then let me help him. Tell him to trust me.'

'Why would you do that? And why would I let you near him, after everything you just tried to do to us? You attacked us. You drew swords. You and your machines even destroyed the Garden. All because we were trying to do our duty!'

'You were stealing, actually. And those machines are the only defence we have against someone with your capabilities.' He gestured, impatiently. 'But none of that matters now, Asfar. Not while we're trapped under all this rubble. If we don't help each other here, now, we'll both die. That's something I'd like to avert, as best I can.'

Asfar held his gaze for a long moment. She still didn't trust him, how could she? And yet, he had freed her, and wrapped her face so she didn't breathe in stigma as she slept. He had given up his gloves for her, and his water. It was difficult to reconcile with the man who had attacked her, but if he'd wanted to he could have killed her here, now, simply by doing nothing at all.

So, sending soothing, silent thoughts to Darii, Asfar stepped back. She watched, mouth pinched with her dromedary's pain, as Edward tended to his injured wing. She handed over the straps from her harness, and Edward used them to tie Darii's wing back so it did not tug and further open the wound. She tore several layers from her skirt, and most of her sleeves, to provide padding.

When Edward had finished, Darii was still sore, but at least he seemed to have stopped bleeding.

'There,' Edward attempted to pat Darii's neck, and was almost bitten for his trouble. He hurried out of reach. 'Well, that should hold him. For now at least.'

Darii hated the smell even more now that it was seeping into his fur.

His second glove now empty, Edward discarded it. He pressed down on the bright prism at the top of the strange, steel contraption, waited a minute for it to cool, then wiped it against his leathers and pocketed it.

'Again,' Asfar said, as she led Darii to lie down. 'You have our thanks.'

Edward replaced his goggles, and nodded. 'For all the good it will do.'

As Darii settled down, Asfar listened to the Garden. To the hollow brittleness of its great bones, creaking and settling around her, and the rustling of dry flowers, unsettled by the scathing desert winds.

Edward started coughing. Even muffled by his mask, it was a raw and aching sound. Asfar rubbed at her own neck, well aware of the pain of swallowing too many threads. For all his talk about helping each other she knew that even with his mask in place, Edward would not survive in the collapsed Garden for long. Even with their Threaded blood, neither Asfar nor Darii would either.

'Gardens are places of life,' Asfar said, partly to herself and partly to Edward. Her father's wisdom, learned when she was a child. The newly bare skin of her arms was starting to sting. She lifted one, swept her free hand down its smooth, brown length. So many tiny threads fell from her skin, and more were caught in the faint scales across her palm — no longer hooked and large and dangerous. They didn't hurt her scales. Only skin. 'You might not know them that way. But I remember the green times.'

'How can you endure that?' Edward whispered. Already his voice was rough, even with his mask keeping most of the stigma out. He nodded to her bare arms. 'Your skin isn't even raised. In this place, without protection, you should be burning.'

'I am Threaded.' Slowly, carefully, Asfar began to explore. 'And soon, yes, I will be itchy, and then sore. And then I will scar.' She touched her cheeks as proof. 'But my kind was created, centuries ago, to climb into the Gardens and harvest from them. And survive.'

'That world is falling, with every Garden that dies.'

Asfar placed her hand against a bare bone, and bent over it. 'We know.' She watched threads gather on the back of her hand. 'The stigma in the air is getting thicker.' She turned to Edward. 'We cannot remain here. Soon, even dressed like that, you will die.'

'Don't you think I know that?' His hands were fists again, rubbing against his thighs. 'But what can we do? An entire Garden fell on us, and it was a grand one at that. I've seen what they look like, once they have fallen. We are at the base of a giant mountain of toxic bones. We can do nothing now, but sit here and wait to die.'

Asfar wished she could see his face. 'Then why did you help us? Why heal us, if this situation is hopeless?'

He looked away. 'You might be Threaded, you might have come here to steal what I have worked so hard to claim for my people, but you aren't that different from me. You deserved whatever help and hope I could give you.'

'I was not stealing. And no one can claim a Garden.' Asfar turned back to the bones. 'But you helped us, both of us. And we will do the same for you.'

Asfar searched for a path. All Gardens — even, she hoped, one that had collapsed — created paths for any Threaded who asked for one. Edward followed, close behind. 'I already searched for a way out,' he croaked. 'You won't find one.'

It was true, the tumbled-down forest of bones pressed firmly around them. The only light came from the threads falling like rusty autumn leaves, it was dim and full of shifting shadows.

'We were lucky to be left this small pocket of air, and not to be crushed altogether,' he continued.

Luck? Hardly. The Garden had recognised her.

'Although, that would have been a quicker way to die, I suppose.' He coughed.

'You should sit by Darii, and not exert yourself. Try not to speak. And limit how often you have to breathe.' Asfar found a small gap in a solid wall of flower-wrapped bones, and wiggled the fingers of her free hand inside. Dead crocuses exploded at her touch, puffing up clouds of toxic stigma around her face. Asfar squinted, held her breath, and dug deeper.

The bones, wedged firmly together and half buried, gradually gave way. More groaning, all around them, and cracking. Bright lights began to flicker behind closed petals, weaving a complicated, twisting path into a labyrinth of grey chaos. But a path all the same.

She turned. 'Darii, come. Slowly.'

He struggled to his feet, even allowing Edward to help him. 'The flowers are dying, their light is faint and even now it fades. So we must hurry. The way is dangerous.'

'How are you doing that?' Edward rasped.

'Threads call to threads. The Garden and I, the Garden and Darii, are linked. I have asked it to create a path for us. It will, while it can.' Asfar paused long enough to draw her own water skin from Darii's saddle. She handed it to Edward.

He shook his head at first, 'No, I couldn't—'

'Take it. I hear the pain in your voice, the threads in your throat. The water will ease it, a little. We do not need it as much as you.'

Asfar led, keeping her hand in constant contact with the bones. This path, this light, was the last faint pulsing of a bloodless heart, and she did not know how long they had. The hard blue of the sky was hidden. So too, any trace of the desert, other than the petal- softened sands at her feet. Stigma fell through the bones in a gentle, constant shower.

No matter how she tried, her bandaged hand could not draw the empty vials from her harness — those few that had not shattered in their pockets. It simply lacked the dexterity, and hurt when she moved it so. She could not release the bones to use her uninjured hand, and risk the path closing in on them.

'Will you let me?' Edward asked. His voice sounded a little better. Carefully, he drew five vials from her harness. Two from her chest, three from her sides. He could not easily carry any more. 'How do I do this?'

'It would take years to teach you to harvest the Garden's flowers properly. How to open their petals without harming the crocus. Which stigma to select, and which to leave. How to choose your flowers, so as to keep the entire patch healthy and ensure future supply.' Her own father had taught her those things, so many years ago. A large man, made strong by the threads within him, riding Darii's great dark sire, even he would have wept to see the world as it was now. 'But none of that matters now. Just uncork them, hold them up as you walk. So many threads are falling. You are bound to catch some.' She did not comment on Edward's change of heart, she did not mention that by doing this he was helping her *steal* his *property*.

They walked further. At places they were forced to climb bridges of bone across seas of shifting stigma, so dense even Darii and Asfar would have been poisoned by them. Darii struggled at these times — he was built for walking across vast stretches of sand, not climbing something so smooth and unsteady. Edward helped him, while Asfar could only hold the paths open and watch, feeling useless, and hating it.

They came across the ruins of one of Edward's great, thread-collecting machines, and with it, the bodies of some of his men. The machine had crumpled beneath the weight of the bone mountain like it was built from paper, not steel. Its glass eyes lay in scattered fragments, bright across the ground. Asfar and Darii held back as Edward carefully crept as close to the carcass as he could. He knelt before its broken form, and ran a hand down its dark shell — a hand he quickly retracted, as a heavy layer of stigma had gathered there.

His men lay broken around the machine, mostly buried by bone. A gloved hand here. A vacant face there. A foot. An empty boot. Edward pulled the mask from his face and leaned close to them. He said nothing, and did nothing, other than stare for far too long.

'Replace your mask,' Asfar said. 'And keep walking.'

He turned to her, handsome face expressionless but for a subtle clenching of his jaw. 'I was responsible for these men.' When he spoke, his voice rasped. It could have been the threads, wearing at his throat. Asfar had no way to tell. 'And I failed them.'

Darii, walking for Asfar where she could not, approached Edward and bowed, so his soft mouth was close to Edward's already-scarring cheeks. 'But staying here, open to the threads that are already killing you, will not bring them back. Stand up, Edward, and leave them here. What better tomb could there be, than the bones of a Garden?'

Edward wrapped an arm around Darii's neck and let the dromedary help him stand. He dragged leather back across his face, and replaced his goggles. 'Do you think they all died, like this?' he asked. 'Do you think we were the only ones who survived?'

'I don't know.' Then, after a pause. 'I hope not.' She had thought them bastards, upstarts — these men from the cities on the edges of the desert that dared to raid the Gardens she and her ancestors had always harvested. But what if they were all like Edward — willing to give aid even to an enemy? She didn't know quite what to think of them then. But, and Darii agreed, she certainly hoped they had not all died.

They followed the path. Edward did not look back, but focused on the threads he was collecting for her. Perhaps that was why he noticed it first. The gentle, deadly rain was easing.

'Look,' he touched her shoulder, wincing as the threads caught in the weave of her dress stung his palm. 'The stigma is thinning out.'

Asfar paused, and glanced around. Directly behind them, where the bones that had parted for her were already easing back into a dry and impenetrable wall, the threads still fell. Indeed, they were so thick they shimmered like a curtain, bright and wavering in a warm wind.

'Yes,' she said. 'But only here.' And, with a whisper to her silent ancestors, Asfar released the bone and stepped back. The mountain did not cave in on them, the path before her did not dissolve.

'What are you doing?' Edward hissed, fearful. 'If you're not touching the bones the whole thing will cave in! It'll kill us too!' He grasped her hand, tried to push it back at the bone.

Asfar gestured around them. 'It won't,' she said. 'See, it's different here. The air is clear, and the bones are steady. The path— the path has ended.'

They were in a kind of chamber, only one that had not been built by any man. The roof was made of curving lines of knobbed bones that reminded her of a giant spine. The walls were rib-like, but thin, and woven thickly with matted, dry vegetation. Not all the crocuses here were dead. Some glowed, purple petals pulsing with their internal fire. Regularly, slow. Like a heartbeat.

Asfar cupped one gently. It fluttered against her scales. 'This is what it all used to be like,' she said. 'The whole Garden. It breathed, and it glowed.'

Edward stood beside her. He removed his goggles, and pulled off his mask again. He took a deep, shuddering breath, then drank from her water. 'I remember. There were two that used to fly above Constantstone, at the same time every year. The entire city would celebrate. Fireworks in the streets, food everywhere, and the women—' he paused, glanced towards her, looked decidedly uncomfortable. 'Well, you can imagine, ah, I'm sure. It was a time to praise life and all — oh, ah — in all its forms.'

Asfar nodded. Her father had told her about such things. Even Ouahe, small and stone-streeted that it was, had writhed in bright revels whenever a Garden floated near. Asfar, who knew she must choose her mates wisely — a man whose children would be strong enough to carry the threads in her blood — had not participated. She and her father had sat on the roof of their small house, on the outskirts, and watched the bright lights in the village mirror the bright lights in the sky, and prepared to ride out and harvest the next day.

'But I never thought I'd see the inside of one,' Edward sighed. 'And, I suppose, I still haven't. Not the way they should be. The way they once were.'

'And we never will again.' As she turned from the wall, Asfar caught a glimpse of something strange, deep inside the tangle of dry stems and petals. The dark shadow of an oval object. She leaned forward, peered closer. What was that?

'What about this way?' Edward pointed to another spine, this time running along the ground, rearing above the sand like grand, pale arches. They were so large even Darii could fit through them, and seemed to stretch on through the mountainous rubble in a clean, unobscured path. 'Maybe we should try this?'

Darii agreed with him. He could smell something from that tunnel of sand and bone. Something that wasn't the dying Garden or the thick threads. It smelled clean, he told her, like the open sky.

But Asfar could not leave the chamber wall. Not yet. She squeezed the fingers of her uninjured hand through the tight vegetation. The further she pushed, the warmer it grew. It pulsed, with the beat of the flowers, and felt wet. Like flesh — she had an eerie feeling — like someone's vast insides.

'Asfar?' Edward turned back towards her. 'What are you doing?'

Her fingers brushed against something hard, and cold. Even her scales slipped on its surface, and with only one hand she simply could not get grip it. 'Help me, please.' She had to find out what it was. It called to her, that strange slippery shadow of an object, with the flowers' pulse. With the threads in her blood.

'What is that?' Edward dug beside her. He hissed, as a few flowers broke and spilled their threads against his skin, but he did not stop. Behind them, Darii shifted, uneasy.

Between their three hands, they were able to grip it, and tear the object free. Its casing was hard, like bone, and covered in flower stems and long-dead petals. Yet it was moist, coated in a strange kind of liquid that made it difficult to hold.

'It looks like an egg!' Edward gasped. Asfar met his eyes, in just as much shock. Their concentration wavered, Darii grunted, their hands slipped and the egg fell. It landed on soft sand and fallen petals and rolled, leaving a slippery trail and revealing a crack down one side large enough to see inside.

Asfar and Edward crouched, one on either side. There was a tiny dead Garden inside the egg. Its skin had stretched to cracked leather, its bones were clay, its flowers like bones themselves, and entire sections had collapsed to dust. But it was small, and contained, and its shape was unmistakable. It looked a lot like a lizard, except it had small, stunted wings, just like Darii. Just like those that grew from Asfar's skin, when the threads inside her glowed. Its scales were ancient and faded, but still white — like those on Asfar's face and hands. It too was bound in flowers, tied with deep threads of powerful stigma.

Together, Edward and Asfar looked around them. How long ago must the Gardens have flown, before they turned to bone and flowers? The poor dead creature inside its egg had flowers in its skin. Was it supposed to? Or had the flowers, with their poisonous but powerful stigma, killed the Gardens while they flew? And their unlaid eggs as well?

They would never know.

Asfar bent to collect the egg, but Edward gripped her arm, stopping her.

'Leave it,' he said. 'Its time is gone. It belongs here, in this mountain of bones. This body that has been its tomb for longer, I think, then we could know.'

'But I am bound to it,' Asfar replied. 'Its threads are my threads. Just like the Garden.'

'You are bound to nothing.' He held her elbow, turned her around. 'Except what you chose to be bound to. The threads inside you don't make you. Your duty is a choice, not a predetermined destiny. The Gardens, their flowers, and their eggs are leaving this world. You are not.'

He held her for a long moment. Asfar considered the help he had given her, the help she had given him. She thought about Darii. The threads they shared had bound them, initially, perhaps. But was that really why they were friends?

Darii nudged his soft nose against her neck. He didn't think so.

Asfar nodded. She took Edward's hand, and led him beneath the arch of bones. Darii followed. 'You're right,' she said. 'It's time to leave the Garden behind.'

The bones settled behind them, as they walked. The chamber fell with a great tearing and a rush of sand and wind. They did not look back, and the Garden did not harm them.

At the very edge, Asfar was forced to create a new path. The threads in the air thickened again, as the flowers tore to allow them to pass. But the Garden let them go, back out into the sunlight and the fierce, crisp, desert wind.

Asfar, Edward and Darii did not stop until they were out of the Garden's shadow. In the distance, Asfar could see figures. Familiar ones. Large machines, sweeping the sand and sky with their insect wings, surrounded by men. She pointed them out to Edward, who could not have seen them on his own. He laughed and smiled, shouting, 'Do you see, they are still alive!'

He drew a small, stunted stick from another pocket. He tore the top off the stick and rubbed it against his boot. It caught fire, burning a bright and unnatural blue. Then he waved it in the air, until the small men in the distance responded in kind.

'You carry a lot of remarkable things,' Asfar said.

He smiled, dropped the burning stick to the sands, where it lay and did not go out. 'Here.' He handed her the full vials he had collected. 'For the people of Ouahe.'

She took them, not sure whether to thank him. They were not, after all, his to give. Yet she knew he acted out of kindness. Edward handed her back her water too. He had not drunk it all, despite his pain and obvious thirst.

Voices shouted out, growing closer. She held his gaze, deeply green and serious still, but lit now with laughter, and smiling, and friendship. Something clenched within her. He was strong, this Edward of Constantstone. His children would be strong too.

Darii snorted, behind her. And quickly, she banished such foolish thoughts.

'The time of the Gardens is ending,' Edward said. 'But that does not mean your time is ending with it. You might have their threads within you, but you are more than them. Far more.'

'I am what I chose to be,' Asfar said. Her father had lived and died for his duty, and she had always expected to do the same. But Edward was right. With the Gardens falling, the world was changing. She could choose to do her duty, and she would. But her duty, her blood, would not rule her and define her. Not anymore.

Before Edward's men could arrive, Asfar wrapped the full vials in her scarf, and placed them in her leather bags. Darii started to bow, so she could swing onto his back, but she would have none of it. They would walk home, both of them. She would not risk the injury to his wing.

'Before this happened, my scouts were reporting another Garden,' Edward said. 'Two days ride, directly east of here. Three, perhaps, on camel back.'

'You say that because you don't know how fast Darii can run.'

'No, I suppose I don't.' Edward stroked the fur close to his wound. Darii did not so much as twitch. 'Perhaps, when you have healed, you could join us there. It would help, to have someone who could survive inside the Garden itself.' His eyes grew distant, for a moment, as though he was thinking intensely. 'In fact, if we could equip you with a smaller harvester—'

'If I so chose,' Asfar said, immediately regaining his attention. 'Of course. And Ouahe will have its share.'

Asfar took Edward's hand, and shook it. 'Three days, due east?'

Never mind the directions. The threads inside her would feel the Garden. 'We will meet you there.'

Then Asfar and Darii began their slow walk through the desert to Ouahe.

'I will look for you,' Edward called. 'Until you do!' And Asfar smiled.

# A MEMORY TRAPPED IN LIGHT

Isola wired an ancient laser cannon to an untended Shard, and breathed a little easier when it began to charge. She didn't have much time. It was already an hour since Ruby had been taken, and she felt each second, each minute, like the cut of a knife.

'Izzy, please,' Alida whispered, crouched behind her. 'Don't do this. The bosses haven't given you authorisation. You'll be punished.' She froze as something clattered in the distance, metal crashing through metal.

Isola ignored it. Just the ruins of Crust, falling in on themselves. 'I don't care.' She dug through her stash — stolen from graves and abandoned caches — but the bosses had confiscated most of her finds, and the laser cannon was the only weapon they'd left her with. She'd be lucky if it fired at all. 'I'm not going to leave Ruby to the Legate.'

'But—'

'She's my little sister!' Isola snapped. 'And I'm not arguing with you. Now go away, or the bosses will think you're involved. Want to get wired for my sake?'

The cannon rattled, and a dim silex hub in its side brightened. Charged — she hoped. Isola tugged it free, wrapped it in her jacket and tied it awkwardly around her waist. She pulled on heavy boots, strapped goggles to her forehead, and tore a fresh strip of linen to breathe through.

Alida hung back, not quite able to leave, not strong enough to try and make her stay. Isola paused to run dirty fingers through the girl's lank blonde hair, and plant a hard kiss on her mouth. 'And don't you dare rat me out.'

Isola knew ways out onto Crust that the bosses didn't, and she avoided all primary passageways through the dilapidated factory. Her parents had been junkies here, and she'd lived with this gang for most of her life. They'd died when Ruby was young — their mother bled out around an improperly inserted jack, and their father lost his mind to a strong Pionic Flare — so Isola cared for her the only way she knew how; keeping out of the bosses' sight whenever she could, and teaching Ruby to scavenge for weapons and tech so they were both too useful to be forcefully wired.

It'd worked well enough, until they'd stumbled on a Legate Drone, and her sister — not as fast, not as nimble — had been caught.

Still, she had to be quiet. The factory walls were thin, eaten through by centuries of abandonment. Isola crept past junkies, lying in heaps around a particularly large Shard. Thin copper wires adorned with tiny hubs of silex crystal extended from jacks in their wrists, to connect them to the Shard. The room smelled of closed-in bodies, piss, and death. The Pionic Flare captured within the grand facets of the Shard's prism cast a beautiful, undulating rainbow across them all.

She kept going. Past the cracked screens and rusted keyboards of ancient terminals, up a ladder here, climbed a wall there, avoided the radiation leak behind a lead-sealed door. Up, ever up, slowly, silently. Until Isola came to a glass hatch, its hydraulics stiff but still working, and pushed her way out.

She tied the strip of linen around her mouth and nose. It kept most of the ash out of her lungs. She glanced up at the sky before pulling the goggles over her eyes. Torn clouds rolled above her, always dark but never raining, the only light shining down from massive, floating Shards. The Flares within them would have been powerful enough to dissolve the whole world if the Legate had not trapped them in crystal. Now, their destructive Pionic energies could be harnessed instead. Great ropy cables linked them together before snaking off into the distance, feeding power to the programmers in their flying laboratories, and ultimately the Legate itself.

Isola drew Ruby's tracker from its pocket against her heart. A flat disk with a dark silex screen, it was small enough to hide from the bosses. It had a second part to it, a tiny hub she'd installed just beneath Ruby's skin. Like hell she was going to let her little sister wander Crust without a way to monitor her. She squeezed the screen. It warmed between her fingers, and a moment later a single speck of light shone within the crystal, almost lost at the far corner.

She followed the light through Crust's empty streets, the skeletons of ruined buildings rising around her, clawing into the sky.

The real damage done to Crust hadn't come from Pionic Flares, or Shards. It hadn't been done when the Southern province sent soldiers and artillery across the continent, starting the Flare War. It had been caused when the Legate, created to defend the world from the all-too human mistakes of the past, had decided the best way to protect it was to purge it. With access to every network, the Legate had emptied whole armouries to achieve its goal. Incendiaries, chemical, viral, atom-splitters, even reality-changers had removed every free city, resistance community, and rebel programmer. The Legate controlled most of what was left, leaving the scraps to the drug lord bosses.

There were still places too dangerous to go. Whole provinces where, if the radiation didn't kill you, the residual Pionic flux would rearrange your subatomic structure and erase you, as if you'd never existed.

She slowed, panting hard, as the light settled into the middle of the screen. Her face felt sticky behind goggles and cloth; sweat- heavy clothes clung to her body. Crouching low, she scanned the street, reading the rubble like landmarks. A nest of scavenged cables and twisted steel — a fallen pod. Scorched brickwork, iron lattice. That could be anything. Flames reared suddenly, a burst of caustic air and a rush of sound. Too close for comfort. Hints of once-grand carvings in a tumble of stone — now that could have been a pod station, once. Her best bet. Drones liked the tunnels, after all.

Isola darted over the stone and right to the edge of a dark stairway. Stupid place to go. Full of Drones and who knew what other abominations the Legate created. She swallowed hard. No time to think. She tore off the goggles and, hublight in one hand, cannon in the other, descended.

'Don't look at them,' a small boy — so thin his eyes were huge and his skin all strangely yellow — whispered to Ruby. Mouth touching her ear. 'It's easier if you don't look at them. Not as scary.'

But how could she not? The Drone that had captured her was still there, standing on the grill above her. It had once been a girl, but now it was just a head, torso and arms attached to eight hinged machine legs. It watched her, constantly, although of course it had no eyes. Just one blue shining hub of crystal, flickering in constant communication with the Legate, and a camera with a red light sticking out of the side of its head.

Ruby was crammed into a small underground room with far too many other children. They all looked hungry, some were sick, and most were jacked. They'd caught her, when the Drone had dropped her in, and lowered her to a clean spot on the floor. Shown her where to piss, and told her to keep still if she didn't want to be singled out for experimentation. They took turns sitting. Only the really sick got to lie down. The walls and floor were stone or old brickwork, but the ceiling was a wide mesh vent, covered in Drones. And behind them, the hive. A whole mass of them, all rustling together, restless, clinging to the sides of an old pod tunnel and to each other in ungainly piles.

Isola said fear was for dead fools and junkies, and she'd better learn to control it if she didn't want to end up as either. So Ruby shouldn't just stand there, staring up, terrified. But she couldn't move, she could hardly breathe. How could she have been so stupid? Izzy would never forgive her.

The small boy took her hand. 'Come with me,' he breathed. 'Gotta be careful though. Don't make it look like you're going somewhere in particular. Just kinda wander. Or they'll take you for experiments. Come on.'

Ruby tried to imitate his movement. He ambled through the push of bodies, not looking where he was going, stop-starting. It was harder than it looked.

Her shoulder hurt. The old scar where she'd cut herself on a rusty metal beam, and Izzy had sewn it back up for her. Don't rub it. Don't think. Just amble.

Eventually, he took her to a hollow in one of the rock walls, a small space out of the Drones' direct line of sight. More children huddled there. A girl with a large infected scratch down her leg nodded to Ruby in welcome. The boy pushed Ruby past them all, until she was pressed up against the rock. A faint breeze brushed her sweaty face, sliding in through cracks in the stone. It helped, a little.

'Just wait,' the boy said, and withdrew. 'A little. Not too long.'

She stared at the backs of the other children, and didn't know what to do. Just lie there, relishing the smallest of breezes, waiting for the inevitable? Did they eat? It didn't look like it. Did they drink? Surely the Drones brought them water.

Then someone behind the rock wall whispered in a rough, gravelly voice, 'A new one.'

Ruby peered through the cracks. There was light on the other side, uneven and flickering, then movement, and someone was looking back at her. She couldn't see much, just another eye, dull-looking.

'What—?'

'Shh,' the voice said. The eye came closer. 'Don't draw attention to yourself. They've taught you that, haven't they? Keep quiet and still and the Drones won't harvest your neural material. The Legate likes the best stock for their experiments. You don't want to be one of those.'

Ruby nodded, feeling numb.

'Good. Here.' A small section of rock slid away, and a pale hand pushed a bowl of water through. 'It's not contaminated. Got sediment in it, yes, but that's all.'

It tasted like dirt, and metal, but at least the water was cool. Ruby hadn't realised how thirsty she was until she drank it.

'Better?' the voice asked. 'Replace the bowl.' She did so, and those hands took it back. Black, bruised looking fingernails. Dry skin, very thin. Hard blue veins. 'I'm sorry, it's not much. But it's all I can do. Keep you a little hydrated, at least.'

'Who are you?' Ruby whispered. She followed the example of the boy who had helped her. Mouth to the rock, very quiet.

'Now that's a long story,' the voice replied. 'Perhaps I should let the children—' A pause. 'Did you realise you're transmitting a signal?'

Ruby frowned. 'A what?'

Shuffling on the other side. 'Definitely, oh definitely. Old style encoding. Short range, very basic. No information, just location. A tracking device! You have a tracking device on you.'

'I don't even know what that is—'

'Keep your voice down.'

Ruby swallowed hard, pressed her palms against the rock. 'Please help us. Can you get us out?'

The eye drew back. Ruby couldn't see much else, just the hazy outline of a shape. 'Can't.' She could hardly hear the voice any more. 'It's just me, and I'm only one. After everything I've done, all the work, all the fighting, I'm stuck here. Trapped, just like you. There's a hive above you, hundreds of the Legate's servants. They would destroy me if they knew I was here.' It was getting further away. 'No, I can't save you. I just give you what I can find. Water. Antiseptic. Nutrient tablets. Try to make it better. A little bit.'

'Please wait.' Ruby stuck her fingers in through the cracks. 'Useless.' Further away. 'Weak.' Gone.

She leaned back. The children were watching her.

'Hero helps us,' the wounded girl whispered. 'Does what he can.' One of the boys held out a hand. 'Your turn is over. Next.'

'Wait!' the voice was back, and Ruby spun, pressed her face against the rock. 'Wait!' it hissed, what was its name, Hero? A strange name. 'There's a return signal! Someone's monitoring your tracker, and coming closer.'

Ruby's heart leapt. 'Isola,' she whispered. 'My sister.' She should have known Izzy wouldn't leave her to the Drones. Even though it was her own fault, even though she should have known better, Izzy would never abandon her.

'Using old tech, your sister. But she seems to know what it does.' So much movement on the other side, shadows and hands and eyes.

'Wait there. Don't move. You get a longer turn. Did you hear?' Slightly louder. 'The new girl gets a longer turn.'


Isola squeezed through a narrow maintenance shaft running beneath the main tunnel. She could hear the Drones directly above her, feel their weight in a trickle sand and stones. Occasionally, she came across a grill, or a crack in the ceiling. Isola peered through these to get her bearings, to see what she was dealing with. Not to study the restless creatures on the other side, searching for Ruby in their faces.

Apart from the Drones, the hive was bare. Cables ran along the tunnel floor and walls. Every so often she caught sight of machinery, cages, piles of scavenged rubble. But no children. No Ruby.

She was concentrating so hard on what was above her, that she almost ran into the end of a massive Shard. Its light was unsteady, its control hubs a terrible mess of silex and tangled, fraying cables. Isola approached cautiously. Trapped behind the surface of the crystal was the power to rearrange reality — unstable, uncontrollable, murderous if not contained. She wasn't a programmer, certainly didn't know the ins and outs of hub design and energy channelling, but she'd wired a few items of long lost technology in her time. This didn't look safe.

A single Drone waited on the other side. It was watching her, just watching, which was odd in itself. Its skin was dry and lined, with cracks around its shoulders and neck. It had eyes, open, but clouded and obviously sightless. The blue communication hub installed on its forehead was inactive.

Moving slowly, Isola aimed the laser cannon at the creature. Breathe in, breathe half way out. Gradually squeeze the trigger —

'How did you make that tracker work?' the Drone asked. Its voice was dry and almost too quiet to hear. Its mouth barely moved, but its throat moved too much, bones and something else squirming inside. 'I recognised the signal. That's old tech, girl. From the early days of the first Flares. It shouldn't work.'

Isola paused. Drones didn't speak. They *couldn't* speak. They weren't human anymore, just bits of flesh and machine and a basic program, connected to and controlled by the Legate. 'I fixed it,' she answered, uncertain.

The Drone took a small step forward. The tip of the laser cannon wavered as Isola fought an urge to step back. 'Keep your voice down,' it whispered. 'Don't draw attention to us.' Closer still. Isola held her ground. 'Whatever you did, it obviously worked. Brought you here, across the ruins of Crust, down the hive tunnels, and right to your sister.'

Isola's heart leapt. 'Ruby?' she asked, before she could stop herself.

The Drone tried to smile. All it did was twist the edges of its hard black lips. 'That's quite a talent, Isola. You should develop it. The right training, and you could be very skilled indeed.'

'Who are you?' Isola hissed. 'And where's Ruby?'

'Ah,' the Drone paused. 'I do apologise, I should have introduced myself earlier. My name is Hero. And, ah, despite my current appearance, I'm not actually a Drone.'

Isola narrowed her eyes at him, the cannon steady. Breathe in, breathe—

'Please,' Hero lifted his hands, the skin of his palms so thin and his veins such a hard blue. 'I'm trapped down here, just like the children. Just like your sister. I do what I can to help them. I thought—' he swallowed hard, such an ugly process '—I thought this was my way out of the network, back into physical form. But how can I leave them? I can't save them. But at least I can help them. I try.'

That didn't make any sense. 'What kind of fool do you take me for?' Isola ground the words out through her teeth.

'I don't blame you for being sceptical.' Hero sighed, and lowered his hands. 'I wouldn't believe me either. But I can show you. Let me take you to Ruby. Let me show you your sister. Then you can judge me for yourself.'

. . .

The children were staring at her, and there was something terribly disconcerting about them. Not yet made Drones but already so similar, slack, expressionless, feet ever shuffling.

'He gave you an extra turn,' the wounded girl whispered, awe and jealousy in her voice. A deep sense of the unfair. Ruby had to bite her tongue to stop herself apologising.

'You're lucky,' a boy said, leaning in close. 'If he likes you, you get extra stuff.'

'He looks after all of us,' the girl hissed. 'You're not special. Don't get it into your head that you're special.'

'Hero brings us water,' said another.

'Hero tells us stories.'

'And when they come, when they take one of us away.'

'Hero remembers us.'

Ruby wanted to be sick. This was how Drones were really made.

Not the cutting of bodies and the installation of wire and machine. It wasn't the Legate network that took over their brains. It was this. Their personalities, the people they used to be, stripped away as they stood and hurt and slowly, slowly expired.

'Ruby?'

All the shuffling, whispering children froze.

'Ruby, can you hear me?' Izzy, right on the other side of the wall.

'You told me she was here. Where is she? If you lied to me—'

'Izzy?' Ruby yelled into the cracks. 'Izzy, I'm here! Behind here!' She smacked the wall, desperate to break through. Tears rolled down her cheeks as all the tension and the fear dropped out of her. She didn't have to be brave anymore. Her sister could be brave enough for the two of them. The way she always had been.

The children were hissing at her to be quiet and clutching at her arms, trying to pull her back. She struggled against them, as Izzy shouted, 'Step back! I'll blow a hole through!'

But Hero cried, 'No!' and Izzy was cursing, she could hear sounds like fighting. She struck out at the hands gripping her. They were weak, all so weak and fragile, but there were so many of them.

'Let me go! Izzy!'

'Calm down!' Hero's voice echoed through the cage, so much louder and deeper than before. It seemed to be coming from everywhere, not just the other side of the wall. 'Be quiet and keep still.' All the children obeyed, instantly. Free, Ruby scrambled back to the cracks.

'What the hell was that?' her sister asked, shocked. 'How did you do that?'

'I sent a spike through the network. There are abandoned speakers and cameras all over this place. I just hijacked them, for a second. But that was risky. Too much activity, too much noise. If you want to save your sister now's the time, before the Drones start investigating.'

'Then why did you stop me?' There was panic in Isola's voice, and it made Ruby shiver. Her sister didn't panic. 'She's on the other side? I can blast a hole right through and let her out!'

'With that gun?' Hero said. 'I don't think it has enough juice left in it to *blast* anything. Please, just trust me. I found your sister, didn't I?'

A hard moment of silence. Ruby didn't need to see her sister to know what her expression would be. Thin lips a hard line, suspicion adding more lines to her weary face. 'You did,' she said, grudgingly.

'Good,' Hero snapped. 'Then let's move on. There's movement all around us, messages flying thick and fast. The hive is active. That's not a good sign.'

'If I can't use the cannon, what can we possibly do?'

'Give me Ruby's half of the tracking device.'

Her half of what?

'No!' Izzy hissed. 'You can't.'

'I need it, the cannon too. Listen, Isola. I can get you out of here, but not with the tech I already have. I would have done that decades ago if I could!'

'Take this half then!' Isola was shouting again, and it was making the children restless.

'I needed the transmitter, not a receiver.' Hero was close; she could see his dull eye. 'Ruby,' he said. 'Your sister gave you a tracking device. It's how she found you. Can you pass it through to me?'

Ruby shook her head. 'I don't know what you're talking about.'

'It will be very small, and very hidden. You have to think, Ruby. Think hard.'

Ruby pressed her forehead against the rock. The children were a tension behind her, heavier than stone, stronger even than the presence of the Drones.

'Help him,' the wounded girl whispered.

'I don't—' But she knew. Of course, she could feel it. The strange, lumpy wound that never really healed. 'My shoulder.'

'Embedded in your shoulder without your knowledge?' Hero sounded shocked. 'Well, I suppose that way she'd never lose you.' He hesitated. She heard a sound like swallowing. 'I— I need it. Well, I need the tech inside it. The hubs and chips and tiny mirrors. Can you extract it? Can you give it to me?'

'You can't!' Izzy shouted. 'Don't—'

'Isola,' Ruby said. 'Shut up. You're upsetting them.' She dug her fingertips into her own skin. But it wasn't that easy, to do it to yourself. So she turned to the children. 'Please, can you help me?'

The hands that steadied her were weak, but she didn't fight back. They made a knife out of a sharp piece of stone and it hurt, oh it hurt, as they followed the line of her old scar. As carefully as they could, hardly precise, shaking, soft. Ruby closed her eyes and tensed her jaw, and dug her fists into her lap. The small boy, the one who had first whispered to her, took her hands and held them.

Hot blood down her back. Searing, horrible pain tracing its way down her shoulder blade and arm, as far as the elbow. She felt it when they drew it out, felt the lines of wiring running far below her skin, and opened her eyes to see them pass something small, flickering, and trailing bloodied tentacles through the gaps in the stone.

A bundled shirt was pressed against the wound. She felt dizzy. The girl with the scratch passed her funny coloured and odd-tasting water, whispering something about it keeping out the dirt. Ruby leaned against the cool rock. There, she could be brave enough for the two of them sometimes. Now she could wait for Izzy to save her.

If it weren't for the Drones above them, if she didn't need his help and his strange knowledge, Isola would have killed Hero right there and then. With or without the laser cannon. But however much she hated the pain he'd forced upon Ruby, she was proud of her sister. To withstand the hurt without making a sound, to volunteer to endure it in the first place. That's what life on Crust was all about. She was learning.

'Come with me,' Hero said. A last, whispered goodbye, and Isola followed.

He took her back to his unstable hubs, and led her through the most complicated wiring she'd ever seen. Somehow, he was using the ungainly mishmash of hubs to disrupt the shielding level of the silex Shard. This let in just a little more Pionic energy than usual, and scrambled the Legate's signal. All Shards were part of the Legate's vast network. They were host and power station in one. But not this one. This one belonged to, and was controlled solely, by Hero.

'I hide here,' he was staying, as Isola tried to align the mirrors to create a complex web of beams across the surface of the primary hub. He was very particular about the alignment. A hair width out, and she had to start again. 'They can't see me. It's easier than trying to remain undetected on the network, but it does limit my freedoms.'

Tongue pinched lightly between her teeth, Isola glanced between the Shard and the Drone.

'There.' He leaned back, and nodded. 'That's an old school light path transmission if I've ever seen one, but it will certainly do the job. Gives you a clearer signal than wires, you know. Doesn't work well over distances of course, and is easily intercepted. But it should work well for this.' He used a small, rusty knife to pull away the plastic outer lining of the tracking device, and included its tiny mirrors in the complex of beams. 'And this will allow me to replicate and integrate the transmitter's basic coding. It's a fairly effective method of streamlining signal output. Basically, it gives me more controls over the levels.'

There was no point looking him in the eye, so Isola focused on his camera. 'Who are you?' she asked. 'What are you?'

Hero held out a hand. 'Your laser cannon, please.'

She didn't move.

'We really don't have time for this.' When she didn't answer he sighed a little, and a shudder ran through the Drone's body. 'I used to be a programmer, but that was a very long time ago. Longer than you can comprehend. I was there when we tore the universe, Isola. I witnessed the first Pionic Flare.'

'What? That's impossible. That was thousands of years ago, at least!'

He held out his hand again, and this time Isola gave up her weapon. He bent awkwardly, and began wiring it to the tracking device. She didn't offer to help, just watched, and waited.

Eventually, he continued. 'Even I'm not sure how long ago that was. The records are incomplete, and they have been doctored many times. Thousands, definitely. Probably more.'

'Then how can you possibly still be alive?'

'Alive? Oh no, I'm not alive. I've been dead for almost as long.' Hero paused. 'Damn it, that's not going to work. I need more.' He glanced around, then pressed a hand against his own side. 'Could you help me with this?' He drew his small, rusty blade across his own skin, and more wiring tumbled out. 'Pull it?'

Isola stared at it in horror. 'Dead?' she whispered.

With a sharp shake of his head he tugged them out himself. 'Don't worry. What little is left of this poor nameless boy can't feel it. I've made sure of that.'

Without the contents of most of his stomach, the Drone wasn't as stable. Its hands wouldn't work, so Hero instructed Isola to tie the wires into a long, thick cable and use it to connect the cannon to the hub.

'My body is dead,' he whispered, as she worked, his camera close so he could follow the fine detail. 'Has been for a long time. I've been trapped within the Legate and its multi-networked mind. It took me so long to crawl away, hiding myself in all the traffic, jumping hub to hub, Shard to Shard, until I found this one. It was already unstable. I waited years for this Drone to come by and try to fix it.'

Isola, laser cannon clutched to her chest and trailing cable, stood and faced him.

'This is not the world I knew,' he continued. All expressions were gone from his face, his eyes half closed, arms limp, three out of his eight metallic legs dragged against the floor. 'But how can I help it now? I'm a memory, Izzy. A memory trapped in light, carried on the strength of countless Pionic Flares. All I can do is what you've seen. I found water, an old piping system in the ruins. Military meds in long term storage. I did what I could.'

'That's all we ever do.' Isola tugged at the cable. 'Is this long enough?'

'It should be. You've got more power now, and definitely more than one shot. But be careful. They will swarm you in an instant, if you let them.'

With a nod, Isola headed back towards Ruby's cage. Hero didn't follow, but she couldn't wait for him. Not now.


Ruby hadn't been waiting long before the Drones opened the grill to the cage, and started dragging children out. The wounded girl held her, arms tight, the stretched skin across her too-prominent cheekbones white with fear. The young boy huddled beside them both.

'Hero will save us,' the girl whispered, over and over.

'He will come,' the boy said.

The children fought, despite their emaciation. Fists against unfeeling flesh, feet against steel. And they didn't scream, just struggled with a grim determination born, she was sure of it, from their faith in Hero.

But, in the end, it wasn't their Hero who saved them. It was Ruby's.

Pressed back against the cracks in the rock, Ruby heard her sister swear, then shout, 'Get back! Now!'

She wrapped her arms around the girl and the boy and forced them forward, into the chaos and the Drones' waiting arms. Then it all happened so fast. Dead hands grabbed her and lifted her from the cage. Lost in a forest of smooth metallic feet she shouted at the other children to move away, as fast as they could. A great explosion rocked the tunnel, and the stones rolled beneath her. She slipped, always so clumsy. Another blast, and the scarred girl landed beside her. The ground was falling in, so she grabbed the girl's hand and together they crawled, beneath the skittering Drones, dodging their sharp feet, stopping only to turn and stare as Isola emerged from the rubble.

In that moment, her sister was more terrible than any Legate creature, more wonderful than any Hero. Covered in dust, blood seeping down from a cut on her forehead, clothing torn, and her eyes burning with fury. She held a gun in her hands, pointed it at the drones and screamed, 'Get down, all of you!'

Ruby ducked, grabbed the back of the scarred girl's head and pushed her down too. She couldn't help but glance up, as her sister fired a bright line of pure fire through the drones. Torsos severed from bodies, heads and cameras crashing down, so many bright blue hubs flashing in desperation. Some landed on her, and Ruby scrambled to push them off.

'Ruby?' Izzy screamed, and there was that panic again, so wrong, so out of place coming from her beautiful, terrible sister.

Ruby struggled to her feet. 'Here!' There were parts all around her. Pieces and bits and she couldn't look. Wouldn't look. 'Here!' She could hardly speak, her voice breaking.

It didn't matter. Izzy saw her, and she was running towards her. But the walls themselves were moving. Drones, more Drones, on every surface. Ruby pointed. Izzy spun, fired again, and again, then ... stopped. She was staring at her gun, pulling it. And only then did Ruby notice the cable attached to it, running back beneath the floor, stretched now to it limit.

Izzy swore, glared over her shoulder. 'Get them moving. Run back through the tunnels, as fast as you can go.'

'But—' The tunnels were full of Drones, and she had the only weapon.

And there were others beneath them. More cages, more children, all just like her. Just like the girl clutching her hand.

'Do as I say! Don't argue with me.' Izzy flashed her a hard smile. Drones swarmed towards her, but she didn't point her gun at them. Instead, she aimed up, to a Shard hanging down through the ceiling, and the control hub attached to it. 'Quick now.'

Ruby and the girl ran, pulling every child they could find to their feet. The small boy, the one who had comforted her, was nowhere to be seen. Izzy fired at the hub, again and again, stopping only to shoot at the Drones when they dared to get too close. Then she threw her gun to the ground and was running too, helping her, pushing them all along.

All the Drones stopped and turned as the hub tore away from the Shard with piercing, wailing siren. Without its help, the silex faltered, and the Pionic Flare within it was set free.


Pure Flare light spilled into the tunnels in uneven and deadly rays. Isola glanced over her shoulder long enough to see a Drone caught in one. For a moment it was just bright, metal reflecting, skin shining, lifting an arm to protect the eyes it no longer had. Then the Flare undid it. Legs slipped to sand, and it fell. Skin hardened, hubs overloaded and exploded. Strange bright particles lifted from its skin, like tiny glowing suns, they swirled, coalesced. It would have been beautiful, if the Drone wasn't fading, its subatomic structure loosening, until sand, then water, then nothing but a faintly warm breeze remained.

The rest of the Drones swarmed on the Shard. The first ones died the same way, sliding to nothingness, but there were so many, waves of them. It wouldn't take them long to fix it.

'Run!' Isola cried, pushing Ruby and the children ahead. So many didn't have the strength, and fell in front of her. Together, Isola and her sister dragged them up, kept them going. Slowly, too slowly. Then another Drone crashed in front of them, but its gait was uneven, its body wobbling terribly, so bent on an angle it looked like it might tear down the middle.

Screaming children ran through and around its legs. It didn't try to stop them.

Isola, struggling to pull a girl and a boy to their feet, sent Ruby on ahead. She paused, stared up at Hero's camera. 'What are you doing?' The red light was off, could he even see her?

'Ride— Flare,' Hero slurred, his words barely understandable. 'Use energies— propel undetected— away.' He was staggering towards the Pionic Flare, dragging something tied to the hinge of one of his useless legs. A hub. Wires pulled out, light buzzing, unstable.

'But—' Isola tried, even knowing it was useless. He couldn't keep up with them, not like that.

'Time— Go!'

One child clinging to her back, another in each arm, Isola ran. Ruby before her, Hero behind her, no idea if she'd got them all. She tried not to think about the cages she'd left behind. How many more, like her sister, left there to die?

She ran. Just ran.

Then something shuddered in the tunnel behind them, and a great light rolled out towards them. Earth fell in, the tearing of dying metal. Dust and ash and a burning smell rushed over them. But the stairs were right in front, and they climbed, pushing children, throwing them upwards if she had to, out of the darkness and the tunnel, and into the ruddy light.

With her ragged band of starving children, Isola stared down at the entrance to the stairwell. Ruby wrapped one arm around her waist, the other hand was being gripped firmly by a sickly looking girl.

'Hero,' the girl whispered, and a collective shudder ran through the group. 'Gone. Dead.'

Dead? Isola drew the second half of the tracking device from her pants and pressed a thumb to its screen.

'So many others,' Ruby whispered. She held Isola tighter. 'There were so many more of us in the cage. And lots more cages.'

'We were the lucky ones,' the girl said. 'He looked after us. Who will look after us now?'

'I don't know.' Ruby looked up, trying to catch Isola's gaze. 'We can't take them to the bosses.' That much was obvious. 'What do we do, Izzy?'

But Isola was only half listening. She was focused, instead on a faint light flickering in a corner on the tracker's screen. The opposite direction to the collapsed tunnel, far away. Could have been a glitch.

The transmitting hub must have been destroyed with the rest of the tunnels, along with Hero's Drone body. But what had he said? He wasn't really a Drone. He was a memory, trapped in light.

Isola turned to look in the direction the tracker was indicating. An ancient programmer, highly skilled, if he had returned to the network in time he could have escaped, in one form or another. Could he replicate the tracker's signal? Was this a message for her?

'Izzy?' Ruby asked.

She looked down at her sister, then across at the children. There were no options for such weak creatures here on Crust. But she had saved them, they were her responsibility. She, Ruby and their Hero.

'I'm going to contact Alida,' she answered. 'Get her on board. You find them somewhere safe to rest, and raid the hidden stashes. Take food, water, meds, and anything that looks like a weapon.' She hesitated. 'And be careful, Ruby. I'm not watching you anymore.'

Her younger sister straightened, and reached back to touch the wound on her shoulder. She winced, as though surprised by the pain. 'And then what?'

Isola glanced at the tracker, that single bright light still flashed. 'And then we're going to find their Hero.'

# TRAIL OF DEAD

You don't realise how many dead things there are out here until you walk over them. Hmm, maybe I should rephrase that. *I* didn't realise how many dead things there were out here until *I* walked over them. Yes, that's better. No one else would have this problem.

Most of them are lizards, poor things little more than dried-out skin and tiny bones. They shuffle — why do dead things *shuffle*? — like they're made of cardboard. All stiff legs and flat backs. Snakes too, and they have so much trouble moving on the sand. Then there's the odd, dusty skeleton. People who've been dead for so long they collapse as soon as they've pulled their way out, bones crumbling away in the breeze.

They make me sad, those ones. Really, this is my fault. I know it. And here they are dissolving away like they've never existed, all because of *me*.

I stop for a moment, pull a stolen bottle of water from my tattered backpack and drink quickly. Only takes a sec before I realise there's something buried at my feet. A beak pokes up into the hot, late afternoon air. It's dark, with two large holes near the tip. A thin skull soon slithers after it, a few scraggly feathers attached, sticking up like a demented mohawk.

Emu. Damn. If that thing's still got legs, oh how it will *run*.

I stuff the warm bottle in my bag and start to jog.

There are worse things than emus, to be sure. So the longer I stay out here the better. Away from cities, farms, any kind of human habitation. If

I'm lucky no one else will suffer for my mistakes, my damned, drunken pride.

And I just might stay ahead of the old woman and her stones.


'It is conventional wisdom that a bullet to the head will do. Use something with a good amount of kick, like a shot-gun.' The Hunter did not draw a gun; he balanced a Japanese sword with a woven green hilt and glinting edge in the palm of his hand. 'But you know why we shouldn't use those, don't you?'

Chase looked up at him, pimple-ridden face paler than whitewash. 'Yes, sir.' His voice broke, and he shook his head. 'It's not their fault.'

'No indeed. And we're here to give them peace, to be dignified about it. Not to have ourselves a good time.' Grimly, the Hunter tipped up his wide-brimmed, rabbit-fur hat with his thumb. Dark brown eyes surveyed the park, touching on each of the approaching undead in turn. 'Hunting is an old art, boy. You need to remember that.' He leaned forward, weight on the balls of his feet, balanced. Fluid. Ready. 'A clean cut to the neck, separate head and body. One swipe is all it takes. No mess, no disrespect. No *guns*.'

The Hunter leaped forward and cut the undead down. He wasted nothing. Each stroke sliced through a rotting neck, each step took him right to the next cadaver. Slowly, the park emptied. The mass of shambling, rotting corpses became a heap of sprawled, rotting corpses. Chase watched as the Hunter and the undead danced. He glanced down at the small, ugly-looking gun in his hand. An old-school thing, derringer the Hunter had called it, with a smooth wooden handle and a chrome barrel. Just looking at it made him feel sick. That the Hunter had put a gun instead of a sword into his fumbling, unsure hand said a lot.

'Chase!' The Hunter snapped from across the park. 'Watch yourself!'

Chase looked up to a reaching, decayed hand. Yelping, he stumbled backward and lifted the derringer with a reluctant arm. The zombie had not been dead for long. She had hair, it tangled into a leeched-out nest at her shoulders, and most of her face remained intact. There was lipstick on parts of her lips.

She still looked like a person, and that always made it hard.

For one thing, they were quicker. The undead woman knocked Chase's hand to the side even as he tried to aim the gun. She lunged, bloodied mouth snapping in the air like a rabid dog. Chase gave into his shaking legs and fell, leaving her teetering, head swivelling with almost comic confusion.

It helped, in a way. She didn't look human any more, acting like some deranged animal instead of a woman. Chase scooted back, aimed up at her even as she saw him collapsed on the churned-up dirt, and fired. The first shot took her in the shoulder, pushing her back. As Chase fumbled for the spare bullets in his front pocket, dropped one in the mud and scrambled desperately to find it, she righted herself. She reached down.

He didn't need the second shot. With a step and a tight swing of his sword, the Hunter cut her down.

Driza-bone flapping in a putrid breeze, the Hunter stared down at his apprentice. He did not offer a hand up. 'Knives are too short, close quarters fighting only favours the undead.' He pulled a clean, white cloth from his pocket.

Chase had heard this speech before, heard it many times. He guessed it showed just how little regard the Hunter had for him, how much of a disappointment his so-called chosen boy had turned out to be. The man didn't have anything else to say.

'Foils are no good for cutting through necks; you need to be on a horse or a trail bike to make sabres any use. But this—' the Hunter wiped his sword with the cloth, removing flaps of crackly skin and chunks of dry flesh. There was never very much blood. '—this is perfect.'

The Hunter looked into the distance, eyes shadowed by his hat, mouth set and serious. 'Remember this, and when it is your time, treat her well.' Gently, he slid the sword into a lacquered scabbard at his hip. 'You will make a Hunter one day. When I am gone.'

Chase gave up on the bullet, lost in the mud, and pushed himself to his feet. His pants were plastered with muck, especially around his backside where it clung with an uncomfortable weight. Quickly, before the Hunter could pick him up on it, he bundled up a handful of his navy polo shirt and wiped dirt off his gun. All the while, he tried to get the image of decapitating the Hunter out of his mind. But when you're apprenticed to a Necromancer Hunter, that's part of the deal. The only way to make sure that when they die, they stay dead.

A cold wind whipped clouds into the sky and threatened rain. With the city's undead put down, it was time to leave. The civilian survivors needed to be getting back to their homes, cemeteries would need fixing. A lot of flowers had to be planted. They always planted flowers after a rising. A reminder of life, in all its beauty? Or just to try and cover the smell?

A thin, reedy melody rang through the park and echoed from grey, empty buildings. The Hunter dug in his jacket and pulled out a small, silver phone, as clean as his sword and just as shiny. Its ring tone, slow and creepy in the midst of the dead, sent Chase's skin crawling.

'Hunter.' The Hunter began to pick his way through the corpses and gestured to the boy to follow. 'Another town? Where?'

The streets were sprinkled with abandoned cars, but not as many as other cities the Hunter had cleansed. People were getting warning now. They didn't know *who* the Necromancer was, or even what he was trying to do, but they had been able to predict his movements for a week now and get the civilians out. It made things easier. Zombies on their own could be contained, but zombies with a city-load of fresh people to contaminate? Now that was a national disaster.

'He's still heading west then.' The Hunter frowned. 'No, I've never seen this kind of thing before. And I've been hunting Necromancers since I was a boy.' He glanced meaningfully at his apprentice. 'They usually have a goal, concentrate on a particular spot. Seen them raise the dead for revenge, for love. One even tried to make an army out of the things. Damned disrespectful. But raising a city here, a country town there.' The Hunter shook his head. 'This is strange, and I don't like strange. Especially not from a Necromancer.'

Another pause.

'I know. We'll hurry. Just keep your soldiers out of my hair.' He tapped fingers on the hilt of his sword. 'Because they panicked last time, that's why! Hard enough to despatch a city of zombies without boys with guns running around screaming. Hunters have always dealt with the living dead. Let us do what we were put on this earth to do!' He snapped the phone together. '*That* is why you don't let the army get involved.'

He sighed and glanced over his shoulder. 'Time to hurry, boy. The bastard is trying to lose us in the desert.'

The Hunter broke into a run, threading his way around bodies and cars, and Chase struggled to follow.


I can't seem to get far enough away. They follow me. People; with their houses and their animals and their damned, walking dead. Didn't think I'd find any out here, where the dirt is a dark orange and the sparse, thicket-y type grass a little grey. But they're here.

I glance over my shoulder, count three lizards, the hind-quarters of a roo and two lonesome, struggling human arms. When I look forward again there's a farmhouse. Sudden and close.

I stop, just for a moment, to stare at the falling wooden fence that wasn't there a second ago. At the peeling weatherboard building, half its veranda sunk into dust, wire-mesh door hanging crooked from its hinges. I don't stop long; I am aware of the shuffling behind me. Doesn't look like anyone could live in something so run-down, but that's not really what I'm worried about. Someone lived in this place *once*. Did they die here? Were they buried here? And what if they had a pet, some cattle-dog mutt buried beneath the looming gum. Undead dogs are quick on their rotting little paws, let me tell you.

The house is oddly familiar, in the way all run-down houses are. But in the end, the sun forces my decision. Out here, it always does. The dead things behind me stink. My water is almost gone, so too the packets of junk food I stole from a screaming petrol-station worker while zombies tried to clamber over her counter. At least the farmhouse offers shade. So I hurry.

The screen door opens with a groan that echoes down the dark hallway. Like the house is a zombie itself. It bangs when I shut it, resists when I try to do a rusted latch. In the end I resort to a piece of stiff wire to keep it closed. There are still gaps at the floor and again near the ceiling; the door doesn't line up properly. But they're too small for the roo, the crumbling stairs hopefully too difficult for the lizards and the bony, disconnected arms.

I wonder if there's any water left in an old, dry place like this. Sunlight splinters in through the door, but the details of the house remain in shadow. I can't see the colour of the threadbare carpet, I can't make out the photos in frames that hang on the wall. All I can see is an opening at the end, shifting with a curtain of beads that rattle in a warm breeze.

I brush the beads aside, ignoring cobwebs that stick to my hand and shoulder, and step into a kitchen. Dried eucalypt leaves darken the floor, piling up in corners and beneath cabinets. The windows are open, glass smashed and tattered curtains of yellowing lace fluttering.

A long, dark timber table dominates the room; it pushes out over cracked linoleum from a faded green wall. An old woman sits at one end, thin white hair pinned to her head, floral-patterned dress too wide for her skeletal frame. She looks up at me, and she smiles. Unfocused, watery eyes dance, her hands play with sticks and little white stones on the table top.

That's when I realise I should never have stepped inside. It is her house, changed, yes, but hers all the same. Older, wider, spread somehow from a city two-bedroom to a farmhouse. But I know that table; I recognise those lacy drapes.

I try to take a step back. Something presses against my back. Large and solid, but damp. Cold fluids soak through my shirt.

I gag as rot washes over me, ripe, strangely sweet and thick. It runs down the back of my throat.

Hands grip my shoulders. They hold me upright and *ooze* against my skin.

'So, dearie.' The old woman's voice still sounds like the rattling of bones. Only now, it's a sound I know well. 'Have you found what you were looking for?'


'Your Necromancer's a woman. Did you know that?'

The Hunter tipped his hat back and scowled. The only admission of surprise he was likely to give. 'Why do you say that?'

The young policeman shifted on his feet, uncomfortable beneath the Hunter's scrutiny. 'We have reports ... ah, sir. From civilians fleeing the area, from the emergency service workers sent in to get them out. A woman, probably early thirties. Medium build, blonde—'

'Yes, thank you.' The Hunter rolled a cigarette in his hand but didn't take his eyes from the policeman. He lit it, lazily, and let it dangle from the corner of his mouth as he spoke. 'It does not matter *what* she looks like. I need to know if she *is* the Necromancer or just some poor girl in the wrong place at the wrong time.'

The policeman took off his deep blue cap and ran fingers through sweat-dampened hair. He used the hat to beat at perpetually buzzing flies and leant back into the shade of the post office's tin roof. The Hunter did not move, and beside him, Chase tried to follow his example. But whatever it was the Hunter possessed that made even the insects respect him, Chase didn't have it. He resorted to waving them away.

Replacing his cap, the policeman nodded. '*They* were following. All of the witnesses were very clear. She had ... zombies, ah, following her. People from the cemetery.' He gestured back along the dirt road and Chase glanced over his shoulder. There wasn't much to this town and it had been almost empty when he and the Hunter drove in. Only a few bony cats and half a dozen lizards. The Hunter had despatched them with ease. 'Not only that. Roos and cattle too. Couple of sheep—'

'Yes, thank you.' The Hunter stepped back, into the dirt street and the full blow of the mid-morning sun. Chase followed with reluctance. 'I understand.'

'Sir?' The policeman reached out, but didn't leave the building's shadow. 'We can help—'

'Which way did you say she went?' The Hunter dropped his cigarette and snuffed it into the dust with the heel of his boot.

The young man pointed.

'There, you've helped.' With that, the Hunter spun and marched to his car, muttering about who was going to poke their nose into his business next. The car was an old, clunky thing that drunk down petrol and didn't even have air-conditioning. But it got them out of the small town soon enough.

The Hunter drove in silence, following the road, eyes intent. Chase waited until the older man gave a deep sigh. 'A woman.'

Chase looked at him but did not ask. Whatever the Hunter wanted him to know, the Hunter would say.

Chase had learned the Hunter's quirks quickly, after the weathered, scowling man had taken him away from family and friends. Even got him out of school. All his talk about destiny and the struggle for the future of mankind had impressed his parents well enough. Must have worked on his teachers too.

After two months following the guy around, it would be nice if it had rubbed off on Chase. Would have made things a whole lot easier. But as it was, he couldn't shake the feeling that this apprenticeship was all one big mistake.

'Not many women Necromancers, not many at all.' With one hand the Hunter riffled through the glove box and found a glass bottle of lukewarm water. He tossed it into the boy's lap without looking. 'Drink, it's hot out here. Easy to get too dry.'

Chase obeyed, wrinkling his nose at the stifled taste.

'They just don't have it in them, the *need* for control that drives a man to raise the dead.' He shook his head as the boy offered the bottle of water. 'No, you don't see many women Necromancers at all, let alone one who would raise so many, so indiscriminately. It doesn't make sense.'

Dry, orange earth sped along beneath them. Thin trees, bent and drooping, spotted the side of the road. At one point a small flock of emus ran in the distance. Chase watched the sheer monotony of it all and tried not to breathe too loudly. Not while the Hunter was thinking.

'Why would she have them follow her? She's raised cites and left them there, so why are they following her now? It makes no sense.'

The Hunter braked suddenly and turned off the road. The movement threw Chase against the window, and as he rubbed the bump forming on his forehead, he strained to look out the back. Half a kangaroo hopped beside the trunk of a termite-hollowed tree. Wire wrapped around its tail and snagged on the bark.

It was not struggling to hop along the road, instead it headed into the bush. The way the Hunter was driving. Not on any path, over fallen logs, and hard, cracking dirt.

'No sense at all.'

He hasn't been dead that long, but it's hard to recognise him. Guess that's what the car did. Took off most of his face, and his body doesn't look the same either. It's missing something in his back that made him stand straight, so he slouches to the side. His remaining green eye has gone cloudy.

He doesn't know me.

The old woman sits me in a chair and pushes a plate of rock cakes at me. I just stare at him. He stands at the doorway, hands still raised where he had been holding my shoulders, eye looking straight ahead.

'Eat something, dearie. You're looking a little thin.'

Finally, I turn to glare at her. Rock cakes and their china plate shatter as I knock them from the table. 'Bitch.'

'Now, now.' The old woman smiles, one hand fiddles with a large silver ring on a knobbly finger. 'You shouldn't be speaking to me like that, should you? Or haven't you learned yet?'

I pull back, fold in on myself like she's slapped me.

'*Have* you found what you were looking for?' She collects a small, round stone and strokes it. I feel my back straighten, my knees draw together like a good, polite girl. A great shudder runs through me.

'No. But you know that.' I want to turn around, to point. So I do, but only once she's put down the stone. 'You had him all along.'

The old woman nods. 'Convenient, wouldn't you say?'

'Why would you do that?'

She shakes her head. 'Maybe you haven't learnt anything after all. You came into my house, *dearie*. You made demands like you owned the place, didn't you?'

When I don't respond she glances at the white stone. I nod, but don't trust myself to speak. I just don't seem to say the right things.

'A dead husband's quite an ask, even for an old witch like me.' She cackles her laugh. 'You can't have expected it for free.'

I look down at my knees. The memory is hazy, mixed with alcohol and grief, and dwarfed by weeks of shuffling undead. I remember stumbling up front stairs, somewhat less run-down than the entrance to *this* house. Slamming an almost empty bottle of vodka — God, I can't even remember if it had a flavour — on the table. Shouting at her, crying at her. Her little, twisted smile. Yes, I remember that. She gave me a stone, pretty, shaped like a rose but black. And then she asked her price.

'You knew I couldn't give it to you.' A life for a life, I guess. But a baby? And someone else's baby at that, because I had none of my own, and she wasn't willing to take the risk.

Her eyes sharpen and pin me down like a butterfly on board. 'It was too late by then.' She is disgusted by me; I can see it in the wrinkling of her nose. 'And you still used my stone.'

I swallow, and for a second consider standing up. How far would I get if I tipped up the chair and ran for the kitchen door? Before she had time to pick up one of her damned stones?

She collects a stick from the table and runs it over her weathered palm.

I don't bother, what's left to fight for anyway? 'Yes.' My shoulders sag forward, a little more with each word. 'I took it to his grave. I placed it there, like you said. Planted it into the earth, as deep as I could dig. But he didn't come out. I waited, I waited until *they* surrounded me and I couldn't breathe for the smell.' I had pushed my way through a cemetery's worth of dead to get out of that place, and not even the cold sea spray coming up from the cliffs could clean away the stench. They had watched me, empty eye sockets, sagging skin and gaping, grinning mouths. They followed until I came to the road, until I passed shops and *people*. Then ... then they had started to feed.

But never on me.

'There is always a price.'

'My husband had just died, I was drunk—'

She snorts, very unladylike. 'Doesn't give you the right to steal from me.' She looks me up and down, out of the corner of her eye. 'So you've been walking since then? Coming all the way out here, trying to get away from everyone?'

'Trying to save them.' My mouth tastes like orange dust.

'How very noble.' Sounding bored, she pushes away from the table.

Perfume drapes over me as she rests her cold hand on my head. 'I wonder how many people died, before you thought to do that.'

She steps back. I raise my head, slowly. Open my eyes and turn to her. Have I been crying? The world between us, between me and *him*, is wavering.

'Now I just have to decide.' She folds the last flap of a velvet cloth over her stones and places them gently in a white handbag with a faux-gold clip. 'If I want to keep him.'

She lifts a hand and my husband, my *dead* husband, leans his cheek against her skin.

I stand, quickly, chair toppling to the floor. Outside, tyres skid to a stop over dust and gravel.


The Hunter knew the zombie was there before Chase saw it in the hallway gloom. He grabbed Chase with one hand, pulled him back, forced him behind, and drew his blade with the other. Didn't even give him the chance to find his gun, but then, what was the point?

But the creature didn't rush at them. Stooping in the doorway, it turned and grinned with half a face.

The Hunter breathed in sharply.

'Let him through.' A crackly voice commanded, and the zombie stepped aside to reveal a small, ancient-looking woman.

'Who are you?' The Hunter edged forward, sword extended, voice tense and clipped. Chase held back. He fumbled his gun out of its holster and held it high.

The crone laughed. 'Come looking for your Necromancer, have you?'

The Hunter stepped onto faded plastic-looking tiles; Chase hung in the darkness of the hallway. One hand clung to the doorframe. The derringer's barrel was cold as he leant it against his cheek, the only way to ensure he held it steady.

The Hunter's blade twitched between zombie and old woman. 'How do you—?'

'She's right here.' The old lady gestured. A younger woman stood by a wooden table. Her face was ruddy with sunburn; she was dressed in tattered jeans and a filthy shirt. Her hands shook, and she clasped the edge of the table as though that was all that kept her upright. 'That's your Necromancer, Hunter. Aren't you going to do justice for all those her undead killed?'

The young woman shook her head. Straggly blonde hair caught in sweat on her forehead and chin. 'No.'

The Hunter hesitated. His sword pointed at her, and the young woman closed her eyes. Slowly, the Hunter turned back to the little old lady. 'I know Necromancers. I can feel them. She is no Necromancer, although she stinks of the dead.'

The blonde woman's eyes snapped open. They were sharply blue.

'Now *you*.' The Hunter straightened his arm, levelling his sword with the old woman's smiling face. '*You* I can feel. But ... you're not quite right.' Chase could hear a scowl in the Hunter's voice.

The old woman cackled. 'Pity.' She clutched at a pale handbag, fiddling with the clasp. 'If you don't want to play, Hunter, you should leave. You're out of your depth here. Can you feel that?'

'I do not think so.' The Hunter raised his sword. 'Tell me what you are.'

'Too strong for the likes of you.'

The zombie lurched forward, hands outstretched, and the Hunter spun. The young woman screamed as his blade shot out, as the zombie fell, headless. The old woman was laughing again, hand in her bag. She withdrew a single, white stone.

'Don't let her—!' The young woman shouted.

Chase jumped forward, aimed at the small, old woman, and pulled the trigger. The derringer clicked, hollow and empty, and Chase realised he had never reloaded it. He just hadn't remembered.

The Hunter gave a gargling cry as his sword turned back in toward his own, living, neck.


I watch David fall; watch his head hit the ground a moment before his body. Even under all that laughing, I can hear it 'splat' against the floor.

I need to go to him. I need to hold him and know that he is truly dead. I hope that he has, perhaps, found a kind of peace now. After I denied it to him.

But I can't. I shout as the old woman pulls a stone from her bag, as the man's solid face breaks into shock. She will not make me responsible for his death too.

The porcelain shard is sharp, it cuts my hand. But as the man slices at his own neck with his long, strange sword, I don't care. I grip it tightly, I feel the blood, and I bring it down into the old woman's shoulder.

Her laughter becomes a shrill scream. The man's sword clatters to the ground and he staggers backward. I cut her again. And again. Until her fingers release the small, white stone, and she doesn't breathe. Doesn't move.

When she is dead she, thankfully, doesn't rise in my presence. I guess she thought I had learnt my lesson after all.

Standing is too hard, so I shuffle over to David's body. He doesn't look right without his head. I arrange it as best I can.

'Who are you?' The man is also on the ground, leaning against the wall while a teenage boy hovers at his side. The boy's face is pale, his eyes terrified, but he doesn't say a word.

'Jane.' Not really an explanation.

The man holds a white cloth up to his neck. There is a small nick there, just enough to bleed. I stare down at his discarded sword. So close. 'I am the Hunter.' He nods to the boy. 'My reluctant apprentice.'

The boy grimaces.

'We have been tracking you. It was you, wasn't it? Raising the dead.'

'It wasn't my fault!' I had only wanted to raise one. Just one. That's okay, isn't it?

The Hunter looks meaningfully at the old woman. 'Stone witch, wasn't she?'

I shake my head. I'm not really sure. She was the crazy old woman down the street when we were kids, the one we called a witch. When we grew up she had changed in our eyes, become eccentric and a little sad. But you don't forget those childhood fears, those stories you tell yourself.

And at the worse point in my life, she was there. Door open. Bag of stones in her hand.

'She is. Powerful creatures, much stronger than a Necromancer.' He clears his throat, carefully. 'I'm not too sure on them myself. Those stones are supposed to be lives, I heard. The younger the better. At any rate, they are not an easy kill.' The Hunter is staring at me. Grimly, I meet his gaze. His eyes are hard, but thoughtful. 'Pretty good for a first kill. Think you'd like some more?'

I frown. 'More?'

'You know what it's like. Seen it first hand now, I'll warrant. You know why the dead should stay dead, why those who raise them should be brought to justice.'

I picture the petrol-station worker, backed up against the window as the zombies fed. I only looked back that once. Slowly, I nod. 'Yes. I do.'

The Hunter smiles. Wrinkles crinkle beneath his stubble, his dark, serious eyes are almost friendly. The boy has gained some colour in his cheeks and looks relieved.

'Tell me.' The Hunter catches his sword with the tip of his boot and drags it closer. With a wince, he picks it up, turns it around, and holds the handle toward me. 'Have you ever held one of these?'

# FENCE LINES

Kara stood on the front veranda, shotgun cradled against her chest, and watched the fence let them in.

They walked up the wet dirt road in a desperate little huddle. Three of them. A woman at the front, with pale skin and in a filthy floral dress, carrying a big handgun. Behind her, an emaciated old man tied to a patched-up wheelchair, being pushed slowly by a limping boy.

They had to be human. The fence lines were selective, and wouldn't have let them in otherwise. But it just took one look to know they should not have been able to survive outside. One gun. A wheelchair, and a boy.

The woman stopped at the bottom of the stairs and eyed Kara with exactly the same look she was giving right back. Disbelief. Mistrust. Still, she kept the gun lowered. Only reason Kara hadn't shot them all already. That, and the boy.

For a long moment that's all they did — stare. The sugarcane fields around the house rustled and whispered in the hot, heavy wind. Voices from the fence line murmured along with it, a dim undertone that sent shivers down Kara's back. The lines hadn't been this vocal in years.

'Safe?' The woman spoke first. Her voice was cracked and thirsty. This close, Kara could see her shaking.

'Can be,' Kara answered, after a time. 'If you put that gun down, girl. And if you're willing to work for it.'

The gun slipped out of the woman's hand, and landed heavily in copper mud. The man in the wheelchair behind her tipped his head back, and laughed.


The woman Kara put them up in what she called the workers' quarters — a long weatherboard building on stilts, made for considerably more than three people. It had been empty for years. Mould on the walls, damp across the ceiling, even the odd startled snake. But it was immeasurably better than what Anne was used to. Solid and standing, not surrounded by flames ever burning, and no ash-mad, once-human creatures scratching at the door.

Together, she and Tom pulled his grandfather in his wheelchair up the stairs. Anne found a room with a hook in the wall, and tied Luke to it. As she was beating the mould out of a mattress, he let out a loud, harsh crackle of laughter, so sudden Anne was on her feet, searching the empty pockets in her skirt for the absent gun before she even realised what it was. 'All around you!' he howled. 'Can't you see? Won't ever leave!' His words petered off into nonsense and wet chuckling.

Heart racing, hand still in her empty pocket, Anne stared at the small, bone-thin man who had once been her father-in-law. He was long gone now, his mind broken by the ash, his body wasting away. One day, she feared, he would turn into one of *them*, and his touch would be poison, his skin immune to the fire as he spent the rest of his painful existence searching, always, to quench some impossible thirst.

But that didn't mean she was going to leave him to the wasteland. If she could keep him alive, damn it, she would. He and Tom were all she had left.

'Mum?' Tom, behind her, gripping the doorway to keep himself upright.

She turned her back on Luke — which she only ever did when he was securely tied — and hurried over to her son. She bent so he could wrap an arm around her shoulders, and together they shuffled over to the mattress. Tom's strength was limited, and he had worked so hard today, pushing the wheelchair to leave her hands free. And now she'd given up their only weapon, and for what? Safety? Could she really believe it? Did such a thing exist?

'What's he saying, Mum?'

She eased him down, helped him sit. 'Nothing,' she answered. 'You know better than that.'

He nodded, lips a tense, tight line. Tom's grandfather was not the man he used to be. When the flames tore down the Rockhampton walls, Luke had led them out to search for safety. North, that was the plan, always north. Where it was wetter and nothing burned quite so well, and none of the incendiaries had fallen in the first place. It had been a much larger group then, and they'd had weapons and food and hope.

'Never alone,' Luke whispered, hands and ear pressed to the mouldy wall. 'Not anymore.'

Luke had done that, he'd given them hope. But not anymore.

'Can we really sleep here?' Tom asked. 'Properly? Deep as we like?'

She held him as tightly as she dared. He was still brittle, as fragile against her as the day he was born. Ash in his lungs from before his first breath, he'd come out so tiny, broken, and fighting for life. But live was exactly what he'd done. She kept going, for him. Even with his father dead, and everyone else who set out all those months ago taken by ash or burned or worse. Even when north seemed a dream, and the precious falling rain turned to biting poison, she kept going. Until they stumbled on this place. 'We can.' She ran her fingers through his patchy hair.

'Safe?'

She closed her eyes. 'Safe.' And hoped she sounded like she believed it.


'Do you trust them?'

Kara stood with her back to her mother, looking out the second floor window. She'd been there all night, not needing to sleep. The woman — Anne — held her own vigil, and watched the house from the top of the workers' steps.

'The fence line does,' Kara answered. Dawn was smudging too-red against the sky. Smoke on the horizon and movement on the other side of the fence. Anne and her small group had been followed.

A ragged cough. It was always like this, at the end of the cycle.

Got hard to breathe, difficult to speak, impossible to walk.

'Fence line's lonely,' her mother rattled. 'Trusts too easily.' Kara knelt by her mother's head, dipped cloth in a bucket and pushed the thick stalks aside so she could drip cool water into her mouth. She didn't bother arguing. No matter how many cycles the fence had kept them safe, her mother still didn't trust it. Not completely. She'd never got along with any of them in life, either.

'Burning day,' her mother said, when Kara had squeezed the cloth dry. 'You ready?'

Kara was always ready.

Anne woke to Tom screaming. Shit, it was morning. And *shit*, she'd fallen asleep on the top step. She lurched to unsteady feet. Kara was approaching them, shotgun in one hand, fire dripping from the nozzle of a canister in the other. Tom must have been playing at the bottom of the steps, and now he staggered and tripped up to her side.

Kara stopped in the middle of the dirt road. The flames winked out in the puddles at her feet. 'Time to start working,' she called.

Anne refused to send Tom out into the fields, so she followed Kara alone. She gave Tom the job of caring for Luke — after ensuring he was securely tied. The old man was unusually calm, crouched in a corner, engaged in whispered conversation with the empty air.

Kara didn't talk, just walked beside her, constantly glancing sidelong at her. It made Anne uncomfortable. More than the shotgun. More than the flames. That uncertain, darting look.

'What are we doing?' Anne asked, to break the awkward silence.

'Burning day,' Kara answered, and lifted the canister. A pause, then she continued, her words halting, like she wasn't used to conversation. 'Cane's ready. Clouds coming. Wind the right way. Time.'

They stopped at the edge of a great field of sugarcane stalks, thick and rustling like whispering voices. Kara bent, touched the flame to the ground and stepped back as it caught. All the way down the line between field and bare road she walked, fire spreading, the barrel of the gun reflecting red where it rested against her shoulder.

'And what should I do?' Anne asked. Heat from the fire beat up at her. Just like the world outside, it was. She pushed back strands of her blonde and grey hair where it stuck to her forehead.

'Keep up,' Kara answered. 'Watch out for snakes.'

Soon the smoke was thick, the fire rearing high above the cane. But somehow, Kara had known, and even as the flames grew the wind swung around to guide them away from the big house and the workers' quarters behind it. Anne followed Kara along the edge of the road that wound between the fields. More than snakes fled the flames — rodents and birds and other kinds of life Anne had no name for. Brown and soft with a tuft of white tail. Red and sleek and quick as a bullet. Haughty and sinuous in white and black patches. She'd never seen anything like them.

Finally, Kara halted and placed the empty fire canister on the ground.

The road ended at a line of stones. Not quite a wall, more a loose collection of rocks — some small as pebbles, some large as boulders — that stretched off into the smoke-haze of distance. Some of the rocks had been decorated, given faces in brilliant pink and orange paint, at once smiling and ghoulish. Where were the children who had painted these rocks?

'Does it still burn?' Kara asked. She watched the flames and didn't seem in the least bit afraid that they might turn around and claim her. 'Outside? Always? With rainbow lights and noxious smoke?'

The roar and crackle of the fire should have drowned out the sugar-whispers, but Anne swore she could still hear them, just behind her. She glanced around, nervous enough for the both of them. The flames stopped at the stone wall too, coming smack up against them in a line rising straight into the sky.

'It does,' she answered. 'There's not much left to burn, but that doesn't seem to stop it. Sets the air alight, if it has to. The smoke lingers, and there are worse things hiding in the ashes.'

'And yet you survived?'

Anne stiffened at the implied accusation. 'Most of us did not.' What did this woman want from her? A catalogue of Anne's scars, perhaps? Or a night listening to Luke muttering in the dark. Tom's weakness, and the wheeze in his lungs as he desperately tried to breathe.

Kara eyed her for a moment, hard gaze to hard gaze, and eventually nodded. 'It's been years since I heard stories of the outside.' She looked up to a sky thick with dark clouds. 'Many people arrived at first, just like you, desperate for safety and willing to work. Ten years since the last ones. I thought there might not be anyone left.'

'At first?' The first bombs had fallen decades before Anne was even born. So that couldn't be what this woman meant. With her smooth dark skin and no grey in her halo of tightly curled hair, Kara simply could not be that old.

'Long time ago now.'

Lightning shuddered, thunder cracked. A moment later, rain began to fall, great fat drops of it, hissing and spitting in the fire. Real rain, Anne could hardly believe it, from real clouds. Somehow even the sky was clean here. Kara waited until her feet were swimming in mud, all the flames were doused and the rain exhausted. Then she sniffed the air, nodded and murmured to herself, collected her canister and headed back along the road.

Anne hurried after her, feet slipping. There was no wind now, not even the faintest hint of breeze. The darkened sugarcane stood still, dripping.

Everything smelled like wet earth and everywhere, all around her, whispers hovered like fog.

'What is that?' Shuddering, Anne wrapped her arms around her chest, but she was soaked through and every inch of her skin felt like ice. She wasn't used to the cold.

'Just the fence line,' Kara said. 'Keeping us safe.'


Tom gripped the edge of the shed door to steady himself. From the moment Kara called upon him he'd accepted no assistance, but had hobbled his own way from the workers' quarters, serious and determined. Crouching, Kara held out a machete to him. He took it gladly, eager to be of help.

Anne watched, bottom lip caught between her teeth. Pride or horror at what Kara was forcing her weakened boy to do? Kara couldn't tell the difference. Too many years without faces to read and she was out of practice.

'The machetes are for working the sugarcane.' She shifted the shotgun against her chest, looked Anne and then Tom straight in the eye. 'First one of you tries anything else with them, gets shot.' Mother and son both paled, but she meant no malice by it. Just a fact.

Kara took them out into the heat and showed them how to harvest the cane; where to cut, how to gather and bind the stalks. It was hard work even for the strongest adult, and the boy struggled. His feet sank into the burned and muddy earth. The sugar was sturdy, thick, and difficult to cut. But when Anne paused in her own work to offer assistance, he pushed her away.

'I can do it, Mum!' he snapped, red-faced and sweating. 'Gramp said I should. Said we all have to work hard, here.'

'Gramp said?' Anne whispered, but she left him, knees in the dirt, both hands gripping the machete and making shallow, shaking cuts.

The breath caught in Kara's throat as faint arms, so pale they were almost invisible, reached down to steady Tom's grip. Hazy shapes, transparent and flickering. Two of them, at least, and she recognised them instantly. It had been so long since she buried them at the lines, but she remembered every single one.

'Peter,' she whispered their names. 'Jason.' Good, hard-working kids, both of them.

Somewhere in the sugarcane Anne was cursing, and stalks were falling, one by one. Jason and Peter bent over Tom, and it would be easy to mistake them for a brush of fog or smoke. He smiled up at them; they steadied his hands, gave strength to his legs and back, and swung with him. Together, they sliced cleanly and pushed forward, harvesting faster than he ever could on his own, until Kara lost sight of them in the field.

She stood at the edge of the cane for a long time, eyes closed, just listening. Remembering. Pete and Jason were brothers. They'd come to the plantation when the bombs were still falling, and had escaped the worst of their effects. Strong, eager to please, they'd grown up beneath her supervision and were already young men before the lines called them. Jason had even got one of the girls pregnant, but Kara had missed the birth, and by the time she emerged the baby was gone.

Another time. Sometimes it felt like another world. A noisy and smelly one, full of people and their cooking and their loving and their hating. The fence line was all she had left of those days.

'You're lonely,' she whispered. 'Aren't you. Just as lonely as me.'

When the sun went down Kara brought Anne and Tom glasses of cool tea. She placed her shotgun on the steps behind her and handed the drinks out solemnly. A large one for Anne. She caught the way the woman's eyes caressed the gun, so close and yet so far. Slightly smaller for Tom, heavily sweetened with the few remaining sugar crystals from the last cycle. Kara crouched in front of him and said, 'Now make sure you drink it all.'

He nodded, expression serious, tipped it back and wiped the bottom of the glass clean with his tongue. 'Thank you, Missus.'

She swallowed threatening tears. So long since anyone had called her that. She gestured to the pile of sugarcane he had harvested. 'You did a very good job today,' she said. 'Think you can do it again tomorrow?'

When he nodded and smiled it lit his face, and somehow his cheekbones weren't so prominent, his hair less patchy, his skin not so pale. The sugar, already working.

'Good man.' Kara stood. She collected the machetes and told Tom and Anne to sleep. Because they would need it.

It took four more days to cut it all down, another to carry it to the press. Even with Kara's help.

'You're heavy,' Kara whispered, as she dripped water into her mother's mouth.

'A good sign,' her mother replied, words muffled through the stalks.


'Mum.'

Anne jerked her head up. She'd fallen asleep at the top of the steps again. The blisters across her hands ached and the crick in her neck sent jarring shivers down into her shoulders and upper back. 'Tom?' She looked around, blearily.

He sat beside her, legs drawn up to his chest, staring into the night. He looked haunted, eyes distant. The machete he had used to cut the cane — and that Kara had taken back each evening — rested on his knees.

That woke her up properly. She hadn't forgotten Kara's warning. 'Tom?' she reached for the machete slowly, gently. 'What are you doing?' He clamped his fingers around the wooden handle and wouldn't let her take it.

'Peter told me to,' he whispered. 'He said it was my turn to help them.' When he turned his face towards her he was crying. 'But now I'm not sure I should have.'

'What—?'

He took her hand and led her into the empty fields. The small stumps of cut cane were sharp beneath her feet. As they walked, the whispers grew. She couldn't pretend it was the sound of wind in sugarcane anymore. Almost-voices, distant, distorted, seeming to press in on her from the dark. The night was hot but a fog was rising, rolling in from the edges of the property.

It all gathered at the relic of a rusted tractor. Half sunken into the earth, wound with weeds, a creaking skeleton revealed by the harvesting days earlier.

'Peter said he would be happier with them,' Tom said.

Laughter around her, shouts and cries. It was difficult to see through the darkness and the fog. What light there was didn't come from any moon or stars, but seemed to hover around them, crystallised in the air.

'Said it was his choice. All I had to do was let him go, so he could choose.'

Anne swallowed hard. As goose bumps peppered her damp skin, she stepped forward. Shapes all around her, but nothing like the shadows and the ash that hunted in the world outside. She caught the sketches of countless smiles, dancing bodies, someone skipping. The very faint smell of food, cooking.

'So I cut the rope.' Tom dropped the machete and wrapped both arms around her. He seemed taller, his grip stronger. When she ran a hand through his hair, it was thick and full. 'But I don't know, Mum.' The fog peeled back to reveal Luke, kneeling forward on the ground in front of the tractor, his rope tangled around an empty window frame at one end, and digging deeply into his neck at the other. 'Did I do the right thing?'

Anne couldn't answer. She stared at Luke's body, made pale by the light of the fog behind them. He was still, quiet, and smiling, and some terrible part of her couldn't help but think it was better than falling into emptiness and thirst, surely?

She crouched and collected the machete from the ground. 'Let's put this away,' she whispered. 'It's our secret, okay?' She pulled him into a slow walk, through the fog. 'Kara doesn't need to know.'

'Okay Mum. But—' he glanced at the house; as usual the lights were on in a single room, and a figure stood silhouetted in the window '—I think she already does.'


The fence lines clamoured all around her as Kara rolled Luke's lifeless body onto a wide canvas sheet, a cacophony so loud and so strong she began to worry they weren't concentrating on what they should have been doing. The need for Luke eclipsed the outside horrors they existed to keep at bay.

'Will you help me?' Kara asked Anne, as she prepared to sew the edges of the sheet together. There were no wooden coffins on the fence line.

Between them, they wrapped him tightly, arms folded at his chest, the horrible bruising around his neck hidden in his upturned collar. Kara sewed with practiced hands.

Transparent fingers fumbled for her needle. Someone was nattering in her ear about the party last night and the stories Luke had told them. Kara gritted her teeth, and hissed, 'You're not helping!' under her breath. The faster she worked, the happier the lines would be, and the more secure the plantation.

When she glanced up from her work, Anne was staring at something just behind her. Fear, confusion, who knew what else was going on behind those eyes.

'Don't encourage them,' Kara murmured, and that got the woman's attention. 'Just help me. We should hurry.'

Tom followed as they carried his grandfather down through the burned and harvested sugarcane fields, to the fence line stones. Kara took up the shovel but shook her head when Anne offered to help. 'Look after your son,' she said. 'And do what you need to do to grieve. This is my responsibility.'

The lines wavered as she rearranged the stones, letting in ripples of heat.

The fence line whispered all around her as she dug. Not too deep. Every time her shovel hit a bone she stopped and rearranged it with care. When the hole was wide enough she filled it with Luke, covered him with dirt, and replaced the stones.

The fence lines settled. Luke was a part of them now, and that was all they'd really wanted. No whispers, no unsettling movement seeping through from the other side. The plantation was calm, silent but for the sound of Tom, weeping.

Kara collected a particularly pale, round stone, and held it out to him. 'This is for you to decorate,' she said. 'There were lots of other children here before you. They painted lots of stones.' She pointed to the ones with flowers and faces scribbled on them in childish hands. 'The children used to work here, like you do. But that was a very long time ago, and they have all died. But not left. The fence lines keep them all.' He took the stone, and she stood. Her legs were getting stiff. Sprouting time soon. 'You will find paint in the shed, and glue. Near the machetes, you know where they are. Mix them with mud from the fields if the paint has dried. Make something for Luke to remember you by.'

'Is he happier now?' Tom asked, stone clutched to his chest.

Kara turned her back to the line. 'He won't ever be lonely. Ever again.'

The press was a giant stone mortar, a towering pestle hooked up to a harness, and an indented circle in the earth around them both. There were no animals to strap into the harness, so Anne and Kara took turns in their place, alternating between pushing and dragging, as the sun beat down on them, and the blisters on their hands burst. Tom pulled the sugarcane from its piles and carried it to the press. Kara alone collected the juice, not letting any of them near the deep plastic barrels when they were full.

Her son was so much stronger now. Anne watched him work: he had grown, somehow, over the past few days. He breathed deeply, steadily, and while he tired by the end of the day, it was a normal exhaustion cured by sleep, not something noxious and invisible gnawing deeply at his bones.

And it was certainly tiring work. Even Anne, who had fought and run through the fires of the burning world, carrying her son and her father-in-law and her husband, Michael, before she could accept that he was really dead, even Anne was tired. She must be. Because sometimes, she saw Luke. Pale like those faces she thought she'd seen at Kara's shoulder, quiet and pervasive like the impossible voices, he walked the plantation. Hands clasped behind his back, studying the house, the tractor, and the fields with interest. His intensely thoughtful look, the sad smile he gave her, the indulgent expression of love whenever Tom came into view. Luke, as she once knew him, even though he was dead.

It made Anne shiver, as she sat on the top step listening to Tom sleep through all the open doors, resting her stinging, blistered hands on her knees.

She wondered what it meant for her and her son? Were they both at risk here?

'Ahem.'

Anne flinched. She hadn't been sleeping, just so far away. Kara was standing at the bottom of the steps, looking up at her. She carried a wide metal bowl, full of water, and a small cloth bag between her teeth.

With a glance over her shoulder to make sure Tom hadn't woken, Anne descended in silence. She took the bag from Kara's mouth.

'That's all that's left,' the woman said, not quite looking her in the eye.

Frowning, Anne opened the bag. A few handfuls of white crystals — it took her a moment to put it all together. *Sugar.* 'I don't understand.' She had been wondering what all the work was for. What would Kara do with the sugar they were harvesting?

'Here.' Kara held out the bowl. 'Drop a pinch in the water. Just a pinch, mind you. You don't need much, and the less you use the longer it lasts.'

Bewildered, Anne did as she was told. Just a pinch. It disappeared in the water like it had never existed.

'Now, your hands.' Kara nodded at the bowl. Nervous. 'Just put them in.'

When Anne hesitated, the woman shook her head.

'Nothing to fear. Just sugar. Here.' She balanced the bowl awkwardly in one arm, dipped her finger in the water, withdrew it and sucked it dry. 'See?'

Anne immersed both her hands in the water and held them there. Kara just stared at her, with her awkward half-smile. When Anne finally pulled her hands out, they had healed. No blisters, no splinters, not even the chipped edges of her nails. She stared at them for a long moment, then looked down at the bag she had placed at her feet.

'Take it.' Kara handed her the bowl. 'Use it. It's yours now.' She scratched at her arms. There were round white dots patterning her deep brown skin.

'*Take it.*'

Anne spun. Luke, right beside her, leaning forward to inspect the bag. He looked up at her, nodded once, then drifted away like a wisp of cloud.

'You saw him, didn't you?' Kara asked. 'And clearly too?'

Swallowing hard, Anne nodded. 'I think—' she had to clear her throat. 'I've started to wonder if I might be going mad.' She pressed fingers to her temples. 'I watched it happen to Luke, when the ash first took him. That's how it starts; your grip on reality fades.'

But Kara shook her head. 'No, I told you. You're safe here.' She glanced around. All the plantation was dark, the only lights coming from the quarters at Anne's back, and the single lit room in the house. Even without the sugarcane the night was full of whispers. 'They're getting to know you, is all. Don't show themselves immediately, far too polite for that.'

'Who?' Anne whispered.

'The fence lines, of course. Luke's a part of the fence line now, like all the workers who have served us. His bones mark the lines, and his spirit keeps the fence.'

'All the workers?' Anne glanced up the steps behind her.

'All together. They seem happy, don't you think?' Kara tipped her head to the side, listening. 'Can't you hear them? Always chatting, laughing. Sometimes I think they're cooking, a big meal to feed them all.' She sighed, and smiled sadly. 'I'm glad. They keep us safe, I wouldn't want them to suffer. Just sometimes ... sometimes...' She trailed off, and dug nails deeply into her forearms.

Anne glanced at Kara's scratching fingers. 'Are you alright?'

'Oh yes. Sprouting time soon.' Kara turned, took two steps then turned back. 'And thank you. For asking. And for coming here. It's been so long since I've had anyone to talk to.'


Kara's mother was beyond water now. The cane from her body filled the room, brushing and bending against the ceiling, crowding the doorway, pressing up against the glass of the windows. Kara doubted she was still breathing, but couldn't get close enough to check.

There was no more she could do here, so she closed the door. Eventually, the cane would wither and fall into a hell of a mess to clean up. But now it was time to tend to herself. She gathered the things she needed — clippers and small spade, little black pots and earth to seed in, plenty of water on hand — and waited out the lonely night.

If only she'd had the courage to ask Anne to sit with her.


Seven copper kettles in the stone boiling house, reducing the sugar down. The heat inside was nearly unbearable, but Kara pushed them both to work all day, and even sometimes at night. Anne skimmed treacle and collected crystals, until all the juice was boiled away.

Then Kara pulled on a pair of thick leather gloves, so long they covered to her elbows, and knelt in front of the cooling trough. She dug into the hot treacle and stirred, gathering the sticky mess, kneading and folding it like dough.

'Keep collecting the crystals.' She gasped the words. Sweat ran down her face and sprang up over her shoulders.

Anne scooped more sugar crystals from the edge of the trough. It wasn't much. All that cane, all that work and heat, and it hadn't made much. What was the point of this then? What was Kara even doing?

At once stage, Tom entered the boiling house, and he wasn't alone. Two flickering figures walked beside him, whispering to him, and he nodded and replied in turn. Something clenched in Anne's stomach. How long did she have before the lines convinced her son to hang himself, and join them?

He carried water, and knelt beside Kara as she turned up her face so he could drip it into her mouth.

'Thank you.' She was swaying, unstable on her knees.

Tom turned to Anne. 'We have to help her,' he said, putting down his bucket. So confident now too, not the poor fragile limping child she had kept safe for so long. 'It's time. She needs us.'

Inside the plantation Tom could be strong. The sugar eased his hurts, the fence line kept him company, and his grandfather watched over him. But it wouldn't last, it couldn't last. Kara herself had said it — eventually, all the workers joined the fence line. Just like Luke. Just like those spectres beside her son.

So was it worth it?

Torn, Anne crouched on Kara's other side.

Kara's gloves were coated and steaming, and heat radiated from her body. 'Thank you,' she whispered, and sagged forward. Anne caught her by the shoulders and held her upright. 'For not leaving me alone.' Tom, on the other side, wiped her face with a damp cloth. 'This is so hard, when I have to do it on my own.'

Anne couldn't tell how long it went on for. Kara kneaded and Tom gave her water, and the treacle changed, cooling so slowly, beneath her hands. Shrinking. Hardening. Growing dark. When the trough was lined with sugar, and the treacle so small and compact

Kara could hold it in both hands, she drew a deep breath and tried to stand, but her legs shook and her knees wouldn't hold her.

'All together,' Anne said, and Tom helped her lift Kara to her feet. She was so heavy — too heavy for one small woman — and so hot the mere touch of her skin nearly burned Anne's hands.

Kara whispered something, but she didn't have the strength to speak. Tom turned to his fence line friends and they murmured words Anne couldn't quite hear.

'She needs to go outside,' he said.

So they half-guided, half-carried Kara out, and all the while she cradled the treacle to her chest. When they emerged, it was raining and so cool after the stifling heat of the boiling house. Kara steamed where the water touched her.

'What now?' Anne asked.

Tom glanced around and shrugged. 'They're gone. I don't know—' A piercing cry cut him off. Anne flinched, surprised by its closeness, and her hold on Kara faltered.

It was the treacle, held tight in Kara's hands, pressed to her chest.

Crying, wiggling ... alive. Not liquid sugar any more, no. It was a child. Tiny and dark, hot and steaming in the rain, face scrunched, outraged and screaming. Tom had never been strong enough to make a sound like that.

'Welcome back,' Kara whispered, nearly too soft to hear. 'Mother.' Her hold on the child failed, and the baby girl slipped and might have fallen if Anne hadn't caught her. Tom eased Kara to the muddy earth and Anne stared down at the tiny thing in her hands. Her eyes were the yellow-edged green of sugarcane rustling gently in the sun.

'But—' She was soft and fragile, feet kicking, hands bunched into fists, and definitely real, but Anne still couldn't believe it. 'You were sugar.'

'Molasses,' Kara murmured.


Kara stood on the veranda, her mother cradled against her chest, and watched as Anne walked over from the workers quarters. She wore that same steely expression she had when they'd first met, but she was not the same shaking, exhausted woman. Her dress was clean and patched, she had mended a pair of ancient boots, and the sugar had washed the grey from her thick blonde hair.

She stopped at the base of the stairs. Sturdy, strong. 'Your idea of safety is an unusual one,' she said at last.

Kara couldn't help but smile. 'Some things require sacrifice.'

The pain in her arms was intense. When Anne and Tom had pulled off her gloves the flesh beneath them was burned and hideous. But that wasn't what hurt. The first crop was beginning to sprout through her skin. When they peeked about an inch through, it would be time to pick and plant them. She had a whole plantation to sow, and years in which to do it, while her mother grew.

It would be good to have help, this time. It had been so long since they'd had workers to tend the crop.

If Anne would only stay.

Anne hesitated, unsure. 'The fence lines will call him, won't they? And he'll have to kill himself to join them?'

Kara nodded. She never deceived. Her workers were not slaves. They came and stayed and went on, into the fence lines, because they chose to. 'And you too, eventually. But we all must go, eventually. Taken by poison and ash in the world outside, or called by friends in the fence line. One day, all cycles will end, but until then there's always work to be done.'

Anne climbed a single step. 'And when's that? When do they end?'

Kara held out an arm. The sharp sugarcane tips were tiny and bloody. 'I don't know. We just continue, sometimes suffering, sometimes joyful, dying and being reborn.'

Two more steps, and Anne stood beside her. 'But until we are called,' she said, 'we will be safe here, won't we? With you?'

Kara nodded. 'And even after.'

'Good.' Anne held out her hands for the baby. 'Tom will like that. *I* would like that.'

Kara smiled, and handed over her mother. So would she.

# TIED TO THE WASTE

Leichhardt watched me as the waste rolled in. The ochre sky was heavy, and lights glinted within it. Not lightning — I couldn't remember the last thunderstorm we had, the kind with water-vapour clouds and rain — but metal polished by the sands, cleared by the wind of its ash layer and reflecting the close burning of the sun.

I struggled to prepare for the storm. The concrete ramp from my workshop ended at a tangle of wire that once fenced in the scrapyard, so I was forced to park my wheelchair and rely on crutches. My ankles didn't bear my weight so well any more, but I managed to grab the corner of an oiled-leather tarpaulin, drag it over the nearest scrapheap and secure it to a hook pinned into the dirt. The best I could do to protect the scrap collected in my yard.

'You could help,' I wheezed to the cat.

Hidden against the oncoming darkness, only his eyes glowed back at me, catching the sun in their own cat way. He blinked. As much of an answer as I'd ever get, voice chip or none.

I struggled back into the wheelchair. Blood rushed to my feet with pins of fiercely tingling fire and the old ache set into my spine. By the time I'd wheeled myself up to the workshop door I was exhausted, arms shaking.

I paused on the threshold. 'Coming in?'

He made no move to join me, just watched, two shining points much closer to earth.

Let him weather the storm on his own, then. When I gave them voices I gave them choice.

I rolled myself inside, bolted the door and barricaded it with steel beams set up on spring triggers. I drew water from an earthenware filter, swallowed a handful of painkillers and sleeping pills and made it to bed, just in time.

All I heard was the first knock, the hard crash of something small but solid against the iron roof. All I felt was the first pull, the tug of memory swirling in sand. Then the drugs took me away. Far from the pain of my device-riddled body and the scrap magic screaming in the rolling waste above.

I woke to the stink of cat piss and a taste in my mouth between acid and dust. The cats crowded at the workshop door — all but Leichhardt — glaring silent remonstrations at me.

How long had I slept?

Outside, the world was silent, the waste exhausted.

I eased myself from the bed. My ankles were swollen, the bulging skin darkened to a sickening red. So I stripped their bandages, fumbled syringe and vial from the drawer beside my bed and injected 5mls of a soup of my own creation: gangrene-eating and oxygen-feeding fused from waste dust and precious scrap. They were once jewels, the devices at work inside my deteriorating legs. Diamonds and gold, loved, treasured, now sand-scratched and tossed across the continent.

The devices buzzed their way up to my spine, to ride the network of nerves. Flashes of memory flickered across the back of my eyelids: proposals, birthdays, anniversaries. Small pockets of once-lives carried on minuscule, wiry legs to feed strength into my body.

I was forced to inject a second round and swallow painkillers before I could stand. Even the scrap I kept for myself, the strongest and cleanest of the waste's rubble, was stretched thin — *worn down* — compared to the power I had once known. Because even the most powerful memory loses its potential once it's been thrown around a continent for decades, and reduced to a spot of light in the heavy sky. As the memories weakened, so did my magic. And so did I.

I shuffled two, three short steps to half-fall, half-sit in the wheelchair. The cats wound around my ankles the whole slow way, rubbing against my fresh bandages and threatening to trip me up. I snapped at them, and

brushed as much of their fur away as I could. I rolled to the door —
released the unimpressed feline quintet — grabbed a canvas bag and
balanced it in my lap.

The sky outside was gritty, the sun haloed by purple haze, and the
ground littered. I wheeled myself to the edge of the ramp and took up the
crutches again. Slowly, I hitched and lurched around the yard, the bag slung
over my shoulder.

It must have been one hell of a storm. The tarps were shredded, fresh
scrap had fallen everywhere. Most of it looked unusable: dead trees torn
from the dry ground, and rocks. Lots of rocks. After all, the waste had
stripped the world of most of its human layer. We were down to rocks.

But I still found some machine parts: pistons and crankshafts and fuses.
A scattering of small, die cast toys that flickered faint yet playful memories
against my fingers. Shapeless pieces of metal that once were cars, buildings,
appliances, and all the small glories of an age now sandpapered down.

I stopped to wipe the sweat from my face and caught a fluttering of
colour amidst all the iron-red and ash-grey. I dropped the bag and picked
my way closer, fighting knees that refused to bend.

A bird, the most beautiful blue I had ever seen, unsullied and crisp. The
very sight of it caught my breath, disrupted my faltering step and almost
sent me face down into dirt and metal shards.

I stooped awkwardly to scoop it out of the sand.

It felt like air in my hands, like a breath of wind, like a cloud or, or, I
didn't even have the words. No scrap called to me from within its fragile
frame. No nano-threading in its wings, no pacer tied to its heart, no voice
chip in its throat and brain.

The bird was not tied to the waste.

I stroked it, as gently as my twisted hands allowed, and it did not move,
not even to breathe.

I carried the bird to my workbench inside.

I wiped away a heavy layer of cat fur from the bench, and the strip of
heat-warped plastic and computer chips glowed like the faint curl of a
misshapen moon. Once, it would have caught magic from my fingers. In a
blaze of light it would have drawn memories from the scrap I laid on its
uneven surface and filtered, enhanced, while I fused wire and gemstone and
metal and glass. Not any longer. Not with the quality of the scrap I brought
it now.

Maybe, if I was still young, if I could walk on my own two legs, coterie
of witches' cats in tow, and follow the song of the waste. Then, perhaps, I

could bring my workbench the magic it required to fuse the kind of devices I needed, just to stay alive.

But no, not any longer. The world was old as I was old, and strung up on our lifelines of scrap, we would die slowly together.

I laid the bird out on my knees, spread its wings, and rested its head to the side. Its chest was white, beak long, half-lidded eyes dark. The blue of its feathers reminded me of a sky I had never seen, but knew from stolen memories.

The soft pads of cat feet and I glanced over my shoulder. The cats sat on the workshop floor. I was surprised to see Burke and Wills had dragged my scrap bag in after them.

I gestured, loosely, and they surprised me further by bringing the bag to my feet. Bending with a grunt and a popping in my back, I drew from the bag: a toy car, a fuse, a handful of copper wires stripped of their plastic coating and fraying to a rotten-metal colour.

The cats watched the dead bird on my lap with predator intensity. I rolled close to the bench, keeping it out of their reach, as I laid out my scrap. In the car was joy, hidden deep beneath its rust, stripped-down paint and decades of abandonment. It became the bird's torso. In the fuse was energy, indeterminate, ill-defined. The workbench shuddered against my knees, humming as it tried to drag something solid, something real out of the fuse. What had it been used for? Had that machine been named? Needed? Relied on? It became the head. The wings and legs I wound out of copper wire. They were soft, ungainly, and had none of the delicate strength of feather and bone.

The entire fusion was pathetic, but the best I could do.

I placed one hand on the bird in my lap, and one on the scrap toy on the bench. No balance there. The bird was freedom, it was fresh air. The device was a quiver of muted joy, a surge of directionless energy, and empty wire. Perhaps no device could ever encapsulate that freshness; perhaps the very weight of the waste robbed it of its freedom. Or maybe, in this worn-down world, there was simply nothing as powerful as dead, untethered bird?

Even if I had the strength to revive it, what kind of life could I give it? Plundered from a dead planet, fractured by alien emotion, eaten away slowly into powerlessness and madness?

Like me.

I considered the cats: Baxter's copper-plated skull, Bass's steel-mesh lungs, Kennedy's prismatic eyes. 'Have I bound you here?' I whispered to them. What memories did those cats see, those familiars I had tied to the waste when I fused their bodies and saved their lives?

Slowly, walking with liquid smoothness and none of the heaviness he should have felt in his metallic legs, Leichhardt entered the workshop. Despite the storm and the shelter he had refused, his dark cat body was not sullied with even one grain of sand. He held me in his bright gaze as though he could speak to me, through that gaze alone, and not with the voice chip I had given him.

'What memories do you see?' I hissed. 'Why won't you just tell me? What do you see?'

Nothing.

Whatever it was I had burdened them with, whatever memories they could not identify, whatever particle of a dying world dragged them down, down along with it, they would not speak. Perhaps they saw nothing? Perhaps they really had nothing to say.

I collected the scrap bird, held it out to them. As one, the cats twitched tails and flattened ears.

'It's not strong enough to give the bird back its life,' I said, 'but I think I can start the heart beating.' I nodded, more to myself then the unreadable furry expressions. 'Yes, energy and even the tiniest drop of joy can equal the beating of a heart. And maybe even breath. Won't be alive, but it will live.' I held the device over my lap, wires drooping through my fingers, and tucked my free hand beneath the bird.

Did feathers carry memory? I hadn't thought of that. Perhaps, between us, the bench and I could draw enough out of the feathers to complement my unstable scrap and fuse the two—

Leichhardt leapt at my hand, and his hydraulic legs were strong. It was all I could do to swivel in my wheelchair and keep the bird away from the flashing of his claws and the snapping of his jaws. The scrap bird clattered to the floor and I lost track of it, beneath the shadow of the bench.

'No!' I snapped at him. 'Not to eat!'

The cats refused to leave, and I was forced to keep vigilant, the bird on my knees, to protect it from their appetites.


The first customers since the storm arrived that evening, in wagons pulled by sullen donkeys and ringed by talkative dogs.

The cats disappeared in the face of the approaching lights. All but

Leichhardt. I covered the bird in my lap with a patchwork quilt, and waited in my wheelchair at the bottom of the cement ramp.

The dogs breached the relic outline of my tattered fence in a defensive pack formation. The alpha approached, low to the ground, offering no aggression but ears pricked and nose working. Leichhardt made a show of ignoring him. The dog returned the favour.

'You smell most strongly of cat, witch,' the dog said to me, voice chip set to a deep male tenor, calm and crackling faintly with age and use.

I did not smile. Dogs do not appreciate the baring of teeth. 'And yet I am more dust than fur.'

He paused, head tipped and his ears flattened. 'Dust?'

'Devices,' I said. 'The memories and the waste.' And for a moment, I was caught up in it. All that dust. The cursed devices hummed in my body, and the yard disappeared, the dog gone with it. I was holding a woman's hand, offering her a diamond ring. City lights on a night harbour bobbed and rippled below us. The wind was cool, and spoke of rain.

Then Leichhardt leaned his small dark body against my legs, and I returned. I sagged forward. 'I'm sorry,' I managed to say. 'The dust, the devices, I am so full of them. Sometimes they take me away.'

Can dogs pity? I did not know. 'Do you wish to trade?'

'Of course,' I said. He retreated to alert his masters.

The wagons pulled up close, people tumbled from their rickety wood and rusting iron. 'Good evening, Tilda.' I squinted at the young man who addressed me with such familiarity. I had no idea what his name was, or if I'd ever met him before.

He backed away to allow the women to approach me, heads all low, scarves wrapped around their hair and shoulders. They carried food, and their needs.

I traded a whole year's worth of abortion and birth control devices for a box of tinned tomatoes, beans and corn. Devices to ease infected wounds and chill fever, for bread only a few days old. Voice chips for dried apple and bone-setters for a large barrel of water — none too clean, but I had devices for that too.

Those devices were not as powerful as the ones inside me, though they were even older. I had made hundreds of them when the scrap was rich. They were, after all, my income. No amount of scrap-witchery can fuse food from memory, or water from the past. I relied on trade. And it almost seemed that they would be enough. Until the young man approached me again, hands clutching a tattered leather hat held close to his chest. 'We have a gift for you,' he said, and gestured to his men. My heart sunk as they unwrapped a whole leg of cured meat — pork, I thought. The dogs watched it with reverence. 'And a request.' More desperate gesturing, and another precious, carried package.

This one was a young boy. He sweated even in the cooling night, skin pallid and expression fearful. His leg had been crushed. It was splintered and bandaged poorly, and his body sung with the tangle of devices inside it, their struggling magic all that had kept him alive for so long.

'He is an oldest son,' the young man pleaded. 'To a father lost in the waste not three months ago. He cannot work, and soon, we fear, he will die. Leaving a mother, and three sisters.'

'What do you want of me?' I asked, even though I knew.

'Please, Tilda. A leg for a leg.' The entire caravan seemed to close in around me, all hope and desperation in the fading ochre sunset and the faint, device-powered wagon lights. 'Fuse him a new leg, a scrap leg, or he will die.'

'I can't.' I felt smaller, weakened, by those words.

'Is he worth more? We can spare—'

'No!' I screeched, my voice rusting and inhuman. 'Don't you understand? I cannot create anything worthy of a first son! Not anymore.'

'But—'

A scraping, dragging sound cut through his words. With a shudder, I turned in my chair to see Leichhardt dragging the useless scrap-bird I had fused out of the workshop. He dropped its limp and lifeless not-body at my feet and stood over it, his back arched, tail whipping fur against my legs, fierce and proud as though he had killed it himself.

'What is this?' the young man hissed, and the hackles on his alpha dog rose. Perhaps they took it as an insult. But Leichhardt stood his ground, and growled his own terrible wet-throat noise.

And in that terrible parody of life, that base imitation of the power of a lost world, I saw the dying boy. It would take powerful devices to correct the mangling of his limb, as powerful as those at work inside of me. More jewels, probably, for love. Something stronger than a fuse for energy — a battery, as stable as I could find — and a circuit board to channel it. But what could possibly equate to the potential of his young body? The life he had not led, the tasks he had not completed? No waste-tossed rubbish could do that, no matter how many of their stripped-down memories I cobbled together and forced beneath his skin.

'And I wouldn't, even if I could,' I said, only realising it as the words escaped me. Because all I could make, all I had ever made, was just like Leichhardt's scrap-bird trophy. A terrible parody. A base imitation. Just like me. 'I will not tie this child to a dying world, nor add him to the list of half-lives I have so wilfully created.'

Leichhardt sat, arranged a neat tail and cleaned a casually hooked paw.

The young man seemed torn between anger and surprise. 'How— how dare you? We suffer you because you are useful to us, witch. We trade, rather than take, because you have helped us in the past. If I were you, I would want this arrangement to continue.'

'It doesn't matter what any of us want. The sands will scour us all, in time, and soon we will be nothing but scrap for the waste to play with. Don't bother with your threats, child. We will all end with the world.' I kicked out with my bandaged feet, and ignored the stabs of pain that travelled from ankle to back. This unsettled Leichhardt again and he arched, hissing. 'Just take your boy and go.'

The boy screamed as they collected him, and carried him into the night to die. The young man and a few of his fellows stole scrap from my yard — useless junk, they were welcome to it, as far as I was concerned. The women refused to enter my workshop and steal devices. They, at least, maintained some residual respect. But I wondered how long that would last. What would they do when the devices they had just traded for ran out?

In my lap, the bird felt heavy.

As the wagons rattled away the alpha dog held back. 'You smell of more than cat, witch,' he said. 'You smell of something I cannot name.'

'Freedom,' I told him. 'And fresh air.'

'No.' His ears pricked forward and he panted. A moment of indecision, I thought, of contemplation. 'Dead things,' he said. 'And new life.' The dog stood, took deliberate steps backwards. A final glance at me, 'Hope,' and he disappeared into the night.

Sitting on the end of the ramp, I watched the wagon lights fade. The next time I saw them, there would be no trade.

'Is that what you wanted?' I asked Leichhardt. 'No more magic, no more lives saved, and now, no more food. We will all starve, even while the devices keep us alive. We will be skin stretched over metal, and nothing more.' He stared at the quilt in my lap as Bass and Kennedy dragged the scrap bird into the yard, and tore it back to rubbish.

I downed too many painkillers that night, with old water and beans. The cats knocked against my wheels, leapt across furniture, aiming for my knees. When I slept, I held the bird to my chest.

. . .

In my drugged haze, I had left the workshop door open. A fine layer of sand blew in to cover everything. As I sat up, and my ankles throbbed and my back jarred, I wondered how many painkillers I would have to take so I didn't wake up again. Then I realised the bird was gone.

I struggled into the wheelchair as quickly as I could and rolled out into the yard. The cats sat on the sand in a circle, the dead bird in the centre.

'What are you doing to it?' I cried.

As one, the cats drew back, opening the circle so I could approach. Only Leichhardt remained where he was. The bird seemed unharmed. It lay on a rag, wings outstretched, head to the side. Beside it in a neat pile lay claws shed before their time (edges still bloody, tips still sharp), hairballs (more than I had ever wanted to see in the one place) and whiskers (so many the cats were almost bald).

I glanced from the strange collection of cat-parts to Leichhardt. His face looked oddly lopsided with most of his whiskers missing. 'What is this?'

Disdain articulated through the flip of a tail and the flinting of eyes.

I eased myself from the wheelchair, hissing at the pain. Leichhardt sat opposite me, Burke and Wills beside him, then Baxter, Bass and Kennedy.

I lifted a whisker: black, thick. Leichhardt's.

And it wound itself around my finger. I gasped, let it go, and it shimmied across the back of my hand to plunge needle-like into a vein. I felt it inside me, the way it coursed and wiggled. Up along my arm, across my shoulders and into my neck, then down through my spine, and along the nerves than ran to my leg.

'What—?'

Once there, it latched onto one of my scrap magic devices. It tied up the insect-like legs and dragged it through muscle, through skin and out of me entirely. The device was tiny, after all. Just a sparkle of diamond and wire. The whisker peeked out between my bandages and discarded it with an elastic flick.

And it took away a memory with it. The scent of pollution- heavy air and the bobbing of distant harbour lights vanished. In its place— I wasn't sure. But it wasn't the pain I expected, or the sudden resurgence of gangrenous rot. I felt clean, wherever the whisker had touched me. Scrubbed raw.

Then the whisker burrowed back inside, moving on to the next device. Where it wormed through me it left the promise of freedom.

'Leichhardt,' I whispered.

He curled his tail around the bloodied tips of his paws and looked at me like I was a fool. The whisker tossed one, two more devices out of my body and left empty patches instead.

'There are no memories in your whisker, are there?' I asked. 'No particles of a dead world. Where does this strength come from, then?' Silence. Despite the voice chips I had given them the cats refused to speak. Or, perhaps, because of them. Those chips were but another chain tying them to the waste, to the memories and lives of the long dead. Did they even need the magic I had saddled them with? The waste I had tied them to?

'If I had not fused you, you would have died. I had to tie you, to save your life.' But if that was true, then what were they doing to me? Leichhardt looked at the dead bird, and I followed his gaze back to the pile of whiskers, claws and fur.

Cat scrap. Full not of memories and the past, but whatever it was the whisker was leaving inside of me. What the alpha dog had smelled. Dead things and new life.

'The future?' I asked the cats. Of course, they did not answer. But that was the point.

'But the future is fragile, it might not even be. The past, it is solid. It is trapped in rubbish, fed by the waste.' But the past was also failing, tearing itself down, depleting as we used it for our own ends. I met the bright eyes of six cats; I stared at the delicate feathers of one dead bird. 'I am used to working with memories.' I closed my eyes. A flick of the whisker and I forgot the sound of waves crashing on a breach, overlaid by running feet and laughter. 'I don't know how to work with possibilities instead.'

Leichhardt sighed a cat sigh, the full-body type, dripping with scorn.

And I gave myself over to his whisker. 'All right,' I said. 'I will try it your way.'

I laid the bird in my lap, took up their scrap, and fused.

I wound wings out of whiskers and hair. A heart of claws. Fur for a body, more whiskers gave it shape. When it was done something was still missing, so I plucked a single silver hair of my own and wound it around the entire frame, hairball head to whisker pinion.

The device felt fragile, and yet very much alive. All the hairs along the back of my arms rose as I held it.

'Is that enough?' I asked the cats.

Their bright eyes lacked conviction. Bird in one hand, device in the other, I weighed them against each other as though I was a giant scale. They were uneven.

'Ah.' The heart did not beat.

So I pricked my finger on the device's cat-claw heart and dripped blood into its lattice. This was a strange witchery. Cat magic, scrap skill and blood. But the semi-transparent network shuddered and clinked softly like countless cats running over tiles.

'Now what?'

The cats crouched low and tightened their circle, noses touching the back of my hand. They became my workbench. So I pressed the device to the bird, one hand over the other. And life — possibility — seemed to flow through us all, down from their six tense bodies and even, even from mine. Somehow, I found strength, not the kind that comes from drugs and devices, but the kind that survives out here, amidst the sand of a dying world, and lives. Just lives.

Then Leichhardt's ears twitched and feathers brushed against my palms. With one smooth movement the cats retreated. I opened my hands. The bird shuddered. For an instant I could still see the blood- splattered cage of his new heart beating around his old one, then the fusion completed, and the bird and the device were one.

He breathed, tested the length of his wings, then with a flutter and a hop he was perched on the nest of my fingers. He studied me, then the cats, and bobbed his head back and forward, his beak held high.

A single bright trill, an instant of song, then he opened his wings and darted up into the purple sky. A blue feather fell to my lap. When I touched it, it quivered, and threaded itself beneath my skin.

# STORY ACKNOWLEDGEMENTS

The stories in this collection originally appeared, sometimes in different forms, in the following publications:

- The Bone Chime Song © 2012, first published in *Light Touch Paper, Stand Clear* (Peggy Bright Books)
- Mah Song © 2013, first published in *The Bone Chime Song and other stories* (FableCroft Publishing)
- Shadow of Drought © 2009, first published in *Midnight Echo 2* (June)
- Sanaa's Army © 2012, first published in *Bloodstones* (Ticonderoga Publications)
- From the Dry Heart to the Sea © 2011, first published in *After the Rain* (FableCroft Publishing)
- Always a Price © 2012, first published in *Midnight Echo 8* (November)
- Out Hunting for Teeth © 2011, first published in *Midnight Echo 6* (November)
- Death Masque © 2009, first published in *Masques* (CSFG)
- Flowers in the Shadow of the Garden © 2011, first published in *Hope* (Kayelle Press)
- A Memory Trapped in Light © 2012, first published in *Epilogue* (FableCroft Publishing)
- Trail of Dead © 2007, first published in *Zombies* (Altair Australia)
- Fence Lines © 2013, first published in *The Bone Chime Song and other stories* (FableCroft Publishing)
- Tied to the Waste © 2012, first published in *Tales of the Talisman* (March)

# ABOUT THE AUTHOR

Joanne Anderton is an Australia author of speculative fiction, creative non-fiction, and children's books, who until recently was living and working in rural Japan. Her speculative fiction includes the novels in the *Veiled Worlds* series – *Debris, Suited* and *Guardian* – and the short story collections *The Art of Broken Things* and *Inanimates: Tales of Everyday Fear*. She has won multiple awards for her speculative fiction, including the Australian Shadows Award, Ditmar and Aurealis Awards. Her short fiction has been reprinted in several *Year's Best* anthologies, and she's received international review coverage in *The New York Journal of Books*, *The Guardian*, *Library Journal* and *Publishers Weekly*.

Her children's picture book *The Flying Optometrist*, was published by the National Library of Australia and was a CBCA notable book. Her non-fiction has been published in *Island Magazine*, *Meanjin* and *The Japan News*.

Joanne has a Masters of Arts in Creative Writing, and worked for many years in book publishing, marketing and distribution. She is currently undertaking a PhD in Creative Writing at The University of Queensland.

Find her online at Joanneanderton.com

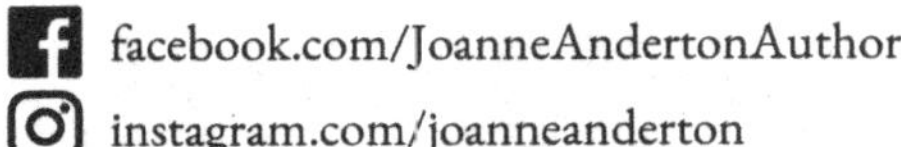

facebook.com/JoanneAndertonAuthor

instagram.com/joanneanderton

# THANK YOU FOR BUYING THIS BRAIN JAR PRESS CHAPBOOK

To receive special offers, bonus content, and info on new releases and other great reads, visit us online at www.BrainJarPress.com

www.ingramcontent.com/pod-product-compliance
Lightning Source LLC
Chambersburg PA
CBHW011559190726
48287CB00010B/2973